MOONLIGHT

MOONLIGHT

MICHELE HAUF

BONNIE VANAK
KENDRA LEIGH CASTLE
ANNA HACKETT
GWEN KNIGHT

MILLS & BOON

Published in Great Britain 2014
by Mills & Boon, an imprint of Harlequin (UK) Limited,
Eton House, 18-24 Paradise Road, Richmond, Surrey, TW9 1SR

MOONLIGHT © 2014 Harlequin Books S.A.

Claiming the Wolf © 2012 Michele Hauf
Courage of the Wolf © 2010 Bonnie Vanak
Her Wicked Wolf © 2013 Kendra Sawicki
One Night with the Wolf © 2011 Anna Hackett
Her Alpha Protector © 2013 Heather Fuller

ISBN: 978 0 263 91386 6

89-0214

Harlequin (UK) Limited's policy is to use papers that are natural,
renewable and recyclable products and made from wood grown in
sustainable forests. The logging and manufacturing processes conform to
the legal environmental regulations of the country of origin.

Printed and bound
by CPI Group (UK) Ltd, Croydon, CR0 4YY

CLAIMING THE WOLF

MICHELE HAUF

A Minnesota native, **Michele Hauf** lives in a Minneapolis suburb with her family. She enjoys being a stay-at-home mum with a son and a daughter. Michele writes the kind of stories she loves to read, filled with romance, fantasy, adventure and always set in France. Though she has yet to leave the US, since her family knows that, once gone, she might set up house in a little French village and never return! Always a storyteller, she began to write in the early nineties and hasn't stopped since. Playing guitar, hunting backyard butterflies and colouring (yes, colouring) keep her creativity honed. For more information on Michele's books visit michelehauf.com. You can also contact Michele at: PO Box 23, Anoka, MN 55303, USA.

Chapter One

Blowing out a breath, Christian Hart watched it fog before him. He stood against the black SUV's hood. He had parked beneath the streetlight posted behind the Lizard Lounge, Paris's resident faery nightclub. Or at least, the club was the closest most would get to faeries without actually stepping into FaeryTown, where the real danger lurked.

It was unseasonably cold for October, but regardless, he didn't wear a coat over the black T-shirt he'd tucked into black cargo pants. A leather holster was strapped across his chest and back, but the pistol tucked under his arm didn't sport normal bullets: they were wooden, designed for stopping vampires. Wood wouldn't kill them, but it would give the nasty longtooths pause long enough for Hart to take them out. If necessary.

It had been some time since vampires had bothered his pack. He missed the action.

Easing back his shoulders, he winced—he was feeling it now in his triceps. *Shouldn't have spent all morning with the punching bag.* He smirked at his wimpy thoughts.

He'd foregone interior duty tonight, letting Tony take that detail, which included protecting their pack leader at close range. The principal, Remy Caufield, had a penchant for shagging faeries, and he would remain inside the night-club that catered to the fey bits of dust and menace until it closed hours from now.

Fine with Hart. Some time alone to let his thoughts wander—hell, who was he kidding? He wanted to be inside, mainlining the thumping beat into his blood, eyeing up the sexy young pretties. He wasn't particular about faeries; he could take 'em or leave 'em. As long as a wolf didn't fall in love with one of the sidhe and attempt to make her his mate—they were ace for one-night stands.

Tony's voice spoke in the two-way curled over Hart's right ear. "Something's going on in here, Hart. Be on the lookout for a tall figure in black."

"What the hell?"

"I didn't have time to assess. I think he planted something on Caufield. Tried to take a swing at him, too. Harm was intended. It's dark in the back rooms. I didn't see his escape. Can you catch him?"

Hart's senses piqued as the club's back door slammed open and out dashed a figure in black, pushing through the crowd of hopefuls who would never be allowed access inside, and hairpinning it to race down the alleyway. He couldn't catch a scent, but he wouldn't lose him visually.

"Got the bloke."

Sliding behind the wheel of the SUV and revving the engine, he rolled onto the street. The assailant achieved good speed, forcing Hart to push twenty kilometers an hour, and navigate a tight Parisian alleyway, to keep up.

It was high time he saw some action. Hart couldn't satisfy his need for adrenaline at the pack compound so he lived apart from the wolves he called family and spent a lot of time in his personal gym. What he needed was a place out in the country to let his wolf run free more often. His very nature demanded it. Yet Caufield was too citified, as was the entire Levallois pack. Though, they did have their darker pursuits.

Hart tried to distance himself from those matters.

Navigating a sharp corner, he saw the person he pursued look back. "Yes, I'm on you, idiot. What are you? Wolf? You should be able to run faster. I'd get out and chase you on foot, but this is more fun, eh? Watching you like a deer in my headlights."

He chuckled to himself, but swore when the next turn found him driving right into three concrete bollards jutting waist-high and designed to keep vehicles off sidewalks. The SUV's chrome bumper just kissed one of the columns. Swearing, he backed up and took the opposite turn.

Heading toward the Seine, he cruised slowly, eyeing up and down the streets. Couldn't have lost him. He should get out and track him on foot, only he hadn't picked up the culprit's scent at the club due to the ridiculous thrill of finally seeing some action.

Suddenly the passenger door opened and a slender figure in black leaped inside. Before he could react defensively, a fist connected with Hart's jaw. He tasted blood and the SUV swerved, but he managed to get it back on track. He was driving parallel to the river, and the traffic before and behind prevented him from stopping.

"So that's how it is, eh?" He gripped the man by the arm, but his clothing was slick, like Gore-Tex, so his hold slid instead of gripping. "You have a death wish, bloke?"

The man kicked, landing the heel of what looked a narrow and feminine boot on the steering wheel. Hart fought to control the vehicle while trying to grab the pistol from under his left arm. His fingers wrapped about the handle, and as he swerved into the line of traffic, he pressed the gun barrel to the man's face where more Gore-Tex fashioned a skull-fitting mask.

With a grunt, the man elbowed Hart's wrist. The pistol went flying and knocked him on the temple. As he shook his head to clear the stinging pain, he noted the three words tattooed on the man's wrist—thought the wrist was bloody thin—then groaned.

"Oh, hell no!" Was it a female? Had to be with such a delicate wrist. But what breed? And to have the audacity to take him on? "Listen, duck, if you've a bone to pick with Remy, I suggest you take it up with him. I'm not trained for relationship rescue."

A heel to his right thigh brought a wolfish growl from between his tight jaws. He grabbed the woman's throat. Before him, a car slowed and he bumped the tail with the front of the vehicle. Adjusting his speed, he yelped when he felt teeth sink into his hand and tear away.

As Hart shook his bleeding hand, the attacker ripped

off the black face mask to reveal a shock of candied red hair and bright blue eyes. *Gorgeous*, was his first thought. *What the bloody hell*, was his second.

She lunged toward him, one hand grabbing the steering wheel and jerking the SUV sharply to the right, toward the river. Then Hart felt the searing, icy pain of fangs sink in at his neck.

No, no, no, no! Not a bloody vampire. And not biting him. The last thing he needed was…this problem.

Dropping the steering wheel, Hart gripped her by the head and yanked. Her fangs tore his muscle and flesh and he yowled and swore. She lunged for him again, attaching her mouth to his bleeding neck like a leech.

"Bloody longtooth!"

He managed to elbow her in the kidney, which detached her just in time for him to feel the impact of the SUV hitting the river guardrail and soar into the air. But he couldn't process the fact that he was airborne and in worse danger than from a mere vampire bite, because the horror of having been bitten flashed red and angry in his brain.

When Hart got brassed off, his werewolf took over. Instinctively, he began to shift. His T-shirt tore at biceps and across the chest. Fingers lengthened, and he kicked off his shoes to make room for his changing feet. His spine cracked and shifted.

The SUV's nose hit the water's surface, jarring them and sending the vampiress flying into the backseat where iron piping left over from a plumbing project at the pack compound clattered. The werewolf he'd become gripped her leg as his hands shifted and talons curled into her flesh. Icy water poured through the open windows, and Hart howled a long and rangy cry that was drowned by the dirty river water.

Now in half-man, half-wolf shape, his brain switched to survival. Trapped within a murky metal box, his limbs shivering from the cold water bath, he slashed a taloned paw outward. The glass windshield cracked as the light from the surface was completely snuffed, save for the small red and blue LEDs glowing on the vehicle dashboard.

Twisting his body, the werewolf pounded again toward the glass and this time the clear sheet sucked inward and the vehicle dropped swiftly. He caught the crackled sheet of glass against his paws and, with a heave, forced it out through the metal frame. Pushing from the seat with his powerful feet, he soared toward the surface.

A paw broke through to the cool night air, and his wolf-ish head followed. Gasping, he eyed the shore, sniffing. No mortals in the vicinity. Kicking his legs, which were encumbered by the mortal pants that hadn't fallen away, the werewolf instinctually shifted as he knew he wasn't designed to swim in this shape.

Sinking in the murky depths, Hart quickly reverted to were-form with a howl that drank in the dirty Seine. Breaststroking, he swam toward the surface and, by fling-ing himself halfway onto the sanctity of a hard surface, landed on the cold sidewalk.

He lay there panting, spitting out the disgusting water, wincing when he realized his left ankle had been twisted and broken during the crash. Already healing, the knitting bone and sinews hurt like a mother.

"Longtooth," he muttered, then lifted his head to scan the river. "Where did you go?"

He suspected vampires were better swimmers than werewolves simply because they didn't have to deal with any shifted body parts, but he watched the deceptively calm surface, mirrored with frail moonlight, for a long time. Nothing broke the water, nor did he spy anyone surface across the other side, or down as far as he could see. They'd plunged in at city's edge. Hell, he suspected it would be a while before rescue vehicles got the call someone had driven into the river.

"One dead vampire is no skin off me," he muttered, then slapped a palm to his aching neck. And yet... "She bit me." He could still feel the open wounds, which meant it was deep, because a small injury should have healed within moments.

If she hadn't surfaced, she must be dead, Hart decided. On the other hand, drowning wasn't going to kill a vampire. And something he'd seen while struggling with the crazed vamp returned to his thoughts.

"That tattoo," he murmured. But a flash second had shown him the detailed and finely wrought words: *come what will*.

Hart lifted onto his elbows and fiercely stared toward the spot where he presumed the vehicle had settled. She was down there. Alone. A just punishment for what she'd put him through.

Shaking his head like a dog to whip the water from his short hair, he growled and smashed his fist against the sidewalk. She was *alone*. And the tattoo bothered him.

Recent? Some weird part of him answered, *yes, it's new ink*. Which meant...

Hart stood and dove into the water.

Danni struggled with the steel pipe that pierced her gut and pinned her like a giant bug to the back seat of the submerged SUV. Upon descent, she'd instinctually started breathing through her nose. She couldn't think how wrong it was she was still alive and struggling. Yet another cool thing about vampirism she had never asked for.

No matter how she tried, she couldn't dislodge the pipe, which had come from the rear cargo area and had wedged in the dashboard. Stuck here forever. Literally.

When would she die? God, she didn't want this. She'd never asked for any of this! The idea of tears made her choke on the water and she wished she could drown and get it over with and done.

When she felt the hand on her leg, she kicked, but instantly regretted the move. Help? Yes, please!

The hand returned and moved along her leg, groping over her limbs. Even with her heightened vampire sight she could only make out shadows and the tiny LEDs on the dashboard. When the hand moved over her hip and slapped against the pipe embedded in her body, she knew whoever it was had determined her dire situation. She landed her hand on his face, stroking her fingers down the side of his jaw and neck, where she felt the serrated skin.

It was him, the werewolf who had condemned her to this watery grave.

You did too, eh, Dan the Man? Would have never landed in the river if you hadn't bitten him.

He tugged at the pipe, and each jerk felt as if her insides were being rearranged by a flunky surgeon. He touched her arm, moving his hand down her skin past her wrist. Placing his palm over hers made her feel as if he were trying to convey something. He swept away, and suddenly she was alone.

He was leaving her? Danni protested with a yell. Stupid. No sound down here, save the gurgling of bubbles still rising from the settling vehicle. And her frantic heartbeats pounding in her veins and ears. She deserved it, she supposed. She had tried to kill him. But only in self-defense.

The hand slapped over her ankle again and he pulled himself inside the vehicle by moving along her body. Fingers pressed gently to her cheek, reassuring, and she moved her hand over his, squeezing. Must have gone to the surface for air.

Now the pipe moved, she could feel every inch as it slowly tugged at her skin and muscles, and hell—who knew—it might have pierced a kidney or her liver. She was still alive by some impossible means that made her want to kick and scream and yell. But she wouldn't. He was helping her. All that mattered now was that she cooperate.

Slowly, methodically, he managed to move the pipe toward the rear of the vehicle. He'd hooked a leg about one of hers, which held him down and his powerful muscles flexed against hers. Another pause, he pressed his palm flat to hers again, and she knew before he left he had to resurface to take in air.

Wolves couldn't breathe underwater? A girl learned something new every day.

Those minutes she lay in the darkness were the longest in Danni's life. Six months ago she'd never imagined this for herself. She wouldn't let this be her end, she was stronger than that. Curling her fingers about the end of the pipe, she felt but a foot left to go, but she couldn't move it herself. Even with the infusion of blood she'd taken in the car, exhaustion coiled about her bones. She couldn't hold her eyes open and let the lids fall shut.

The next time she opened her eyes it was to thin moonlight upon silver waves as she was being pulled ashore. Her body landed on a hard surface and she choked up water endlessly.

"Gotta get out of here," a male voice with a British accent said near her head. "I can hear sirens now. I'm sure neither of us wants to talk to the police. Trust me, eh?"

Danni's eyes closed as she felt her body lifted and tossed over the burly wolf's shoulder.

He walked the half mile home with the vampiress flung over one shoulder as if she were a sodden sack of laundry. He only encountered a few odd looks at the half-clad, soaking wet man as he went along the way. He growled at an elderly gentleman who'd suggested he take his antics to the privacy of his own home. The French were such snobs.

Hart dropped the vampiress onto the ceramic-tiled floor inside his apartment, not wanting to lay her on the suede sofa. Without a glance behind him, he aimed for the bathroom, striping off his wet pants and the few remaining shreds of his shirt. Walking right into the glass-walled shower, he turned on the hot stream. "Bloody yes, I needed that."

Ten minutes later, he grabbed a towel and wandered out to the living room to find the vampiress alert, crouched against the door and flexing to stand as he approached. She put up her fists, as if ready to go a couple rounds with him.

That gave Hart a mirthless chuckle. "Feisty longtooth, aren't you? Here." He tossed her the towel, and she pressed it to her gut, which didn't bleed anymore, but then, he hadn't expected it to. "You healed?"

She nodded.

Anger returning in a whirl of energy, he fisted the air as if he'd just laid the punching bag flat. "What the hell are you about? Going after my principal, then nearly drowning me? And this?" He slapped the side of his neck where the bite wounds had finally healed, yet had marked him forever in ways no wolf could comprehend.

"Just doing as I was ordered." She straightened, lifting her chin defiantly.

Despite her bedraggled, wet-rat appearance, her eyes were bright blue and her thick lips were jeweled with water that dripped from her candy red hair. The dark clothing clung to a long, narrow frame defined by lean muscle.

Hart's first assessment of her stood: gorgeous. Yet deadly. And too cocky for a vampire standing before a wolf who could shear her head from her neck with one flick of his wrist.

"Why did you do it?"

"Do what?" Hart snapped, pacing before her, unsure yet

if he should get out the stake he kept in a kitchen drawer—
he'd lost the gun in the Seine—or shove her out the door
and wish her good riddance.

"You saved my life."

He flung a hand outward, dismissing the heroic deed.
"Wasn't like you were going to die."

"No, but I would have been stuck down there forever."

"Yet still alive. So there. I didn't save your life."

She heaved out a sigh and nodded. "Either way, I owe
you one."

"I don't need a favor from a longtooth, thank you very
much."

"I know. You hate me. I'm supposed to hate you." She
lifted the clump of her wet hair and squeezed the water
out onto the floor. "What's your name?"

He snarled, thinking she had some nerve. By rights he
should bring her in to the compound to let the pack serve
her the justice they saw fit.

I'm supposed to hate you. Like she wasn't sure whether
or not she should?

"Hart," he offered briskly. He never used his first name;
Christian was too sissy. "You can take the towel with you.
Just get the hell out before I decide to serve you as chum
for the pack."

Wrapping the towel about her shoulders, she opened the
door. A sigh preceded her darting glance at him. Sadness
wafted through the air and permeated Hart's chest. He felt
the hit directly and sucked in a breath.

"Name's Danni Weber," she said. "Tribe Zmaj. I know
it doesn't change things, but…sorry about the bite. I was
in survival mode."

With that, she closed the door, and Hart let out his breath.

"Sorry? About changing my life forever?" He grabbed the nearest thing—a pillow on the couch—and hurled it at the door so hard the seams split and out spilled thick white stuffing.

Hart slapped a palm to his neck. The wound was achy and hot. He would have preferred death over a bite, any day.

Chapter Two

Danni stood naked before the mirror mounted on the back of her bedroom door, inspecting her smooth stomach. Gliding her fingers up the skin, taut with underlying muscle, she frowned at the absence of a scar below her ribcage. That her body healed at an insanely fast rate did not cease to bewilder her. It was unnatural. Wicked. Perhaps even demonic.

Truth was, it was vampiric. And thinking the V-word ignited a wrenching twist in her gut. She hated what she had become. Or did she fear it?

A little of both, for sure.

Pressing a palm to the mirror she opened her mouth and watched as she willed her fangs lower. It didn't hurt, but accompanying their descent, she felt a strange tingling for fulfillment, to satiate her needs with blood and sex. Another wicked, demonic thing that had become a part of her life.

It was all Slater's fault.

She'd not called him this morning to check in. Revealing her incompetence wasn't so much a risk to her status in the tribe as it would be to her brother's neck. Literally. No, she had to avoid Slater for a few days until she could again put herself near the pack leader, Remington Caufield. And this time she wouldn't screw things up.

The sticky tracking device had slipped off her finger before she'd gotten it on the principal. And the device being miniscule, she hadn't a chance to find it in a dark nightclub. She'd fled in a panic. The pack wolf who had pursued her—Hart—had been a surprise.

This lurking about and spying business wasn't her thing. Though tribe Zmaj seemed to think it was. As a former soldier, Danni could reconnoiter a site, sneak up on the enemy, and had even begun training to scout out landmines. Getting close to a werewolf to plant a tracking device? So out of her comfort zone.

But she had to do this. She must not fail a second attempt. Or David, her brother, would suffer for it.

She tapped her fang and sneered at her reflection. "I won't let this happen to you, David. If it's the last thing I do."

Hart plowed a right hook into the punching bag, held by fellow pack member Tony Santenolli. The wolf grunted and let go of the bag, stumbling backward.

"Hart, I think you've got it. You got something anyway. Why so angry?"

Angry? Light on his feet, Hart dodged side to side, fists wrapped in tape up by his face in defensive position, before he swung again, and sent the bag flying toward Tony's growling face. He wasn't angry. He was…

Hungry. For something he couldn't quite name. Not food, that was sure. The hunger had been gnawing at him for days, since he'd woken the morning after his swim in the Seine. And yet, that deep, dark twist in his gut and curdling at the back of his throat did have a name. It coiled in his nostrils, drawing in Tony's musky, metallic scent from beneath his skin.

Blood.

"I'm cool," Hart huffed. He delivered another iron blow to the bag and felt the sting in his forearms. The best way to avoid the truth? Beat on something.

"Yeah? Well, I'm wrecked, man. You're beating me bloody." Leaner, and not as dedicated to the gym but still a powerful force, Tony shoved off from the bag and swiped a hand over his sweating brow.

"I don't see any blood on you. Come on, bloke!" Hart delivered a high kick to the bag with his bare foot. Mixing in Muay Thai with standard boxing moves was his thing. He loved the martial arts workout and never missed a day. "Give me a challenge!"

Tony waved him off and grabbed a water bottle from the weightlifting bench.

It had been three days since Hart's plunge into the Seine. He'd thought to walk it off, get on with his life. He'd detailed his chase after the vampire assassin to his principal, but had left out the part about her being a female—and biting him. Pack Levallois would banish him if they knew he'd been bitten. Which is why he had a workout towel draped about his neck right now. The bite mark had scarred and had not gone away as most wounds did within hours.

And every day he felt it more. The gnawing hunger. The deep, gut-clenching desire to sustain himself on a substance no sane wolf would consider. Werewolves didn't need blood. His breed lived alongside mortals, and to each his own. But consume their blood for survival? Hell no.

The day Hart started drinking blood was the day he gave it all up. He had a good life. He worked hard to protect the pack and in turn was surrounded by the family his soul required. Someday he hoped to take a mate and begin his own family. It was all he needed.

Damn it! Everything he needed was now thoroughly shagged thanks to—her.

"Stupid vampire," he growled, as another punch pummeled the sand-filled bag.

"What was that?" Tony set aside the water bottle.

"Nothing. Get out of here, man. I'm almost finished. Thanks for sparring with me."

"No problem. You going to the games tonight?"

The blood games pitted two half-crazed vampires against one another to the death. Right now? Hart would love to see a vampire get its throat ripped out as a small means of recompense against the travesty committed against him. But if he smelled blood, let alone, saw it fly through the air and stain flesh, floor and walls? He'd lose it.

"Nah. Have a…date," he summoned.

"Cool. Talk to you later."

Date? He punched again, this time feeling the bones crunch in his knuckles and wincing through that small pain. Who the hell was he trying to fool? He had a date with the weights at his home gym because if he didn't find a focus, his mind and body would stray toward the hunger.

Wicked, unnatural, wrong—*so wrong*—hunger.

As it stood, he wasn't sure he could make it home, walking the streets filled with innocent mortals, smelling the hot blood gushing beneath their skin, calling to him, beating, pulsing, thumping…

"Aggh!" Hart kicked the bag and the chain snapped, sending it flying. It hit the wall, and knocked a hole in the plaster.

"Exactly how I feel." Like a hole had been kicked in his gut. And the only way to fill it required a dark deed. "I have to resist."

Her best bet was to return to the Lizard Lounge tonight. From the intel tribe Zmaj had obtained about pack Levallois, Remington Caufield frequented the place. Danni had to use caution inside the nightclub. Supposedly faery dust was dangerous to a vampire. Getting some on her skin would give her a contact high, and the place had glittered with the stuff. She'd suit up in head-to-toe Gore-Tex again and cross her fingers the second time proved the charm.

Masculine clothing was sort of her thing. Wearing form-fitting workout shorts, which reminded her of men's boxer briefs—she loved them on a man—and a military-issue tank top, Danni leaned over the kitchen counter. The tiny tracking device was stuck to an adhesive tape she could wear inside the wrist of her glove. Slater had provided her with three. Because he'd suspected she would need the extra chances? The man was a self-possessed asshole whose crooked snarl always sent a chill up her spine. Yet his bite was frustratingly erotic.

Setting the glove aside, she turned to go gather her work clothes, when someone pounded on her apartment door.

Grabbing the nearest weapon, a bowie knife she'd been sharpening on a whetstone earlier, Danni stepped lightly and cautiously to the door. Could be someone from the tribe, in which case, she'd keep the weapon in hand. No love lost with any of her tribe mates.

Tightening her jaw, she leaned forward and turned the knob, stepping back and raising the blade to attack.

She lowered the blade, her jaw dropping as well.

In the doorway, palms to the white-painted wood frame, leaning forward and huffing as if he'd run a marathon, stood the werewolf who had rescued her. Hart. She'd never forget that name. It was ironic on this beefy hunk of wolf. And yet, she suspected she was more wrong about the irony than she could ever guess.

"What the hell?" She stepped aside as he plunged forward and landed on the sofa, hands to the back of it to support his weak stance. Had he run here? "How did you find me?"

"Followed your scent. It's strong. And the big surprise is it runs through my system now. I can suss you any-where. Weird." He turned, leaning against the sofa. His muscle-strapped chest heaved and he seemed to relax as he took in the room, the bare white walls and furniture, and bright red pillows and rugs that popped like bloody stains. "Danni, right?"

"I'll give you two minutes, wolf." She thrust the blade up under his chin. The man didn't flinch, yet his gray-blue eyes grew serious and his breaths calmed to silence as if a ninja preparing for the kill. "What do you want?"

"What I want is the craziest thing," he said. "And you are the one who gave me that insane want with your bite. Danni, I have the blood hunger."

"Yeah? Well start snacking, big boy. There's a whole world of mortals walking around with blood running through their veins. Bonanza!" she said, though the idea of making a feast out of mortals didn't sit well with her. She was discreet and only fed once a week, and never killed.

"You did this to me!"

"Hey, it's not like you're my bitch now, so quit freaking and man up."

"Man—? This is not normal. It's an abomination for a werewolf to have this feeling. I crave, Danni."

"Already?"

"Yes. Fuck!"

He stood and Danni took a step back. He was slightly taller than her six feet two inches, but his imposing shoulders made her feel like an All Hallow's skeleton standing before a Mac truck.

He grasped the air and winced. "It's a deep, feral craving. Right here." A fist pounded his gut. That was about where the blood hunger originated, though she tended to feel it a bit higher— "And here." His palm slapped over his heart. Okay. So the guy got it right. "And it's…hell, I thinks it's sexual."

"Sounds about right. Blood and sex usually go together.

Go find yourself a mortal and sink in those fangs. You got 'em, just like me. Yours are probably thicker—"

He grabbed her arms and squeezed so hard she couldn't maintain control of her grip, and she dropped the bowie knife at their feet. "I can't harm a mortal. I would never—this isn't natural for me, Danni, don't you understand?"

She nodded. For as little as she had learned about the various paranormal breeds over the past few months, she was aware wolves depended on humans the least of them all. And a wolf with a blood hunger was off-the-scale wrong.

"Like I said that night, sorry," she said and shoved at him, but he wouldn't release her. His musky scent wasn't entirely offensive, yet her instinct to get free was stronger than her desire to lean closer to his smell. "Let go of me!"

He maintained hold. "You do owe me one."

"What?"

"After I pulled you from the Seine you said you owed me one." He released her. "Well." He spread out his arms, his eyes slinking appreciatively down her skimpy attire. "I'm here for the one."

"You want to stave that craving on me?" She straightened, hooking her hands akimbo. No one told her what to do. Okay, so they did if they were vampires. But a wolf?

Danni ran her tongue along her lower lip. On the other hand, a bite always felt so damn good. She hated when a tribe member bit her because that wasn't her choice, even though it ended in bliss. But this man? A wolf. Such a fierce and powerful creature. He needed her. How awesome was that?

You hold the power over him now, Danni. Might return the power and confidence the tribe robbed from you.

And he wasn't bad to look at. Handsome, in a bulky, tough guy kind of way. She liked them brute and manly. Give her a soldier over a GQ model any day.

"Danni?" His accent was British and he spoke differently than she expected.

"For a guy who's all muscles and punch," she said, "you speak softly."

"Yeah? Well maybe I should shout so you can hear what I'm saying. I'm hurting here. And you have to know how it brings me down to stand before you—a vampire—and ask for such a thing."

"Then why not go to one of your pack mates?"

"And risk them discovering I've been marked by a vampire? I'd rather die. I wish I had died instead of you biting me."

"Flattery." It was an easy form of defense to go for the snark.

"I know you were in fight mode. I'd have done the same thing in an attempt to save my arse. I blame you and I don't. It's been done. Now I need to deal with it."

"And you need my neck to deal?"

"I don't know who else to go to."

He sat on the sofa arm, head bowing and shoulders rounding. No man should be reduced to such a cower. Especially not this one, whom she suspected had never bowed before a woman for a favor, ever.

"It aches. I can't think of anything but blood, of tasting

it. It's tearing me apart fighting it, but I know I'll go mad if I don't fulfill this craving."

Yes, he probably would pop a mental chord or two if he resisted too long. Danni remembered when the blood hunger had overtaken her. She had screamed and begged for blood, an appalling thing. The wolf's insides must be burning, his skin sensitive to the slightest touch, and his senses picking up everything, her heartbeat, the gush of her blood, the heat of it and the vanilla scent of her skin.

Torture had never been her thing. But to suddenly hold the cards over a werewolf? This was too rich. Maybe she could use his weakness to get to the pack principal? Bargain with him. A bite for information?

Danni strolled before Hart, assessing his beaten posture. Sweat trickled down his face, pearling over the stubble darkening his jaw. His mouth, open and breathing heavily, appealed to her. Now she was vampire, plain old mortal men didn't do it for her. Not the ones she used to date, anyway, and they had generally been strong, macho soldiers.

What could be more challenging than a werewolf? A man who, by nature, hated her breed, and would likely tear out her throat if she let him near her? She might die in his arms, and it—this horrible life she'd been forced into— would be ended. Nothing wrong with that.

Except that would leave David a sitting duck for tribe Zmaj.

Right. She couldn't give up so easily. Hell, giving up was not her thing. *Come what will*. And today, what had come into her life was a desperate, starving werewolf.

"Hart," she said, garnering his attention. His eyes resembled an icy winter sky, gleaming yet troubled. A nick in his left eyebrow made her wonder who had hurt him so seriously it had actually scarred the wolf, and if he'd enjoyed the challenge. He had, she knew. This man would like a good fight. She'd given her best when they'd been battling in the SUV. And she had scarred him as well.

Points for the vampire? The win didn't feel right.

"Come here," she said, placing her feet square and exhaling. Drawing in a breath tightened her abs, and her core felt solid, steady. Preparing, she gave herself one last moment for retreat, to lunge for the bowie knife and shove it into his gullet.

"Will you…" He stood, his hands out, palms up. "Help me?"

"You know what you're getting into, wolf?"

He shook his head. "Everything has gone pear-shaped. I don't know anything right now but blood. I can smell yours. It's sweet, like vanilla cream. I think it'll taste like a treat, and I want to rip out my heart for saying that because it's too wrong."

He turned away from her, his shoulders shuddering as he resisted the instinctive pull. Fists hard at his sides, the wolf gritted his jaws.

Danni sucked in her lips. He was in real pain and determined to fight this. Knowing that he wasn't as tough as he appeared, her heart pulsed for him. And she wanted to make it better.

Sliding a hand along his arm, she moved her fingers over his massive biceps and tight, sinewy forearms until she reached his hand. Opening his palm, she placed her palm against his and closed her eyes. Wrists parallel to one another, his pulse beat against hers, his skin too hot. He exhaled against her shoulder and dipped his forehead to rest against it.

"No turning back," she said. A tilt of her head exposed her neck and veiled her hair over a shoulder. "You tear me to pieces, wolf, I will fuck you up."

"I won't hurt you," he whispered. "Won't try to, anyway. Danni." His fingers shook as they stroked the skin on her neck. "It's strong, your pulse. Calls to me. And your skin against mine is like a normal touch, but ten times more real, if that makes any sense." He growled and made a painful noise. "My fangs, they hurt to come down. Thicker than yours. It's going to hurt you."

"Just do it!"

Chapter Three

Grabbed about the waist by Hart's strong arm, Danni's bare feet left the floor. The wolf clutched her chin, forcing back her head—and then the intrusion. Hard, thick fangs opened her skin in a painful piercing. Heat, light, terror, passion. Danni moaned. This was how it felt when the piercer grabbed the skin and shoved in the belly ring without a numbing agent. Hart held her in a powerful clutch and growled as he slipped out his teeth and sucked in her blood.

The hand at her jaw slid down over her breasts, clasping, clutching. He squeezed her body against his, kneading her into him as he fed upon her. It felt too good, and painful, and blissful, and never stop, *never stop, never stop...*

Danni closed her eyes and coiled forward, suspended in the werewolf's clutches as he feasted upon her. His erection, hard like the steel pipe that had penetrated her, crushed against her hip, and she wanted to grab it, squeeze it, and this time allow it inside her willingly, but she was flying into the swoon right now and nothing else mattered but surfing the pleasure of his wild and wicked kiss.

The hand at her breast massaged and tweaked her nipple, which rocketed all sensation to the stratosphere. Danni slapped a hand over his, encouraging him to continue, to punctuate this embrace with the rough command of his sensual desires.

With a hiss, he pulled his mouth away from her neck. Eyes wild and blinking, the wolf stumbled backward, Danni still in his grasp, and he sank to the floor, sliding against the sofa, holding her clutched tightly to his chest, as if she were a favored doll.

"Oh, yes," she moaned against his panting chest, her breathes coming quickly and her fangs descending. She wanted to reciprocate the bite, she needed to feel the river of his hot blood in her mouth, but a little voice held her back. *Let him process this. Don't push him over the edge.*

Hart moaned like a man who had climaxed, and indeed, she knew the act of taking blood was very close to orgasm, and she oftentimes achieved a similar high. Sliding her hand over his hard-on, he groaned, hugging her closer, while his body shuddered in reaction to her ministrations.

"Now the sex," she whispered, and without his permission, unzipped him and slid her hand inside his pants to find the impossibly hot, steel rod that strained for release. "You ready for this, wolf?"

"Fuck," he murmured, still lost in the blood swoon. "Ready?"

Blood stained his mouth, yet she kissed him deeply,

driving her tongue over his teeth and tasting her blood, his sweet breath, his panting desires satisfied. Her hand wrapped about his cock, her fingertips did not touch. Big, swollen, and like molten coal. She wanted to burn herself on the source of his heat and dipped her head to lick the head of him.

"Danni." He shifted his hips and gripped a wodge of her hair. "Hell yes. This is... So much to process. Your blood..."

"Stay in the swoon, Hart. I want to explore the big bad wolf. Got a problem with that?"

"No," he croaked out. He lifted his hips when she tugged at his pants, pulling them down to his thighs. Commando beneath; she appreciated the easy access.

Kneeling before him, she took him into her mouth to the rousing sound of his moaning approval. Sweet and musky mixed with a tendril of spicy cologne. She reached low to cup his heavy testicles. His fingers gripped her hair tightly and followed her rhythm, not pushing or forcing, which she appreciated. One of his hands tugged the tank top over her breasts, eager now.

Surfacing from the swoon, he was finding his bearings, and she sensed his switch to the hunger for her body, as opposed to her blood. He pinched her nipple and she nipped the head of him, eliciting a groan. Working her hand up and down him swiftly, she glided her shoulders up, and he found her breast with his mouth and sucked her hungrily.

"Yes, hard and rough," she encouraged. "Don't hold back, wolf."

Dipping her head aside his neck where his scent was

deliciously strong, she had to caution the need to sink in her fangs. She'd love to taste him again, but she decided to give him this one. A freebie. For now.

"Christ, you're amazing. You're going to get me off again...." He clutched her by the hips as her hand worked faster and faster. "Never thought I'd do this with a vampire...."

Yeah, rub it in that she was a longtooth. Right now, Danni didn't care about their differences, because they were too much alike. They needed, and perhaps for the moment, they two were the only in the world who could fulfill each other's intense and wanting desires.

Hart cried out hoarsely and came, spilling over her hand, his hips thrusting upward. He swore in the good way most do when they climax, and then grabbed her by the neck and pulled her in for what she thought would be a punishing kiss—until his mouth landed on hers so tenderly, so sweetly.

Melting against his body, which shuddered with the after-tremors of climax, Danni pulled up her knees to snuggle tightly to his heaving chest. His shirt was soft and worn, and it felt good against her bared nipples as he kissed her slowly and deeply, reverently. Making her his. Showing her a tenderness she wagered none had ever won from this brute wolf before.

Falling into his kiss, she wasn't sure she'd ever experienced such a perfect moment of connection, of taking in each other's breath and sighing softly in reply. Fast replacing the thrill of the almost-sex they'd just had was a desire to remain snuggled against him and seek protection from forces she could never completely escape.

"You've destroyed me, Danni," he whispered into her mouth. "I hate you for that." And he hugged her to him in a way conflicting with what he'd said.

He hated her. As he should.

Danni could not summon an ounce of hatred for this hard wolf who had softened in her embrace, and who she couldn't imagine letting go of ever again.

Hate her? If only.

Hart watched Danni stand over him and slip the tank top off over her head. Then she slid down the tiny shorts that had hugged her muscled thighs possessively. When they reached her heels, he tugged off the bit of fabric as she stepped out of it. His eyes traveled her impossibly long legs to the sensual curve of her knee bones where he'd have liked to plant a kiss if he weren't so stymied.

He'd consumed this woman's blood, and then she'd jacked him off. What a bizarre and amazing thing. It had felt tremendous. A new kind of adrenaline rush that no amount of time in the gym could match. Someday, in were-wolf hell, he would burn for this. But until then? This wicked simmer heating his skin and pounding his pulse was worth the impending flames.

Following the inner softness of her thighs with his gaze, he lingered there at her mons, which boasted dark hair, not the bright color as that on her head. Her belly panted and Hart's eyes skipped to her full, heavy breasts that had tasted like sweets filling his mouth. And there, a trickle of crimson spilled over the top of one breast, and he followed the trail to the side of her neck where her skin opened in two wide holes.

He swished his tongue across the enamel of his upper teeth, the canines thick and sharp, shocked he'd actually done it. Yet, now that he assessed the moment, the craving had subsided. He'd fed the gnawing, insistent hunger, and it had felt *good*.

Danni leaned forward, her take-me-on cherry hair spilling over the telltale sign of his brutality. "Come on, big boy. We're just getting started." And the nude nymph strode away, down the hall to, he presumed, the bedroom.

Turning and going on one knee to follow the sexy sashay of her tight arse, Hart vacillated between racing after her with his pants spilling about his ankles, or turning to dash out the front door which was only six feet from where he knelt.

A wise wolf would get the hell out of here. Never return. He'd done the deed, now he needed to move beyond, figure out what came next for a werewolf who had consumed blood as a means to satisfy a craving.

And yet, Danni's derriere was perfect. He could place a hand to each side and squeeze, hard. He wanted to follow the curve of it with his tongue and glide along the smooth line of her spine. He wanted to taste her, to eat her, to devour her—but only her skin and her sighs and her moans.

No more blood. *Stop thinking about blood*. Could he chase away thoughts of blood by indulging in the decadent pleasures her arse offered?

Licking his lips clean of the last traces of wicked crimson elixir, Hart bounded down the hallway, kicking off his shoes and pants as he did so, and swung around the doorway into the afternoon coolness of a dark bedroom decorated in deep purples and bright reds. No decorations beyond the color though. The whole apartment was Spartan, which was odd for a woman. He liked the unexpected surprise of her.

Danni sprawled forward onto the bed, wiggling that sweet arse in invitation, and peering back over her shoulder. "You still hungry?"

"Not for blood." The words spilled from his lips. "No more. Can't. Can never—"

"Don't sweat it, Hart. I'm talking about a different kind of satisfaction." Twisting, she sat and spread her legs, drawing a finger down her toned stomach and along her thigh. "Come on, wolf. Taste all the places on me you haven't yet discovered."

Now that was an invitation he couldn't refuse.

The wolf started at her ankles, licking his way slowly up her sweat-pearled skin. When he arrived at the inner curves of her knees, Danni squirmed and rolled to her stomach, granting him easy access to a spot she had never realized was so sensitive. It was almost like he was licking her between the legs because the sensation of his touch skittered up her inner thigh and hummed there at the V of her legs. Her core spun dizzily and she gripped the crisp white sheets and bit the corner of the pillow.

Vanilla scented the room from organic oils she kept in open jars on the dresser. It cast a hazy mellowness over all.

Lost within Hart's attentions, she couldn't remember a time when she'd been without care or worries. In the moment now. Some kind of dream she'd thought long lost to her.

Hot tongue snaking its way higher, Hart stroked along the curve of her derriere, and she lifted her hips, coaxing him to explore wherever he may desire.

"Spread your legs," he rasped, the commanding tone gentle but irresistible.

He liked to be in control, and she had no problem succumbing to his demands. Still lying on her stomach, hips lifted, she slid her knees wider and nestled her cheek against the pillow.

The intrusion of his finger into her pussy stirred a humming moan from Danni's throat. She wiggled her hips, pressing backward to sheath him as far as she could manage. His thumb slipped over her clit, and his rough knuckles teased at the sensitive length of her folds.

"More," she pleaded.

"Two," he said, and eased another finger inside her. He kissed across her ass and tickled the indented dimples of Venus with his tongue, his palm rough but seeking as it glided her spine. "Or maybe three? Mmm…"

Rocking back and forth, slicking herself upon his fingers, she fell into a giddy, blissful reverie she never wanted to leave. A fang tore the pillow case and she giggled, but the giggle quickly turned to a wanting moan as he punctuated his entrance with a determined focus on her sensitive clit.

"Hart, fuck."

"Yes, I'm fucking you. Though I prefer the term shagging. You did want this, yes?"

"Yes. Feels so good. Want to…"

His voice whispered near her elbow, his tongue lashing out to trace her skin. "Want to what?"

He filled her and dizzied her senses. She was close. Every part of her hummed, preparing for release. "To bite you," she gasped. Her fingers curled into the sheets and she cried out in orgasm.

The burly wolf behind her slid close, his thighs hugging the curve of her bottom, and as his fingers slipped from her, her body spasming to hold him inside, he slid in his cock, and beat out a new rhythm against her shuddering body. One hand clutched her breast, holding her to his hard chest as if there would be no escape, the other dragged fingers through her hair, twisting her head aside to receive his quick kiss to her jaw. He pounded against her, driving, seeking, dashing to the teasing, rushing edge of oblivion.

Gripping her tightly, to keep her, to control her, Hart suddenly burst into his own orgasm, which renewed the delicate shimmers and squeezes of after-orgasm in Danni's body. Together they collapsed on the crinkled sheets, side by side, spent, but nowhere near exhausted.

Danni twisted her body to hug her breasts against her werewolf lover's heaving chest. His gasps hushed over her mouth, her neck, her shoulders.

"So good," he muttered.

She traced the scarred bite mark on his neck, and he bit

his lip, moaning. "Hell, what was that?" he said. "It feels like you are stroking my cock when you touch me there."

"I own you," she cooed. Well, maybe? She wasn't sure what the whole biting a werewolf thing implied, beyond giving him the unnatural blood hunger. But only her touch on the scar would give him pleasure, and right now that felt like ownership to her. "And I need you again."

Fangs descending, she dove for his neck, right over the scars, and sank in the pin-sharp tips.

Hart growled and shoved her roughly away. His skin tore and it hurt her fangs as they left his neck. He gripped her jaw and shook her head. "No! Never again, you sneaky longtooth."

The cruel epitaph brought Danni down from the pleasure high like an SUV crashing into the river's moon-mirrored surface.

"You've already marked me once," he insisted. "Isn't that enough?"

"But you know the blood and sex—"

"No." He pushed away from her, reeling, to stand beside the bed. His body glistened with perspiration, his muscles hard and defined from exertion, and his bold cock stood proudly, ready for more action. "I can't do this. This was… wrong."

He grabbed his pants and stuffed his legs into them then looked around for his shoes.

Danni sat, wiping the trickle of his blood from her fang. It hurt still. If he'd been rougher, he might have yanked out her fang. Mean old wolf.

Mean old wolf with whom she had thought she was making a connection. What was wrong with her? Oh, right. Wolves and vampires didn't play nice together. It's what the tribe had taught her.

So why did she feel as though that was the biggest lie ever?

"I shouldn't have come here," he said, pulling the dark T-shirt over his head and tugging it down to greedily hug his pecs. His glance lingered on her skin, his eyes softening as he licked his lips. Part of him was still lying next to her, his skin melding to hers, taking from her and giving as good.

"But you were craving," Danni said softly. "You needed me. I helped you, Hart."

"Help?" He compressed his lips and shook his head, looking ready to punch something as a fist formed. "Because of you I now crave blood. Blood! And blood mixed together in some kind of weird sex act."

"This wasn't weird. You enjoyed every minute of it!"

Hands flattening in the air before him, he bowed his head, giving his anger a moment to settle. She hoped.

"I'll give you that. The sex was ace. But that's the point. I enjoyed it, Danni. And I enjoyed drinking your blood and that is not right in my book!"

Charging out of the bedroom, the wolf left her there, sprawled on the bed, hair tangled and body still weak from the heady, muscle-wringing climax. When the front door opened, then slammed, Danni winced, and buried her face against the pillow. Tears didn't come. She'd never been one to cry. Dan the Man was tougher than that.

But this once, she wanted to know what it felt like to cry and release the hurt from her heart that had been coiling there for half a year.

Chapter Four

Hart marched down the hallway and punched the elevator button. Slamming his palm against the white marble wall panel, he growled. He shouldn't have stormed out of Danni's place like that. He'd left her all gorgeous and naked with cherry curls spilling over her delicious breasts and wondering what the hell was his problem.

But she shouldn't have tried to bite him again. Did she not understand the serious results of her bite? Hell, did it matter anymore? He'd succumbed. Against better judgment and reasoning, Hart had answered the compelling call to drink blood.

And what did that make him now? Certainly not a werewolf in the usual sense. He'd become something different. Changed. Not right. A creature his pack would sneer at and walk around in a wide circle. The pack would oust him if they ever learned about what he'd done.

He needed the pack. They were family. An anchor to this realm of mortals amongst whom his breed were forced to survive. Both his parents were dead and he had no siblings. He'd been raised by the pack after Remy had found him wandering the forest edging Bristol, a sixteen-year-old who'd been fearful to go near the city lest he shift without warning. Remy had dreams of living in the cosmopolitan city of Paris, so they'd packed up and headed east and started what was now pack Levallois.

He'd learned a lot since then, and though he'd never call Remy a father figure, the man had been kind to him and taught him the ways of his breed. Hart knew nothing else. If he were not surrounded by his kind he would become lost, angry, rage amongst those who could not understand him. He'd return to the forest, that sixteen-year-old boy, fearful and uncertain of what the world would throw at him next.

The elevator doors slid open, but Hart remained in place, and pressed his forehead to the paneled wall. A tilt of his head spied her door, painted red to match the odd spots of color in her white living room. Like blood on skin?

Why couldn't he leave? It shouldn't be so difficult to put distance between he and a blood-sucking vampire.

Yet something about Danni snagged his attention like a fish to the hook. Something beyond the blood and fangs and the fact she had tried to kill him. Something…soft and needy. Sexy. Strong. Wanting. She'd curled herself against him more than a few times, as if seeking protection, a safe place to be. It twanged at his heart, and tempted him to think about her, to recall their lusty tangle in bed, the fervent sounds she'd made as she climaxed. She'd been wild beneath him, yet had melded into his embrace, willing to let him master her. Danni had abandoned her tough exterior to be soft for him.

Hart shook his head. He needed to get out of here before he talked himself back down the hallway.

First, he needed to figure out if he was going to crave blood again. He needed…something he felt course through his system as if one of Danni's sighs brushed over his skin. Connection? Touch?

No, a good session with the punching bag will knock some sense into you, bloke.

When Danni's door opened and she rushed down the hall, he winced, wishing he'd gotten on the elevator when he'd the chance. And then he did not.

"You following me?" he asked.

Standing there in her body-hugging shorts and top, she equally embodied strength and weakness, and all Hart wanted to crush against his chest and never let go.

"Why can't you leave?" she defied with a tilt of her head.

And that was it, wasn't it? Why couldn't he leave?

Turning, crossing his arms over his chest, Hart drew his eyes over Danni's body. Her nipples were as hard and tight as she held her jaw. Those rigid abs would put an athlete to shame. And her hair had been dipped in candy, yet was soft and fluid, capable of entwining about a man's—no, he wouldn't think it.

"Do you know why I rescued you?" he asked. "Why I worked so hard to get you out of the vehicle when I could have left you at the bottom of the river?"

"Hell if I know. I tried to kill you. And worse, I bit you."

"This." He grabbed her wrist and turned it upward. There the words tattooed on her skin read, *come what will*. "I saw this while we were fighting, and remembered it when you were underwater. Vampires don't get tattoos because they heal too quickly, pushes the ink out even as the tattooist is working. Yet this tattoo was clear, modern, and maybe new. I knew you couldn't have been vamp long. Am I right?"

She shrugged, wrapping her free arm defensively across her stomach. "So?"

"So, in that split second of indecision, my heart said, 'She doesn't know what she's doing. She didn't want this.'" He dropped her wrist and looked aside. So difficult not to pull her against his thudding heart and kiss her until their pulses synched. "Am I right?"

"Surprisingly so. You got all that from a flash of tattoo while we were struggling in a fast moving vehicle?"

He shrugged. "I'm a quick study. Pick up details most others miss."

"And yet you didn't know I was a woman."

"Okay, you got me with that one. You being a woman surprised the bloody hell out of me. So what's the deal with you? You haven't been vamp long, have you?"

"Six months. I didn't want this nightmare. I was forced."

"Then what were you doing in the nightclub trying to get close to a pack principal? Do you have any idea how dangerous that was? Talk to me, Danni."

"Does it matter? You're leaving. You're disgusted by me—"

He gripped her shoulders. "Not by you. Never by you. What we just shared? That was incredible. It's just…"

"I know. The blood. Which, in case you haven't figured it out by now, is sort of a necessity when dealing with me."

"Yeah, I get that. And apparently me, too, now." He rubbed the heel of his palm over his temple. "I'm lost here, Danni. I have to quit blaming you for biting me. What's done is done. So what's next? Am I going to need to drink blood often? I don't want to go after mortals. That would kill me. But could I drink your blood? All the time? And that assumes you'd even let me."

He exhaled, and as he leaned forward into the breath, Danni slid her arms around his neck and pressed her body to his like he'd wanted to do moments ago. Felt too good for a burly old bruiser like him to fall into a gorgeous woman's tender embrace, but he wouldn't—couldn't—resist.

"I like you, Hart. More than I should. I'll help you figure this out, if you want me to."

Nodding, he laid his head on her shoulder. Wrapping his arms about her, he pulled her into his world, knowing it would never again be the same, yet hoping she might ignite the spark that would light his way. He wasn't too proud to admit he didn't want to go it alone; he needed her direction.

"Come back inside," she whispered. "We'll talk."

"I have to return to the pack. Need to check in with Caufield and see what's on the schedule for the night. I'm security. Can't be avoided."

"What about this?" She tapped the scar on his neck and Hart shivered at the minute erotic thrill tracing over his flesh. "If they see it...?"

"They'll not be pleased. I'll have to hide it until I suss things about the new me." He kissed her. Her mouth opened for him, giving and taking no more or less than he desired. And curse him, but he desired her. "Can I give you a ring later?"

"Don't call, just come over. I'll be waiting for you."

He wasn't needed for guard duty tonight, yet Hart had gotten an earful from Remy as the pack principal had sat behind his big mahogany desk toying with paperwork. Hart could never decide if it were a ruse to make Caufield look important, because what the hell kind of paperwork did a principal need to do?

They were on the lookout for the vampire who had attempted to assassinate Remy, he'd learned. Assassinate? He didn't think Danni had gone so far, though he'd not asked her exact intentions. She was tough and could hold her own against him, but to *slay* a werewolf? And in a nightclub with guards close by? It didn't fit. But Remy seemed to like that idea, and the pack was circulating word to be on the lookout for a tall vampire dressed in black.

That basically described ninety-percent of the longtooths skulking about Paris. But with his night open, Hart knew exactly how to spend it. And that involved finding a tall vampire who may or may not be dressed in black.

Danni rubbed essential oil on her wrist. It was light and tinged with the scent of spring freesias. It had been a long time since she'd gathered fresh flowers into a bouquet. When a teen, and she'd lived in the US with her family, she'd fancied going into the Weber family's greenhouse business. That was until she'd dated a guy who'd served in Iraq for three deployments. She'd been impressed with his patriotism and utter drive, and had realized it mirrored her own.

After they'd broken it off she'd enlisted. She'd served a deployment in Afghanistan, and had been thinking to sign on for redeployment six months ago when she'd stumbled into Slater in the Exsanguine nightclub while on a trip to Paris. He'd seduced her, lured her to his lair, and hadn't flashed fangs until she'd been lying beneath him, blissfully satisfied. He'd transformed her against her will. Only months later had she pieced together that Slater had been on the hunt for someone like her. Tough, skilled in military training, and alone in the city, away from her family.

The tribe had set her up in this apartment, given her spending money, and generally left her to live and learn. Yet tribe Zmaj did expect her to do their bidding—at the threat of her brother's life.

If she could return to the teenaged Danni and turn her head away from the lure of the military, and the one night in Paris she'd gone out to have drinks and scam on all the sexy men, and instead pick up a pot of soil and fertilizer, she would in a heartbeat. She'd wanted the world once. Now she only wanted her soul.

She hadn't lost her soul after becoming vampire, only, it had been irreversibly damaged and altered beyond recognition. Danni still existed inside this body somewhere. But some days she felt she was losing grasp on the mortal she had once been. She now used other mortals to survive. How wrong was that?

A knock at the door startled her from wiping the kitchen

counter. She'd spent the afternoon baking and the kitchen smelled sweet and chocolaty. Tossing the wash towel into the sink, she pulled her hair forward over a shoulder and checked her clothes. A dusting of flour whitened the hem of her dress, and she frantically wiped it away as she walked to the door. Yes, a slim, fitted jersey dress because she'd wanted to look feminine tonight. Because, hope upon hope, she'd expected company. And hell, she could do the girlie look when she wanted to. Though she was barefoot, high heels were not her thing.

A froth of yellow daisies greeted her in the open doorway, and above that bouquet, Hart's smiling gray-blue eyes.

Danni's heart skipped a beat at sight of the flowers. No guy had ever... Sudden memories of her family's red-and-white painted greenhouse, lush with flowers and shared laughter, threatened to bring an impossible tear to her eye.

Hart sniffed the air. "Is that...?"

"Brownies, fresh from the oven. Want one?"

"Want one?" He dropped his lower jaw. "Uh, yeah?"

"Come sit down and let me treat you. The flowers are pretty."

"I picked them up at a cart by the river on the way here. I don't think I've ever brought a woman flowers before," he said thoughtfully. "These seemed to call out your name. Just silly daisies."

"They are not silly." She took the bouquet and, realizing she didn't have a vase, put them in a glass water pitcher and filled it with cool water. "Thank you. This is the nicest thing a guy has ever given me."

"Can't be true. You must receive gifts from guys all the time."

"Nope," she said abruptly, and pulled out a knife from the drawer. "Guess I'm not worth the effort."

"You're worth my effort." He slid onto the barstool and watched her carve up the pan of brownies.

"And why is that? First you save me from a watery hell, and now flowers. What next?"

He shrugged. "Diamonds?"

Danni tilted her head expectantly.

"I don't know why I said that. Sorry. Diamonds are out of my price range."

"Mine too. Though seriously? Give me a cool leather wristband cut with skulls and I can so rock it."

"Not a frills and lace kind of girl, eh? Though that dress looks amazing on you. Your body is so hard and toned." An approving growl rumbled in his throat.

"I'm former military. We don't do the frill."

"Military? Impressive and believable. You've been trained. Gave me hell in the car the other day."

"Yeah, well, we've moved beyond that, right?"

"Absolutely."

"So, these are my mother's recipe. They'll knock you off your chair." She slid a double-size slab of gooey, moist chocolate onto a plate, along with a fork, and set it in front of Hart.

He made to pick it up with his hands, but she waggled a finger at him. "Nope, what you have there is a heavy-duty Weber brownie. Meant to be eaten with utensils."

Conceding with a tilt of his head, he picked up the fork,

but before digging in, he asked, "Why do you have brownies? I thought vamps…?"

"We don't eat. I know, it's torture to bake and fill the house with this delicious aroma—but not. Brownies were my favorite treat when I was mortal. Now I make them every so often to smell, and, you know, remember."

"I think I can understand the part about missing things and wanting to remember them. They do smell great." He forked in a bite, and then another, and followed with a close-lidded moan. "Oh, Danni, these are ace."

"Does that mean good?"

"Oh, yeah. And they're thick and chewy, like my mum used to make. Mercy." He forked in another bite, and went for another.

She pressed her fingers to his fork. "Slower. Please? Tell me what it's like."

His brow raised and he nodded in understanding. Forking in a bite, Hart chewed the morsel slowly, again, closing his eyes and shaking his head. "The perfect blend of chocolate and chewy that sort of melts in my mouth, yet isn't so gooey it gets stuck in my teeth. And no frosting. Frosting always ruins it."

"I know, right?"

"And look! You gave me an edge piece." He grinned, ear to ear. "I love the edges. You're so good to me."

She propped her chin in hand and watched him devour one piece, and when he pushed his plate toward the pan, she served him another. The look on his face was blissful, orgasmic as he savored the sweet treat, drawing the fork out slowly. With each bite, he shook his head in reverence and smacked his lips more than a few times.

"Walnuts," he muttered between bites. "I love walnuts."

"You can come over for brownies anytime, Hart. Watching you eat them is almost better than sex."

"Whew!" He set the fork on the empty plate. "If you'd have said it was better than sex, I would feel greatly incompetent right now."

"Oh, never, lover. Sex with you is on a scale I don't think has been designed yet."

"Speaking of sex…" He waggled the scarred brow.

Danni lifted her head, suddenly aware of things outside her apartment. Her hearing had increased since her transformation, and she now heard footsteps striding down the hallway. A familiar tingle shivered up her neck, and she knew.

"You have to leave." She grabbed Hart's hand and tugged him off the stool. Where to go? The apartment didn't have a back door.

"Why?"

"He's coming."

"Who?"

She shoved him toward the patio door. Outside, a narrow balcony about a foot wide and railed with wrought iron, jutted over a small, enclosed courtyard below.

"Someone from my tribe. You can't be here. I was supposed to bring him information on your pack. Can you climb up on the roof?"

He leaned over the railing, eyeing the roof above with a

twist at the waist. "Yes, but are you sure? Are you afraid of him? I should stay here and protect—"

A knock on the door sounded.

Danni shoved him outside completely. "Just make yourself gone."

She turned and rushed to the door, pausing to eye the patio doors to ensure Hart could not be seen. He wasn't there. Must have jumped or climbed to the roof. Another knock was cut off as she opened the door and smiled at Slater, the tribe's resident recruiter and token bad guy. He went by a last name, but she'd never heard his first name, and had no interest in getting chummy with the guy who had maliciously selected and stalked her, bitten her and changed her religion forever. Good thing she'd been baptized. Holy objects couldn't harm her, yet the idea of it gave her a shiver.

Slater strode across her threshold, having received the ever-damning invite the day he'd bought her the apartment—and now the invite would hold forever. The spicy scent of his cologne should have had her swooning, but it only sickened Danni. Clad in gray Armani, a smart pair of aviator sunglasses propped on the top of his immaculately coifed head, he sniffed and wrinkled his mouth.

"Brownies?"

Should have gotten rid of the plate and fork on the counter. Hell.

"You eating, Danni?"

"I uh…it reminds me of…better times." She rushed to the counter and grabbed the dishes, sitting them in the sink. "I nibble. Don't you miss mortal food?"

"It's been so freakin' long. Last time I ate, the Nazis were occupying Paris."

She'd never asked how old he was. Most vampires in Zmaj reminisced about the seventeenth and eighteenth centuries.

"So how did things go?" he asked, but she knew he was baiting her, fishing for the truth. He always knew things and waited for her confession.

"I had an issue," she said.

"Yes, I've heard." He sat on the sofa, crossing an ankle over his knee and stretched his arms across the back. "Come over here where I can see you, Danni. We need to talk."

Meekly, she wandered before the sofa, but when she got within his sight she lifted her chin and stood proudly. He may have been able to bring down her confidence, but somewhere inside, her soul was still fighting. She could take this man. She was Dan the Man. But he held a wild card that gave her good reason to hold her punches.

"Remington Caufield has put word out an attempt was made on his life by a vampire."

"There was no assassination attempt," she defended. "That's not what you requested."

"You must have scared the wolf. But you didn't get the info, right? The location of the warehouse?"

"Not yet. I wasn't able to plant the tracking device."

"Not yet," he repeated glumly. "I thought you'd be better than this, Danni, I really did. Inadequate comes to mind. Got something to show you."

He reached inside his suit coat and pulled out a glossy

photograph and held it before him so she had to bend forward to get a good look. Controlling her breath, she stopped the urge to scream at the sight of her brother's smiling face.

"Did you know he's vacationing in Belize?"

She didn't. She'd tried to keep as far from David as possible since her transformation. She knew Slater was keeping tabs on him. To keep her in line.

"Don't you fucking hurt him, Slater."

"You do your job, and your brother will be fine. What the hell? Is that a bite mark on your neck?"

She slapped a palm over her neck. Apparently being bitten by a werewolf left a telltale mark. It should have healed by now.

Slater chuckled. "'Bout time you came around, sweetie. Thought for sure you were going to starve yourself when I first transformed you. Now you're taking as good as you're giving. Good for you. Live the life, I always say. Although...am I interrupting?" He looked about and down the hallway. "That bite mark looks fresh."

"He just left," she managed with a shrug, her palm still pasted to her neck.

"I see. You're spending your time with a lover when you should be working." Slater stood and tucked away the photograph she wanted to grab and keep for herself. He had no right touching an image of one of her family. "Two days," he said. "Get the information, or you'll have to deal with me and my bites." He flashed a fanged smile. "I know you like my fangs, sweetie. But next time? I won't be so gentle. In fact, I'll tear out your carotid if you fail me on this job. Ta."

And he strode out, leaving the door open behind him.

Danni slammed it and beat her fist against the wood. She bit her lip, then winced because a fang cut the thin skin. But at the moment, pain was better than the hurt in her heart…and the awful image of having her carotid torn from her neck.

She had to get the information the tribe wanted, or David would never forgive her for not protecting him from the fate Slater promised.

Chapter Five

She turned to find the werewolf standing outside the patio door, hands fisted at his thighs, and a focused look pinning her through the heart as if with a stake.

Hart could give her the information she needed to save her brother. But that would mean using him for a means she wasn't comfortable with anymore.

Danni rushed over and opened the door. "Did you hear?"

"He's threatening you with your brother's life? Bastard. Is he the one who changed you?"

"He is. He has a sort of control over me. You've seen how tough I can be. But around Slater it's difficult to raise my voice, let alone a fist."

He pulled her into his arms and stroked her hair. "What can I do to help you, Danni? I want to protect you. And if that means protecting your brother—"

"It's too much to ask. I can't. I won't." And yet... "They

need the location of the warehouse where pack Levallois holds the blood games."

"Ah."

Ah, indeed. She bowed her head to Hart's broad shoulder. This man smelled musky and cool, like the wind and sex. Like everything she never knew she wanted until now.

"I can't give you that information," he said.

"I know. You'd betray your pack."

"Then what will you do?"

"I'll figure something out."

"You can't go sniffing about the pack again, Danni. Remy has a high alert out for you. Though, he has no idea you're a woman. I led him to believe the vampire I pursued was a man."

"Thank you. But I have to do this for David, my brother." She stroked the bite scar ruching his neck. "I feel awful about this now," she said. "You're too kind, Hart. Nicest guy I've ever met. My bite must have been the cruelest blow."

"I'm tough. " He clasped her hand and kissed her knuckles. Bowing his head to her neck, he kissed her below her jaw so close to the scar he'd left there. "But I think you soften me. That may be a good thing or a very bad thing."

"I'm pinning it as bad. You need to stay strong for your pack. I don't want to make you weak. Do they know you were bitten?"

"No, but I can't hide it much longer. I haven't given thought as to what I'll do without a pack."

"We have a lot to think about."

He dove into her hair, nuzzling into the thickness and

grasping it to smooth along his cheek. She loved him lingering in her, taking her in, devouring her with his senses. She wanted to do the same with him, to learn him completely, and then start over and learn him again.

"Let's stop thinking," she whispered against his ear, dashing out her tongue to tickle the lobe. "Make love to me, Hart. If you forgive me, and feel you can trust me, show me. Surrender to me."

He dropped to his knees before her. She stroked his mouth, his lips soft and thick, and he tongued her finger.

"I'm yours," he said. Spreading out his arms, he opened himself to her. "Body and...we'll see what happens from there."

She lifted a brow.

"There's a lot involved with having sex with a werewolf, you know. A fine line between mating and sex, if you know what I mean. Your bite bonded us in a strange way, but not like my breed's mating bond. That involves you getting busy with my werewolf."

"That would bond us for life?"

He nodded.

"I'm not ready for that, Hart. I just want to have sex and enjoy the moment."

"Then let's get that dress off you."

The sky had darkened quickly, and rain pattered against the tiled roof. Danni had opened the bedroom window because she loved the sound of rain, and the occasional sprinkle on her sex-heated skin felt like faery kisses.

Skimming her fingers through Hart's short, thick hair,

she thrust her head into the pillow and widened her legs, allowing him access to do as he pleased. And the wolf did what pleased her well. His tongue touched her in ways that ignited the fiery tingle over and over, and when she had climaxed so many times, her breaths coming out in quick gasps, she could but loosen her muscles and accept his unrelentingly sweet torture.

She would never tell him to stop. She was not a fool.

Sometime later, she found herself curled against his body, her head bowed to his softly haired chest, and her knees against his stomach. Wondering what he would look like, feel like, in werewolf form put the question at the tip of her tongue, but she didn't want to ask him to shift, and decided she would see him that way when he trusted her.

Hart kissed her hair and stroked it across her back. "You want me to close the window?" he asked. The rain still sprinkled the bedside, and while the sheets weren't wet, they were getting moist.

"I wish we could have sex in the rain," she whispered. "I want to feel the cool water dribbling over my skin while you pump inside me."

"You have a balcony back here. Isn't it one of those little private courtyards below?"

"Yes, but my neighbor's window is six feet down and to the right. She's old, but curious."

"Let's give her a show."

"Hart." She laughed and bit at his stomach but did not use her fangs.

"I'm serious. It's past midnight. She's probably sleeping, and it's only a half moon on the other side of the building."

He slid off the bed, and his body was silhouetted by the pale moonlight he seemed to think was not shining on this side of the building. His erect cock jutted up, ready and willing. He held out his hand to her and something akin to starshine glinted in his eyes. "I dare you."

"Oh, now you've done it. Dan the Man can never resist a dare." She stood and accepted his hand.

"Dan the Man?"

"That's what they called me in the service. I once crossed a minefield to bring the crew sandwiches on a dare. Could have blown my leg off, but instead I served up the salami."

Hart waggled his hips, which set his cock swinging. "Speaking of serving long thick things you like to taste…"

She grabbed his cock and tugged him outside onto the balcony. They had but a foot of space and the outer wall was smooth fieldstones. Rain spilled through Danni's hair and down her shoulders and back, lifting shiver bumps on her arms, yet she tilted her head, opening her mouth.

"You are a goddess," he said, clasping a wet nipple and squeezing it. "And she is sleeping because there are no lights on in the window below."

"All the better to watch the horny neighbors," Danni said. She licked the raindrops splattering his shoulders and followed them down his tricep and around to the thick nugget of muscle bodybuilders would kill for. "Let's put on a good show. This may be the most action she's seen in decades."

Hart lifted her and she wrapped her legs about his waist, snuggling her mons against the head of his cock. He didn't push inside her, and she liked that he'd learned that about her. She loved it when a man rubbed his cock against her clit. She came much easier with direct contact there than by internal stimulation. All her nerve endings seemed to grasp out greedily and take in every slip and slide and grind. *Gimme, gimme, gimme*, her body whispered. And oh, her werewolf lover gave.

Kissing his lower lip, she lingered there, sucking it in and tracing it back and forth with her tongue. He tasted like rain and salt, and still a bit like the brownie he'd had as a snack a while ago after they'd paused to recoup following their wild gyrations on the bed.

Slicking her fingers through the hair on his chest, she found the hard, tiny nipples and pinched them. Hart growled into her mouth and rocked his hips, rhythmically dragging his swollen cock over her clit.

"I love it when you hurt me," he murmured.

"You do have a tendency toward rough and hard," she agreed. "But you can be oh, so gentle, too. Bruise me, lover," she said. "Let me feel you hard between my legs."

Her shoulders hitting the fieldstones, he supported her against the wall, and increased the rhythm of his hips, sliding against her, teasing her to a shuddering, jittering tangle of nerves and tingles and tightening muscles. Her toes curled over the iron railing and she tilted her hips forward, matching his glide. Hands gliding to his neck, she bracketed his jaws and tilted her head as her fangs descended. She wanted the bite. To bring this climax to a new peak.

When he noticed her struggle, without stopping the motion of hips and cock gliding and sliding and luring her to the edge, Hart nodded, yet it was a weird mix of up and down and side to side.

"What does that mean?" she entreated breathlessly.

"It means…I don't know! I'm so close, Danni. And so are you. But your fangs…the sight of them. Bloody hell." The thick canines lowered in his mouth and he twisted his head as if fighting it, his neck muscles tight and stiff—and then he grinned, relaxing. Surrender. "Yeah. Let's do this."

She required no more permission. Lunging forward, Danni sank her fangs into the hot, wet heat of Hart's neck, in the same spot where she'd first marked him. He growled the deep fuck-yeah growl that usually came when he was *this close* to orgasm. Pulling out her fangs, Danni slurped his purling blood. Sweets for the vampire.

I could do this forever—be a vampire. I could accept it finally. But only with him.

But would he be there to make that happen?

With one final thrust of his molten hot cock against her mons, Hart's teeth entered her neck, and the universe collided with her soul and lured it to a bright and perfect place navigable only by her and her werewolf lover. It hurt sweetly until he pulled out his fangs, and they fed upon one another, there, pinned against the outer wall, the rain splashing their bare skin, and the moon winking over the rooftops.

Yes, forever sounded right.

The sweet, metallic taste of blood on his tongue did not disgust him. Hart closed his eyes and rolled to his back, his palm sliding down Danni's cool belly to rest upon her neatly-trimmed mons as she lay sleeping beside him.

He'd jumped, diving deep into the murk once again. But this time he saw more clearly. He no longer feared what he could become. Because whatever he did become, he'd deal with it. Taking Danni's blood, and in turn, she taking his, was indescribably erotic and about the most amazing thing he'd ever experienced. It was like a runner's high mixed with the ecstasy of orgasm and one's tenth birthday when they got the motorized mini race car they'd always wanted.

So damn cool.

Which meant, he was going to have to get his ducks in a row and figure out what came next with the pack. Alliances had shifted since he'd met Danni. And he liked the side he stood on now. Sure, they hadn't known each other long, but he was in it for the ride, no matter how long it lasted.

And if they mated? Nothing would please him more.

Hart dressed and gave excuses for having to leave. He had duties to the pack, and he didn't want anyone questioning his alliances until he'd worked out his story.

Danni couldn't protest that. She hoped he returned quickly. In his arms she felt safe. It was weird because since Slater had changed her she'd thought to never feel that way again. And who would have thought she would know such a feeling with a werewolf?

Stranger things had happened, but this one was the good kind of strange.

"You going to hang around here today?" Hart asked as

he pulled his shirt on. Danni suspected he was wheedling around to see if she had plans to spy on his pack.

"Yes, wander about the house. Naked. Thinking of you."

"Naked, eh?" He leaned over the bed and kissed her stomach. "And when you think of me, while you're naked, will you do this?" His fingers strayed between her legs.

"There is a chance."

"Then I already regret having to leave. I'd like to watch you thinking about me."

"Hurry back and you might get your wish, lover boy."

"I will." He kissed her again, then pushed from the bed and left the room.

Danni listened as the front door closed and her heart fell. She did have other things to do today and it involved things she was wiser not to tell Hart about.

Chapter Six

Hart knocked on Danni's door, and while he waited, he sniffed the roses he held. Red, because he thought the color signified romance or passion, but more so because he'd been fascinated by the velvety thick petals. He'd like to lay Danni down on these petals, spread across the bed, and make love to her slow and easy until they lost track of time and knew only the sounds of one another's heartbeats.

Silly thoughts for the tough-guy werewolf bruiser? Probably. He'd never let any in the pack know he'd been smitten by a pretty set of legs and pearl-white fangs.

But it was more than that, wasn't it? Beyond Danni's obvious beauty, and the compelling allure of her bite, something more kept Hart returning to her arms and thinking of her when he was not in those arms. She had become a part of him, literally, because her blood was inside him, as was his inside hers. But that wasn't the deepest most intense reason that found him waiting impatiently before her door right now.

While he felt he filled some part of her wanting soul, he knew she had stepped into the part of his life he'd never realized was wanting. He *needed* to be with her, plain and simple. All the time. Watching her, admiring her, learning her, knowing her. Kissing her. Loving her?

He shrugged at his thoughts. Maybe. He couldn't claim more than a few romantic flings, all of which, he'd thought to be in love, and maybe he had been. Love occurred over and over in a person's life. He believed that. But to know the love was meant for you and to hold it gently yet firmly enough not to let it slip away? Now that was the challenge.

Another knock, and he listened carefully but didn't hear anyone inside. She said she'd be home all day and he'd hoped to catch her in the act she'd alluded might happen when she was thinking of him. Even if he missed it, he would request a private show. Was that what she was up to right now?

Smiling at that thought, he tugged out his cell phone. No messages. And he didn't hear any moans on the other side of the door. Maybe she'd stepped out for a few things?

He tried the doorknob. It was locked, but he didn't want to stand around in the hallway waiting. And maybe he could enact his plan to spread around the rose petals?

Slipping out a credit card from his wallet, Hart jimmied the lock, and stepped inside the quiet apartment. Before he could close the door, his phone rang and he eagerly answered, thinking it was Danni. "Hey, sweetie."

"Dude, that is so wrong."

Shit. "Hey, Tony, what's up?"

"I didn't know you had hooked up, man."

"I uh... Well, you know, I have my flings. Why the call?" He rapped the bouquet of roses against the back of the sofa, thankful he'd not gone into some sappy *I adore you and want to watch you masturbate* greeting.

"We got the vamp who was creeping around Remy. And get this. It's a freaking chick."

Hart's pulse stopped, cold and dead as a corpse. The roses scattered at his feet. Grasping the air with his free hand, as if trying to catch himself from a fall, he shook his head. "When did that happen?"

"Few hours ago. We found her snooping around the compound."

Oh, Danni. He clutched his aching chest where his heart pounded for escape. She'd told him she couldn't give up because of her brother. He should have given her the information she needed. That would have kept her away from the compound.

"Hart?"

"I'm here. What are you going to do with her?"

"We tossed her in a cage. Will make for some excitement in a few weeks after the UV sickness kicks in."

The blood games. Bloody hell. No sane punishment for a woman, let alone, a vampire of any persuasion.

"I should be the one to interrogate her," he summoned quickly. Anything to put him close to her, to gain control of this crazy turn of events.

"Maybe. Hart, you didn't know the vamp you pursued was a chick?"

"The suspect was wearing all black, including a skull mask."

"Uh, sure, but—"

"I'll be there soon, Tony." He slapped the cell phone shut and turned to find a man he recognized standing in the open doorway to Danni's apartment. "Slater."

Rushing the vamp, Hart grabbed him by the lapels of his expensive suit and slammed his spine against the door frame. "You bastard! You did this to her!"

"Chill out, wolf. What the hell is a werewolf doing in Danni's home?" He cocked a sly look toward the floor. "With roses?" His slimy gaze moved up Hart's form and landed his neck. "Ah, you've been bitten. Romancing the fang, buddy? No wonder Danni failed this job. She's been playing for the wrong team—" His last word was cut off with another slam against the frame.

"You changed her against her will, and now you threaten her brother's life to keep her in line." He rammed a punch into the vampire's gut and the man bent forward, groaning. Gripping him by the hair, Hart slammed him backward again and fisted his jaw.

Slater yelped and spat his blood at Hart, hitting him on the cheek. The smell of it made him growl. "Rough me up, man. You're signing the brother's death warrant."

"You!" He kneed the vamp in the thigh to effectively pin him. "Will not go near David Weber. Danni has been taken by pack Levallois, and they are going to use her in the blood games."

"No way. I never wanted that for her."

"Yeah, well you sent her in to nose around the pack, what did you expect? She wasn't cut out for what you commanded of her. She's too new, barely comfortable with vampirism. Arsehole."

"Apparently she's comfortable enough to claim herself a wolf."

He slammed a fist into the vampire's gut for changing Danni against her will.

"From this moment," he said forcefully, "you will leave her alone. She's out of your tribe, got that? Danni no longer does your dirty work."

"Who's going to stop me?"

Hart gripped the vamp under the jaw and closed his hand over the windpipe. Wouldn't kill him, but the man sputtered and clawed at the wall behind him as he lifted him from the floor. He willed down his canines and watched the vampire's eyes grow wide at sight of the thick teeth.

"My bite will not get you off," he said. "It'll tear out your veins and rip out a big chunk of your face. Want to try me?"

"Fine! She's out of the tribe. She's worthless anyway."

Hart slammed the vamp hard against the wall, making him choke up more blood. "And if you harm one hair on her brother's head I will rip your head from your neck. Tell me you understand, longtooth."

Slater nodded, wincing as blood drooled from his mouth. "You going to get her out of the games?"

"What happens to Danni isn't your concern anymore." He shoved the vamp out into the hallway, and Slater caught his palms against the opposite wall. "Get the hell out of my air. I'm feeling the werewolf wanting to get loose."

"The bitch is all yours."

"And her brother?" Hart called after the vampire's retreat.

"Never heard of him. Just keep your damned pack from using our tribe members for their sick games, will you?"

If he had such power, Hart would do that. "I'll try," he muttered, and turned to pull Danni's door shut.

Danni paced the cell from the concrete block wall to the double set of bars separating her cell from the next, which was empty. It smelled like sweat and piss down here. One other vampire had been contained two cells down from hers, but he lay on the floor, face down, arms prostrated. No shirt, and his pants were torn to his knees, revealing wicked boils on every part of exposed skin. Every time the UV lights switched on he'd yelp and hiss as his flesh bubbled. She'd only been here a few hours, but she dreaded that sure and painful future.

What a fool to have been grabbed. Tribe Zmaj would never find her now. Slater could care less, she felt sure. She was lost, an unwanted creature plucked from the streets, as invisible as the homeless, and as reviled. No one would look for her.

Rubbing the tattoo on her wrist, she smirked at the words. Come what will? Uh-huh. Well, they wouldn't bring Dan the Man down that easily. She still had some fight left in her. If she went down, she was going to do it with fangs embedded in some werewolf's neck.

Her only hope was Hart. Would he question her absence when he returned to her apartment? She hoped so. But then came the hard part. She'd never expect him to go against his pack and request her release, or even attempt to save her.

The steel door at the top of the basement stairs opened and footsteps shuffled down the concrete steps. Turning and crossing her arms, she would not give them the pleasure of seeing her weakness or fear.

"Make it quick," a man said to someone else. "I got a lunch break in five minutes, and I don't need to spend that babysitting you and the vamp."

A throat cleared and Danni lifted her head. Not going to play their games. Fuck 'em all.

"You found her outside the compound?"

Hart's voice. *Oh yes!* Danni cautioned herself from spinning around and rushing to the bars, eagerly stretching out her arms to him.

"Tony got the jump on her. She's tough, but when threatened with a stake they always crumble. Ha! Crumble into ash, get it? I kill myself."

Out the corner of her eye, she saw the idiot wolf who had tossed her in this cell. Roughly, shoving her to land on her knees and palms, scuffing the skin bloody. He'd made smacking kiss noises and had spat on her.

"Turn around, vampire," Hart said. His voice was steady, calm. He hated her. He had to. "I need some information about why you'd risk your life approaching the pack, twice over. What is your mission?"

He knew what her mission was. Something was up.

Tilting back her head, and rubbing her hands up and down her arms, Danni resisted turning. But if she didn't look at him now, she may never see him again. What color were his eyes? Gray-blue. But could she recall the exact shade now? And his mouth, full and soft; would she ever recall the curve of it as he marked his territory across her skin, or the dark stubble that shadowed his jaw and roughly tickled her when they kissed?

Look now or never again.

Turning, her head bowed, Danni thought she heard Hart exhale. He gripped the iron cage bars and she wanted to grasp his fingers, to touch his warmth, and remember how gentle her mighty wolf had been with her.

"Name," he demanded.

"We got her stats," the other said from the shadows by the stairs. "She's with tribe Zmaj. We're sending scouts out after them. They think they can mess with us? Ha!"

"That's a stupid move," Hart said to the other. "If Caufield thinks he can continue with the nasty blood games he has to lie low, like I always tell him. If he starts a war with the vampires it'll all get blown to hell. Do you want the Council on our arses?"

Good play, Hart. The Council was tightening the reins on the vampire/werewolf relations. That was all Danni knew about the ruling group who oversaw the paranormal nations.

"I don't know nothing about the Council, man. Hurry it up! I'll be at the top of the stairs." The werewolf trudged up the stairs.

And Hart reached through the bars, his fingers grasping. With his other hand, he put a finger to his lips to silence her. And when Danni put her hand in his, she felt everything they had shared the past few days and saw in his eyes what she needed to know—she was still his girl.

"I'm going to get you out of here," he whispered. A glance to the stairs, and then he placed his palm over hers. *I will return.* "Be strong."

She nodded. When he pulled away and walked up the stairs, she felt the first teardrop splash her cheek.

"I thought so," Tony said as he eyed Hart curiously, his focus going to his neck where Hart knew the man saw the bite mark. He hadn't buttoned the shirt, knowing he'd have to face the cold hard facts sooner rather than later. "Remy wants to see you again, man. Right now."

Remy Caufield stalked up to Hart as he entered the office, and slamming a palm against Hart's jaw, tilted his head roughly aside. The keen-eyed principal sneered. "You've been bitten. And you weren't planning on telling me? It was the one we have below, wasn't it?"

Exposed, all sorts of excuses started forming in Hart's brain, and then he shoved them all away. He was no man to lie. To get out of a tough situation he always used his fists. But a fight wasn't going to protect the girl this time around. Above all things, he must protect Danni. He could care less what happened to his own hide.

"She bit me that first night I pursued her. In the middle of a scuffle."

"So you didn't ask for it?" Remy's eyes widened, assessing, and then he nodded. "You would never do that, right?"

"No, I didn't ask for it, but I've since drank blood. The craving was strong. I couldn't—" Perhaps he could have. No, he would never lead the principal to believe she'd forced him to anything. "—*didn't* want to resist."

"Fuck. I thought I taught you better than this."

Remy shoved a hand through his hair and paced before Hart. He was a small man, but smart and strong, despite his size. Hart could take him down in an instant, but he would not. He respected the pack principal even though he didn't agree with everything Caufield felt was best for the pack. "You're tainted now, Hart. You know what that means."

Head bowed and hands clasped before him, Hart offered, "Sorry. If I could change things I would."

"You can go and stake that vampire bitch right now. Maybe that'll stop your blood hunger?"

"I don't think it works that way. And I wouldn't dream of harming Danni Weber."

"Is that so? Why is that?"

"I've learned a few things about her. She was forced to spy on the pack. They're threatening her mortal brother if she doesn't do as the tribe commands. She's an innocent in this mess."

"Innocents don't rip out one of my pack member's necks and change them to something—Christ. You know what this means? Tony!" Remy huffed and slapped a hand onto Hart's shoulder. "Sorry about this, but I have to stand for the pack. And we can't have a tainted wolf living amongst us. Tony, take him below and lock him up. We'll set him lose later tonight after the banishing."

The banishing.

Hart winced as Tony tugged him toward the door, yet he went freely, unwilling to resist when he deserved what was coming to him. Banishment was no picnic. It would scar him physically. But emotionally? He had no idea what to do with himself if the pack banished him.

At sight of Hart being led toward the cage opposite hers, Danni gripped the iron bars. He walked inside the small cell of his own free will, and watched as the other wolf locked him inside.

"Sorry, man," the wolf said, and turned to spit at her. "Bitch ruined our best wolf."

"What the hell?" she asked after the stairway door had slammed shut. "Hart?"

"They know I've been bitten and the principal is brassed off over the whole situation. They'll banish me later. Remy wants me tucked away down here for safe keeping until the pack can sharpen their talons and gather the wolfsbane."

"Wolfsbane?" That didn't sound good. Danni swallowed a reedy moan. "This is all my fault! Look what I've done to you."

"Danni, I wish you could get beyond that."

Get beyond ruining his life? Was the wolf on something? Maybe the UV rays they kept flashing down here had affected his thinking.

"Right now," Hart said, "we have to worry about how we're going to get you loose." He tested the bars, wincing as he pulled at them and they didn't move. "Made to keep in vampires. Very strong. Iron strafed with titanium, I'm sure."

"Yes, but what about a fully shifted werewolf?" Danni offered absently, stunned he carelessly disregarded his own danger.

He tilted his head, eyeing her with a sexy grin that melted her core and made her want to kiss him. "You may have something there."

An electronic sizzle preceded the metallic clank of the overhead UV lights being switched on. The vamp two cells down yelled and moaned as his skin sizzled under the deadly rays. Thrusting her hands over her face, Danni cried out too. This time it hurt. The light felt stronger than a thousand suns and her skin burned.

"I can't let this happen to you," she heard Hart say. "Take this!"

The sleeve of his shirt landed on the base of the outer bars of her cage. Danni crept over to it.

"Put it over your head and cover as much of your skin as you can. Crouch down. I'm going to get you out of here, Danni, if it's the last thing I do."

And the wolf howled, declaring to all who would listen he would not be silenced.

Danni pulled the shirt over her head but her bare legs were exposed still and the pain was fierce. She panted and crouched, trying to protect as much of her body as possible. Behind her, she heard bones crack and Hart's growling moans as his body shifted. Peering out from under the shirt, she watched her lover shift into the half man, half beast werewolf within seconds. She had hoped her first sight of him like that would have happened in a different situation, in a more trusting atmosphere, at the least.

But she couldn't argue the appearance of her rescuing knight, once again.

A slash of his talons across the wall cut the concrete block into dust. The werewolf charged the iron bars, gripping them, and they bent.

The heat on Danni's legs seared into her veins, and she gasped as her thoughts blacked out.

Chapter Seven

Danni woke in her apartment, lying on the sofa, a half dressed man standing over her, his gray-blue eyes intense and worried. Relief spread though her like a swig from a whisky bottle. "You got me out." She pulled Hart down to kiss, but after a mere touch of their mouths he pulled away.

He paced before her, shaking his fists near his thighs. "I can't stay. I just wanted to make sure you woke and are okay."

"I'm good now I'm home. But your pack—what will they do to you?"

"They let me escape too easily. I suspect they'll be tracking me soon enough. I have some clothes in your bedroom." He marched into the room and called out to her. "I have to go back!"

Danni sat and smoothed a palm over her forearm, which was tender to touch. The UV lights in the compound had given her a nasty sunburn, and she wondered how long it would take for her superfast healing capabilities to kick in. Didn't matter right now.

Hart strode out, tugging on a T-shirt. She grabbed his shirt tail and stopped him before he could touch the doorknob.

"You can't go back. They'll kill you. Then they'll come after me."

"They are not going to touch you ever again. I'll talk to the principal. I'll make sure pack Levallois forgets Danni Weber exists."

"Even if that was possible, what about you?"

Hart sighed, heaving out his broad chest. "I've been bitten, Danni. In their eyes I don't belong in the pack anymore."

"Then stay here with me," she pleaded. "Start new."

"Doesn't work that way. The pack needs to have their blood, so to speak. I've been slated for banishing." Taking her hands in his, he kissed the palms of them, nuzzling his face against her warmth. "If I let it happen, then we can be free."

"But you mentioned wolfsbane. Won't that kill you?"

"Not if I'm lucky."

"Hart." She bracketed his face with her hands and kissed him long and deep. She'd thought to have lost him while surrounded by iron bars in the pack compound. Now they had a second chance. Would that chance be taken away as quickly as they'd earned it? "I need you to return so I can fall in love with you."

He took her hand and opened it, palm up, and pressed

his palm over hers, their silent language between one another. "I'll return. I promise."

Remy Caufield had listened to Hart's request they forget the female vampire's transgression against the pack in exchange for his willingly submitting to the banishing. While Hart knew he didn't have a leg to stand on with that argument—the banishing would occur whether he submitted or not—he hoped a glimmer of compassion resided within Caufield.

"She did you no harm," he reminded as the principal paced before him. Hart had been shackled at ankle and wrists the moment he'd stepped onto the compound's grounds. Silver, wrapped with leather. The thin manacles would contain him without killing him. "She won't come after the pack. I've made sure her tribe drops her. They were the force behind her spying. If anything, tribe Zmaj is the true enemy."

"Are you in love with a vampire, Hart?"

"I, uh…" Didn't think so. *I need you to return so I can fall in love with you.* On the other hand, hell yes, he could love her. He'd begun to consider mating with Danni. That was as extreme as it got in the emotional department, and he wasn't about to turn away from it. "Does it matter? After tonight, Christian Hart does not exist to pack Levallois."

"True. I hate losing my best man."

Hart shrugged. "Tony is a good guy. He's loyal, too."

"You've some integrity, Hart. Talking up your successor while your future lands in the crapper. That's what I always liked about you. You've grown into a fine man—and yet... You seriously crave blood?"

Hart nodded. "It's pretty intense."

"That disgusts me."

As it should. But it no longer disgusted Hart, and that was all that mattered to him.

"Leave her alone, please?" Hart asked.

With a nod of his head, Remy silently consented. Then he set the two guard wolves to take Hart to the room where they held the blood games.

The stone walled room smelled of blood and not in an appealing way that Hart could get behind with his new-found craving. He was unshackled, and when the guard wolves shoved him toward an iron frame riveted into the stone wall, Hart said, "No. I don't need to be bound." He gripped the iron bar mounted a foot higher than his head.

The wolves looked to Remy, as other pack members entered the room. The principal nodded. "Leave him as he wishes. He won't run."

Behind him, Hart heard the pack begin to shift to werewolf form, and he knew he was not allowed that same blessing. No, not a blessing. He must take this in were form. It was one small mercy against the wolfsbane. If he were in werewolf shape, the wolfsbane could prove deadly. In this form? It may cripple him, and would most certainly scar him.

When the growls and low murmurs of a dozen pack wolves loomed behind him, Hart squeezed the iron bar hard and centered his thoughts on the one thing he wanted most—Danni. Then he abruptly blocked her from his mind.

The last thing he wanted to associate with banishing was the soft and lovely woman who had stolen his heart.

"Begin!" Remy commanded.

The first set of talons slashed Hart's back, carving into his flesh and nicking bone in the process. The wolfsbane the wolves would carefully dip their talon tips into burned like acid. He grit his molars and growled, fighting to contain a yell. Nothing in his life had hurt worse.

The second wolf stepped forward to deliver another knee-bending blow. Hart huffed and clutched the iron bar so hard, it bent. Another, and another. By the ninth talon, his blood spilled down his back and soaked his jeans. The wolfsbane felt like fire from Hell.

The final wolf, the pack principal, stepped beside Hart. Huffing and panting, Hart lifted his head proudly and met his former leader's gold, wolfish eyes with his own. Caufield slashed his talons across the back of Hart's head, forward over his ear and neck, and drew it out through his cheek.

Releasing the bent iron bar, Hart fell to his knees and caught his palms on the floor puddled with his blood.

The day after Danni had been rescued from the pack compound by Hart, she paced the floor of her apartment before the patio doors. Outside rain pummeled the city, and she was thankful for the lack of sun—and she was not. Rain reminded her of making love with Hart. Would they ever be so close again? It had been over twenty-four hours since he left her for his banishment.

"Where is he? He doesn't answer his phone. They've killed him, I know it."

Clutching her fists to her chest, she felt what must have been the thousandth tear fall across her cheek and regretted ever wishing she could cry. She needed to know Hart was alive. If he didn't ever want to see her again, she would have to deal, but she couldn't begin to get over him until she knew he was safe.

She couldn't return to the compound. That would be suicide. She couldn't contact her tribe because Hart had told her to stay away from them. He'd made it clear to Slater he was to stay away from her and David. Yet her new freedom came at an insurmountable price.

Over and over this morning, she'd gone through possible scenarios for banishing. It could not be good, certainly not pleasant, and definitely painful.

"Oh, Hart, please be safe."

At the very least, alive. The pack wouldn't kill him for something she had done to him, would they?

They kidnapped vampires and forced them to fight to the death, of course they would be sanguine about killing one of their own.

On the kitchen counter sat a mixing bowl and inside of it, two uncracked eggs. She'd briefly considered going through the mundane motions that usually made her feel better. But really? Not this time. Brownies were not going to save her man.

A knock on the door set the hairs on her body straight up. Danni ran and opened it to find Hart standing there, his grin slightly crooked, but he was smiling.

She leaped into his arms, wrapping her legs about his waist and hugged him tightly. Cheek pressed against his neck he felt warm and inviting. Alive.

He walked inside and closed the door behind them, leaning against the wall, not letting her go, and whispering gentle things like, "I missed you. I'm here. I'm never going to leave."

"I thought you were dead." She clung, unwilling to let go for fear he might slip away. "You didn't answer your phone."

"I needed to…heal a bit before I saw you. Danni, look at me." He set her on the back of the sofa, and only then did she finally look at his face.

His bright gray-blue eyes fixed to hers. His mouth was that soft thickness she loved to feel pressed against her mouth, her skin. But there, at the corner of his lips, the skin tugged toward his cheek. And she traced the thick, angry scar slashed from mouth, across his cheek, over his ear, and cutting through the side of his skull. Another dashed his jaw, red and vulgar in its thickness. And at his neck, yet another.

"Ohmygod. What did they do to you?"

"I'll heal, but the scars will remain. Wolfsbane," he said. "It's not a werewolf's favorite herb."

"But—so cruel." Her fingers shook as she reached for the scar at his jaw. He did not flinch from her touch. He wanted her to look at him, to see him now. Changed. Altered. *Because of her.* "Doesn't change things between us," she said bravely.

Did it? No. He was a handsome man. The scars? They

were ugly. Angry. But they proved his honor. He had purposefully returned to the pack, knowing this would be his fate, because he'd wanted a clean ending between them, and he'd wanted to ensure her safety.

"Does this mean I get to fall in love with you now?" she asked.

He bowed his head and looked aside. "Can you love this, Danni? The scars aren't going away. I'm forever marked."

"I think it's too late to ask that." She stood and kissed him. Their bodies melded together, finding a place they'd created with their heartbeats. "Because I already love you. And I think you've taken these awful marks because you love me."

"Hell yes, Danni. I love you."

"Then tell me we can be together."

"Always. You really love me?"

"Yes." She kissed the scar on his cheek. "Oh, how can I heal you?"

"Your touch makes the pain go away. Your love will keep it away. God, Danni, I want you to be my mate."

"That means me and you, forever?"

"Yes. Is that something you can imagine? The two of us? Maybe get a cottage out in the country. I've been craving the fresh air and some land to let my wolf out to roam."

"Sounds amazing. Can I plant a garden?"

"You like to grow things?"

"My mortal family owns a nursery. I've always wanted to do the same. It's a missed dream, you might say."

"Yes, to a garden."

"And yes, to letting the werewolf run wild." She kissed

him and had to caution herself to do so gently because she sensed his wounds did still pain him, no matter what he said. "So if I'm your mate…" She knew how it worked with werewolves, and mating was serious bonding stuff. "Does that mean…?"

"You'd have to let my werewolf shag you, which could get hairy and a bit, well…vigorous. More so than usual. Still interested?"

She licked her lips and tilted her head, gazing into his gorgeous, giving eyes. Placing her palm flat against his palm, she said, "Sounds like a dare I can't resist."

A month later, Danni strode down the gravel road, which curved before the little château Hart had found for them on the outskirts of Toulouse. They were a long way from Paris, and she didn't miss the big city at all. An old vineyard fronted the property, and Hart had big plans to resurrect the vines and learn about crafting wine. Though the snow had begun to fall, Danni was already dreaming about the garden she would plant behind the château come spring. She'd plant flowers to attract butterflies and bees, and vegetables so she could cook stews and tarts for her lover.

She found she had but to drink from a mortal only every other week, so a quick trip into the city was required, but she also got some grocery shopping done at the same time. Domesticity felt marvelous, and her future looked incredible. While she mourned her mortal family, she had decided it best to never see them again. David might accept her truth, but she didn't want to burden him with that. The Webers would believe her dead, a girl gone missing while on vacation in Paris, which was going to be tough enough for them all.

A brown wolf loped across the field toward her, tongue lolling after a long run through the nearby forest. Danni bent to greet the gregarious wolf as it trundled over and licked her cheek. She smoothed her fingers through its coat, noting it had grown thicker for the winter months. He toppled her onto the snowy ground.

"All right! I surrender. But I don't have a stick to throw, you silly wolf.

The wolf tugged at the hem of her shirt, carefully, yet she got the message.

"You think so, eh?" She sat and brushed the snow from the elbows of her sweater. "It's getting cold out. How about I meet you out back and we can get busy in the mud room?"

The wolf barked and took off toward the château.

And Danni stood to walk back home and rendezvous with her lover, who would be in werewolf form and waiting by the time she reached the château. When shifted into werewolf shape, Hart was half man, half wolf, and horny as hell. Surprisingly, he took her as gently as was possible in that form, and had never once accidently clawed her. They had bonded for life, and Danni couldn't wait to have his babies.

Increasing her pace as she neared the house, Danni pulled off her sweater, exposing her bare skin to the chill air. Her nipples tightened. Arousal warmed her skin. She walked through the front door, dropping her sweater, and unbuttoning her jeans as she raced toward the mud room.

Hart's howl echoed through the plastered walls of their

new home, setting an old iron chandelier to a titter. Licking her lips, Danni slunk into the mudroom, and touched the furred shoulder of her werewolf lover.

"Just you and me, my big bad wolf." Her fangs lowered as the wolf turned her around and pushed her against the wall. She'd bite him soon enough.

And then he would bite her.

Life could not be more perfect.

* * * * *

COURAGE OF THE WOLF
BONNIE VANAK

Bonnie Vanak fell in love with romance novels during childhood. While cleaning a hall closet, she discovered her mother's cache of paperbacks and started reading. Thus began a passion for romance and a lifelong dislike for housework.

After years of newspaper reporting, Bonnie became a writer for a major international charity. She travels to destitute countries such as Haiti to write about famine, disease and other issues affecting the poor. When the emotional strains of her job demanded a diversion, she turned to her childhood dream of writing romance novels.

She lives in Florida with her husband, Frank, and two dogs, where she happily writes books amid an ever-growing collection of dust bunnies. She loves to hear from readers. Visit her website www.bonnievanak.com or e-mail her at bonnievanak@aol.com.

Chapter One

Just another day in a tropical paradise filled with demons.

Right.

If only it was just a typical day and not the very one he'd been dreading.

Ambling backwards on the roadside, Michael Anderson scanned Florida's Alligator Alley for a silver Lexus. As always, Sabrina Kelly was late. The Draicon werewolf would be late for her own funeral.

The thought sobered him.

Minutes later, Michael pushed a hand through his long, ragged hair as Sabrina's car pulled off the road. He breathed in her scent of fresh lavender as the Draicon werewolf hurried toward him. Dressed in a pink sweater set and a floral skirt, she looked like spring. Cut razor straight, her black hair swung just below her jawline. Wide, sea-green eyes shone with intelligence.

When she threw herself into his arms, he hugged back, feeling a lump rise in his throat. The vision came to him again. Blood. Death. Sorrow.

Michael set her back down on her feet. As much as he wanted to use his powers as an Immortal Justice Guardian to direct destiny, he could not. Punishment would be severe if he broke Guardian laws. He'd already broken a big one to buy Sabrina time.

Years ago, when he was still a Draicon werewolf, he'd made a promise to keep her safe. The burning need to protect her had never stopped. It wasn't love, but a fierce admiration of her strong spirit and honoring the deep friendship they'd shared in the past.

"Why did you want me to pick you up on this road? Forget how to dematerialize?" she asked.

He shrugged. "I like walking. And I thought it would be nice to ride with you in the Lexus to your grandparents' anniversary party."

"You knew I was taking the Lexus and not the Expedition? Oh, of course, you know everything." She shook her head. "Even what type of underwear I have on."

"I don't know everything."

When she turned, he flicked his fingers. A microburst of air sent the fabric swirling upward.

"White lace," he noted with a grin. "Very nice."

"Michael!" she scolded him with a smile.

A faint blush raced across her cheeks. It was like watching the sun chase away the night. Enchanted, he watched her moisten her pink lips. What would her petal-soft mouth feel like beneath his as he took her, hard and fast?

He swallowed hard at the startling, sexual thought. Sabrina was off-limits.

He was a Phoenix, an Immortal Justice Guardian who'd died and been reborn to his powers. Michael patrolled the earth, doling out justice and destroying predators of paranormal creatures. He'd succeeded at his job until a year ago, when the Hellfire demon Ambrosis slaughtered Sabrina's parents and five siblings as Sabrina tried to save them. Her family had been heading to visit her grandparents when the demon attacked them as they took a brief respite from driving.

If he could, he'd die to keep her safe. But he couldn't die again. Sabrina had to face her own demon. Guardian laws demanded he must not interfere.

"Let's go," he muttered.

The sun sinking toward the horizon warned they were running out of time.

Inside the car, his senses drank in her scent as if he were still a Draicon werewolf. Trees, palms and scrub brush passed in a blur as the car sped toward Florida's west coast.

"Michael, you're the only friend who still bothers with me. Thank you," Sabrina told him.

"I'm not just your friend, Brie. I've watched over you since I became a Justice Guardian. You've shut yourself off from the world."

She blinked hard. "If not for you, I'd never have done this. I can't bear the memories."

White showed on her knuckles as her fingers tightened on the steering wheel. "All I can recall is fighting. Pain, and then nothing. Nothing except waking up to see my family was dead."

"You still don't remember what happened to you?"

"It's a blur, except I have the scar to remind me. I have nightmares about Ambrosis, and this voice keeps telling me I must have the courage to face him again. But ever since I lost my family, I'm terrified of something else happening."

Michael looked away. "You should pay attention to your dreams. Often, they contain messages."

She inhaled deeply. "Dreams are just dreams. Let's not talk about it. It's hard enough for me to drive on this road again. I haven't been this way since Ambrosis killed my family."

A fist of guilt slammed into his guts. He stared out the passenger's side window.

I'm sorry, Brie, but I must do this. It's my duty as a Justice Guardian.

Familiar landmarks appeared on the roadside. Sabrina's hands shook. "This is the place. If I'd never insisted on Dad stopping so we could hunt in the swamp, they'd still be alive. I'm going to speed up...."

"Pull over," he told her.

"Here?"

"Now."

Blood drained from her face, but she steered the Lexus onto the narrow shoulder.

"Stay here," he ordered, hating her fear, smelling it like burnt wood.

He got out. Clouds the color of lead hung low in the

gathering dusk. He breathed in the fertile scent of dank earth. The task before him lay on his wide shoulders like twin weights. A haunting loneliness gripped him.

He hated this part of the job.

In the canal paralleling the Alley, an alligator swam by in silence, its eyes peeking through the dark brown water in cool indifference.

Michael vaulted over the chain link fence, and walked a path through cypress and pine trees until he reached a tree island surrounded by shallow swamp water. At the northwest side, he touched the earth where a great battle had been raged. Sorrow squeezed his insides.

From his backpack, he withdrew a single white gardenia, the blossom fresh and preserved by magick. He laid it on the ground where the blood of Sabrina's family had been spilled.

A mocking crow cackled overhead. Michael fisted his hands as he walked to a small pool. No animals ever drank from this vile water—the home of Ambrosis. Michael had imprisoned him here after the battle that claimed Sabrina's family.

Hellfire demons were attracted to paranormal beings possessing enormous integrity, strength and courage. They siphoned off those qualities for energy then killed the victim.

Beneath his palm, the dark water rippled. His immortal senses "saw" Ambrosis. With his index finger, Michael traced a sacred pattern in the muck below the shallow water. The ground vibrated.

An eerie, haunting scream rent the air. Disturbed by

the sound, a great blue heron resting in a nearby cypress tree flew off.

The face of Sabrina's nightmares appeared in the pool. Nasty laughter echoed through the swamp. The demon vanished below the water.

It was done, consequences be as they may. His duty as a Guardian was fulfilled.

"Forgive me, Brie," Michael whispered.

He stood, dusting off his hands on his jeans. Shouldering his pack, he headed toward Sabrina's car, but not before the earth gave a mighty shudder and the demon's triumphant roar echoed through the silent clearing.

Chapter Two

Ribbons of violet and rose laced the skies over the tranquil Gulf of Mexico. Palm branches fluttered in the cooling breeze. On the sand, a man drove a tractor, picking up turquoise umbrellas and chair cushions. She'd been here a full day, yet could not relax in the serene tropical atmosphere.

Sabrina braced her hands on the hotel railing and stared down at the Tiki Bar three stories below. Her grandparents' gray-haired pack mingled with each other, clinking glasses as they watched the sunset.

Her grandparents waved up at her. Intense feelings rushed through her as she waved back. Losing her family had left her cold and empty, as dead as those she'd lost. But when she'd emerged from her car, her grandparents engulfed her in hugs and kisses, reminding Sabrina that she was still loved. She hadn't seen them since losing her family. Nathan and Martha were the only family she had left and she would never allow anything to happen to them.

Michael stood in the circle's center. A hank of dark brown hair hung over his forehead. He wore a blue-and-red Hawaiian shirt, navy shorts and nothing on his feet. His long, leanly muscled body was tall, filled with enormous strength and his face had a hard edge about it, contrasting with a mouth almost too sensual for a man.

When he was still a Draicon werewolf, Michael's eyes had been brown. After he became a Justice Guardian, his eyes burned a silvery blue, hinting at his enormous powers.

Sabrina's hands trembled. Flutters in her belly intensified into something deeper. *Okay, you're smitten with a guy who's not only immortal, but can kill everyone here by blinking.*

She'd been friends with Michael all her life, ever since he was a Draicon werewolf farming the land next to her pack's. His sunny smile and boyish charm masked his quiet strength and fierce loyalty. But her girlish crush on him was useless. Sabrina had resigned herself to adoring friendship.

Shortly after her eighteenth birthday, Michael died while fighting a demon that tried to kill her. He was reborn as a Phoenix, a Justice Guardian.

Sabrina rubbed her clammy palms, stepped back into the room. She closed the sliders and shivered. Ever since her family's death, it seemed like she could never get warm enough.

She went downstairs.

Approaching Michael, she spotted the red-and-blue

phoenix mark on his throat. Clutching a sword in its claws, the bird rose from a bed of ashes. The symbol of a Justice Guardian.

Sabrina accepted the imported beer Nathan handed her. The beer tasted like cold, wet ashes. Ever since surviving Ambrosis' attack, food and her favorite beverage held no appeal. She shivered again.

Her grandfather swirled his scotch and soda. "Brie, we're celebrating life, enjoy yourself. Liven up!"

Martha kissed her cheek. "I'm so glad you're with us, honey. It's a miracle you're here. How about running with us later?"

"I don't feel like shifting, Grandma," she said. "The last time I did, my family died. They died despite the fact..."

She didn't finish, knowing her words would accuse the Phoenix standing next to her. The Gray Wolves looked troubled, as if she'd dropped a bomb into the middle of their merriment.

Michael gently clasped her wrist. The contact was electrical, making her shiver with pleasure this time. He led her to the lee of a sturdy palm. Beyond the gently sloping beach, the sun descended into green Gulf waters. Pregnant with rain, purple clouds scudded across the distant horizon.

"Brie, tell me what you want to know. I've only been waiting nearly a year for you to ask."

Silence draped the air between them. Finally, she summoned her courage.

"You've saved thousands of lives. Why couldn't you save my family?"

He glanced away. "I tried, but Tristan locked me in a

cell. I knew what would happen, but my mentor said I could not interfere with destiny."

She blinked away hot tears. "I thought you forgot about me."

The silver blazed in his blue eyes with fierce intensity. "Understand this. I'd never forget about you."

"I wish I had died that day. At least I'd have been with my family."

The beer bottle flew out of his hand as he hugged her in a grip that sucked away her breath. Michael set her back, his expression grim. "I sense your fear, Brie. What's wrong?"

"I had a hallucination yesterday about Ambrosis. This voice kept telling me I had to fight him like I had before or something horrible will happen. I feel like I'm losing my damn mind. It took everything I had to risk coming here, but I didn't want to disappoint Nathan and Martha."

"Maybe it's a warning."

Sabrina lifted her troubled gaze to his. "I can't face Ambrosis again, Michael. He killed my whole family because I insisted on hunting through his territory."

"You didn't know it was his territory," he said gently. "Hellfire demons attack for the pure joy of killing innocents. You fought him with everything you had."

"And now I'm terrified of him. What if he kills someone else I love?"

She glanced at Nathan and Martha. "All I have left are the Gray Wolves. They can't fight back, they're elderly and not strong enough."

Michael's jaw tightened. Not a good sign.

"You did lock Ambrosis away, right?"

"The demon will only arise when I release him," he agreed.

"Good. I'd die if anything happened to my grandparents and I don't have the strength to fight anymore."

"You have enormous inner strength, Brie." He cupped her cheek. "I believe in you and I always will."

The contact between them felt sizzling and intense. Sabrina put her palm on his chest. Feeling the heavy muscles there, the silky hairs springy to her touch. She slid her fingers across his firm chin, the dimple clefting it, up to the soft texture of his lower lip.

Tracing his mouth, she murmured, "You deserve someone to take care of you, Michael. Don't you ever get tired of saving the world?"

He quivered beneath her touch, studying her with hot intensity. As she reached up on tiptoes to kiss him, Michael stepped back. For a minute his eyes mirrored her own longing. Then they shuttered.

"Don't, Sabrina," he said quietly. "We can't do this."

Humiliated, she turned her head. Why couldn't she ever stop reaching out for him? "Sorry to bother you," she muttered.

"Brie, you never bother me."

Two hands settled gently on her shoulders, turning her back to him. "I just don't want to hurt you. I'd do anything to keep you from being hurt."

Kissing him and finding out he didn't feel the same sexual attraction would hurt, she admitted. She'd already lost far too much. Emotional distance was necessary. He was an immortal who could break her heart. If only she'd found her destined mate, she'd have someone to help her regain her life.

"I suppose I should go back to finding my destined mate. I've even slept with a few Draicon just to see if they were the one." Sabrina intended her bold confession to serve as a jab for Michael's rejection.

She heard Michael let out a low hiss in response and then raised her chin.

"I don't sleep around. That's not me. But sometimes I get so lonely…." Damn. She hated saying this, hated the thin, trembling tone of her voice.

"You're never alone, Sabrina."

His reassurance nearly broke her. She shoved the beer at him. "I'm going for a swim."

She felt his gaze burn through her sweater as she headed upstairs to change.

Minutes later, she stood at the diving board. The tangerine bikini was old and she wished she'd bought a one-piece. Slashed across her belly was the angry pink scar left by Ambrosis when he'd tried to gut her.

Sabrina went to dive.

The pool went dark red as it filled with blood.

She pitched in headfirst. Coldness and death washed over her. Sabrina kicked upward, her eyes tightly shut. She broke the surface. Treading water, she opened her eyes.

The bodies of her parents, brothers, sisters floated in the viscous liquid.

A high scream tore from her throat. Then the images

disappeared, replaced by children laughing and splashing in the clear blue water. Sabrina blinked.

I'm going crazy.

She flailed her arms again, saw Michael looking at her.

Help me, she mouthed silently, before submerging into the depths.

Chapter Two

Ribbons of violet and rose laced the skies over the tranquil Gulf of Mexico. Palm branches fluttered in the cooling breeze. On the sand, a man drove a tractor, picking up turquoise umbrellas and chair cushions. She'd been here a full day, yet could not relax in the serene tropical atmosphere.

Sabrina braced her hands on the hotel railing and stared down at the Tiki Bar three stories below. Her grandparents' gray-haired pack mingled with each other, clinking glasses as they watched the sunset.

Her grandparents waved up at her. Intense feelings surged through her as she waved back. Losing her family left her cold and empty, as dead as those she'd lost. When she'd emerged from her car, her grandparents folded her in hugs and kisses, reminding Sabrina that still loved. She hadn't seen them since losing her

Chapter Three

After surviving a vicious attack by a Hellfire demon, Sabrina was drowning in eight feet of water and struggled to break the surface for air.

She felt strong arms grasp and haul her upward. And then surfaced with a series of violent coughs. Air sluiced through her lungs in biting gasps.

Michael towed her to the edge, climbed out and hoisted her from the pool as if she weighed no more than cotton candy. Her grandparents hurried over.

Sabrina couldn't stop shaking. Michael held her, smoothing back her hair as Martha wrapped a towel around her. "Easy," he murmured. "It's okay now."

Nathan's eyes went wide. When he saw she was all right, his shoulders sagged with obvious relief. "Honey, I thought I taught you better than that when I gave you swimming lessons. I hate the idea of losing you again…it kills me."

When he was still a Draicon, Michael's eyes had been brown. After he became a Phoenix, his eyes burned a silvery blue, hinting at his tremendous powers.

Sabrina's hands trembled. Flutters in her belly intensified into something deeper. *Okay, you're smitten with a guy who's not only immortal, but can kill everyone here by blinking.*

She'd been friends with Michael all her life, ever since he was a Draicon werewolf farming the land next to her pack's. His sunny smile and boyish charm masked his quiet strength and fierce loyalty. But her girlish crush on him was useless. Sabrina had resigned herself to adoring friendship.

Shortly after her eighteenth birthday, Michael died while fighting a demon that tried to kill her. He was reborn as a Phoenix, a Justice Guardian.

Sabrina rubbed her clammy palms, stepped back into the room. She closed the sliders and shivered. Ever since her family's death, it seemed like she could never get warm enough.

She went downstairs.

Approaching Michael, she spotted the red-and-blue

"The pool... I saw bodies. My family," she whispered.

Michael gave her a long, thoughtful look. "What do you remember about their deaths and your attack?"

The familiar red haze fogged her brain. Cold seeped into bones. "I can't remember!"

He wrapped the towel tight around her. "Let's get you warm."

Sabrina leaned against him as he guided her up the stairs. In her room, he turned on the shower and gestured her toward the bathroom. But when her knees sagged, he undressed her and gripped her shoulders gently.

"Can you stand?" he asked.

She couldn't allow herself to be weak. "I can do this. Thanks."

A breath hissed out of him as he glanced at her naked body. Michael muttered a low curse and left.

The hot shower chased away the icy chill penetrating her bones. When she emerged, clean clothing sat on the counter.

After dressing, she found Michael on her sofa. Sabrina sat beside him.

"I can't go on like this. I feel as if I'm coming apart. These hallucinations are more frequent."

"Have you considered they're not hallucinations, but something else? A manifestation of the past?"

"Or the future? I'm not a precog. I wish I were that strong."

"You are. You battled a Hellfire demon with only werewolf magick, except you forgot the details."

"Meaning I have lost my mind?" She gave a brittle

laugh. "I don't know where I belong anymore or if any of this is real."

His gaze was steady as he regarded her. "You're here now, with me. This is real."

The promise of sensual pleasure shone in his eyes. Reading his expression, Sabrina moistened her mouth. Instinct told her Michael wanted her as badly as she wanted him. Maybe they could be more than friends.

Go with your gut.

When he bent his head toward her, she leaned close. Warmth poured through her. Every cell tingled with awareness and anticipation. He was going to kiss her, finally. She closed her eyes, waiting with breathless eagerness.

And felt him pull away.

For years she'd fantasized about his kiss. Now she sensed his hunger, felt her own, yet he still pushed her away.

"Michael, what's the deal? You keep acting like you want to kiss me. Why can't you kiss me? This is so unfair."

"I'm a Phoenix, assigned to watch over you. We're forbidden from sexual intimacy with our charges." His voice went husky with desire. "If I were still Draicon, you'd be naked in my bed right now."

So her instinct *was* right. He did feel attraction for her. For the first time, she felt hope. Sabrina pressed her palm against his muscled chest. "So is this rule the only reason you avoid kissing me?"

"That and the fact that I'm an immortal and my desires run strong. You might not be able to take exactly what I want to do with you."

At the hint of dark passion in his voice, the space between her legs became swollen with need. "I want you, Michael, I've always wanted you. Even before you became a Guardian, I thought we could have something between us. This is so frustrating."

Silver flashed in his eyes as if his powers surged. "I'm sorry, Brie. I forgot myself. Around you, I have the tendency to lose control. I want..."

She touched his mouth. "Want what?"

He stood up, every muscle rigid. "Wanting and having are two separate things."

She watched him pace to the doorway, his hand on the knob. "Good night, Brie. Get some sleep...and try to remember what happened when you fought Ambrosis. It's more important than you realize."

Before she could puzzle over his words, Michael vanished.

Sabrina tossed and turned all night, giving up the fight to sleep as dawn broke. After showering, she took her coffee onto the balcony. A warm wind blew off the Gulf, sending lacy whitecaps tossing their heads. The sky was a sharp, clear blue.

Sitting on the sand with his back against a tall palm tree, Michael watched the waves. He looked like an ancient god observing some solemn rite, with his legs crossed, his eyes closed and palms open to the sky.

Something was wrong. The air felt thick with a menace she'd felt before.

Sabrina went inside and dumped her coffee. The feeling of unease flowered. She ran downstairs to her grandparents' door and banged hard.

No one answered.

Panic bloomed hot and sharp in her stomach. She raced to the office. A smiling girl in a tropical print shirt was tapping on the computer.

"Can I have the key to Room 103, please? My grandparents aren't answering, and I'm afraid something happened."

The girl tapped a few keys, frowned. "There isn't anyone registered in room 103."

Now the panic tasted like hot gunmetal. Sabrina swallowed. "That's ridiculous. Your computer is malfunctioning."

"Our system is fine," the clerk insisted. She gave Sabrina a level look.

As if Sabrina were nuts.

Michael must have answers. He stood up as she approached, brushing sand off his long legs.

"Something really weird is going on," she burst out. "The front desk has no record of Nathan's registration."

"Nathan's not here, Brie."

Her heart thudded violently. Ignoring him, she ran to the glass sliders of her grandparents' room. Sabrina fisted her shaking hands. Something foul and dangerous tainted the air. She gave a violent tug at the door and it slid open.

"Brie, listen to me…"

Sabrina ran inside.

The room had a small kitchenette and separate sitting area with a large-screen television and a king-sized bed. No sign of occupancy, but the stench of sulfur and decay made her gag. Sabrina clapped a hand over her mouth. Hair rose on the nape of her neck as she saw a small white card on the bed.

Her knees went weak as she read the card: *If you want your grandparents to live, come to the Sand Dollar swamp at midnight and summon me for the Demon Challenge. Otherwise, they'll die slowly and painfully, just as your parents did.*

The card spilled out of her opened fingers as she stared at the signature.

Ambrosis.

Chapter Four

Sabrina had until midnight to face her worst nightmare. A tight fist of fear knotted her stomach. She stared at Michael entering the room. "You took care of Ambrosis."

"Let's go back to your room. The stench is too strong in here."

Michael was too calm, as if he knew something. When they reached her room, he pointed to the couch. "Sit, Brie. We must talk."

A fleeting thought came to her. "You set him free! Michael, oh God, how could you?"

"I had no choice." Layering through his solemn voice was a hint of anguish. "It was my Guardian duty to release Ambrosis."

"He killed my family. And now he'll kill my grandparents." Guilt and fury collided together like waves crashing onto the beach. "You bastard, how could you do this? How can you hurt me like this?"

Michael closed his eyes. "I had to, Brie. Listen to me..."

Sabrina set her jaw like granite. "The hell with you. Rules can be broken and you choose to follow them instead of helping me."

Silver blazed in his blue eyes as he opened them. Michael pointed to the couch and said in a dark voice, "Sit down."

A little afraid of his power, she sat. He joined her, gathering her hands into his. When she tried to jerk away, he clasped her hands tight.

"I'd never do anything to hurt you, Brie. Trust me. Your grandparents are safe for now. They're at the condo where I'm staying with members of their pack. I transported them there and shielded them with magick before Ambrosis could track them here. However, even my powers can't protect them after midnight, when the Demon Challenge you issued takes precedence. If you don't summon him, Ambrosis will find and kill them."

Her heart thudded a staccato beat as she stared at his somber expression. "I don't understand. What Demon Challenge? This is crazy, I'd never do such a thing!"

Michael rubbed his thumbs over hers in a calming gesture. His touch felt like a soothing massage, erasing her tension. It was deliberate, she realized.

"A year ago, when Ambrosis attacked, you issued a Demon Challenge by saying, 'I'd spend eternity trying to destroy you, just give me the chance.'"

Horror stole over her. "Those are the words you said

once when you were Draicon. You're telling me I did the same thing?"

"Yes. Once you issue a Demon Challenge, you paralyze the demon, allowing a Guardian to trap him. You have a full year to reorganize your life. After that, the Guardian appointed as your mentor must release the trapped demon. If you don't summon the demon to fight him again, he is free to capture and try to kill anyone he chooses." Michael's jaw tightened. "Meaning, he can choose anyone you care about."

"I don't remember any of this!"

"After you challenged Ambrosis, you blocked that memory. I tried everything, stirring your memories through dreams and even hallucinations. I told you the truth once, but you blocked that out as well. Nothing worked. Your terror paralyzed you, Brie. You've had a year to face your fear and prepare to confront Ambrosis, but that time has run out."

The red curtain always fogging her memories lifted slightly, allowing her a peek at the past. Sabrina blinked away tears at the vision of herself standing before Ambrosis.

Abruptly the curtain dropped, replaced by pain spiking her temples. "I had a year...and I spent it not seeing my grandparents, not living, just cowering?"

Michael looked away.

"I'm a damn coward."

"You suffered an enormous trauma. You had the courage to issue a Demon Challenge. Few do that, Brie. You can find your courage once more," he insisted.

"Maybe Ambrosis is bluffing. He wouldn't want my grandparents, they're old and he could barely siphon anything from them. Maybe they won't die."

His expression darkened. "I've had visions of your grandparents dying just as your parents and your brothers and sisters did, a future that can only be changed by your actions."

Her stomach felt like someone had stuffed it with ground glass. She wrenched away from his comforting grip. "This can't be, how can this happen to me? Why would I issue a Demon Challenge, knowing the consequences? You told me what happened to you!"

"Because you have so much inner courage, you risked everything to defeat Ambrosis and have the chance to fight him again. You had the enormous strength to stand up to him, Brie."

"I can't do it again, I just can't."

"You will." A slight smile touched his mouth. "And this time, kick his ass straight back to hell."

"No, Michael. This is hell." Sabrina studied her slim hands, doubting they could be used to fight a powerful entity. "If I don't fight him, my grandparents will die."

"Find the courage you displayed once. I know you still have it." He ran his thumbs over her clenched fists. "That which does kill us makes us stronger. When I summoned Icktys, I'd spent a year in absolute rage because I felt cheated. The demon stripped me of my life and finding my destined mate. The anger consumed me. I had to overcome my fury to take him on again."

"And look what happened. You died! Fighting such a powerful demon is suicide."

Releasing her hands, Michael stood and paced to the sliding glass doors. "You do know why a Hellfire demon targeted you, Brie? Ambrosis wanted your bravery. When he wiped out your family, he sucked away it away, leaving you a ghost of yourself."

His frank dismissal outraged her. She bounded off the couch. "I'm not weak."

He smiled. "I know. Now go prove it. Conquer what you fear most."

Sabrina uncurled her hands, trying to see herself fighting Ambrosis to save her grandparents. Fear squeezed her throat as if someone tightened a noose around it.

"The first step is shifting into wolf. Try it," Michael told her.

She hadn't shifted in a year. She closed her eyes, summoning the power. Clothing melted away as her bones lengthened, her body became wolf.

Senses flooded her as she lifted her muzzle and smelled Michael's delicious scent of leather and pine. Her hearing was sharper, her body ached to break free and run.

Baring her teeth, she growled. Michael studied her.

Suddenly he vanished. In his place was an eight-foot-tall demon with gray skin. Silver claws sprouted from its long, spindly fingers. The demon advanced.

Sabrina ran into the corner.

Ambrosis vanished, replaced by her beloved Michael. Ashamed, she shifted back, clothed herself with a hand wave. Her skin went clammy and cold. Sabrina rubbed her shaking arms.

"I can't do this," she burst out. "Not as a wolf or in human form."

His gaze was level. "If you want your grandparents to live, you must."

Chapter Five

Fighting in a humid Florida swamp was not how she envisioned her beach weekend.

Sabrina shifted into wolf form to get a better sense of the surroundings. Thick brown mud sucked at her paws as she slogged through the dank water. Sharpened senses picked out old guano from nesting wood storks, heard small animals darting into the undergrowth. She smelled rain dampening the distant air.

Suddenly a new, disturbing scent surfaced. This scent tasted sharp and metallic. The smell of her own fear.

Her tail went down. She turned, baring her teeth and growling, when the Hellfire demon burst from between two cypress palms.

Terror seized her. Animal instinct overrode human control. All she could think about was running from danger.

Sabrina darted for a fallen tree, digging frantically for a hiding place.

"Oh Brie."

Michael shifted back into his true form. Once again, he'd turned into a replica of Ambrosis as a test. Shame filled her.

Sabrina shifted back, rubbed her arms. Even her thick sweater and jeans could not provide enough body heat.

"Concentrate, Brie. If you can't fight him as wolf, then you must use all the strength of your human self. Find an open area where he can't corner you. Take the advantage when you summon him."

Dusky shadows began to drape the grayish Spanish moss dripping from the cypress tree branches. Pink streaked the overhead sky. Sunset. She had less than six hours to find her bravado again.

"I haven't mustered the courage for a year to summon this demon, so what makes you think I can do it now?"

"Because you must."

"Thanks a lot. You're some help, telling me to pick a position. Why can't you help me?"

Anger simmered in his eyes. "I'm trying to, within the parameters of my limitations."

"You're an immortal Justice Guardian. I guess your limitations are pretty big."

Earth around her exploded in a shower of dust. Tree branches overhead burst into flame. A cold wind blew out of nowhere, combing through his long, dark hair.

Just as quickly, the fury died. Sabrina studied him calmly as the flames went out and the wind diminished.

"That was impressive. Not the powers. I know all about those. I'm talking about the emotion."

Understanding dawned in his eyes. "You said that to provoke me."

"Because you're such a serene voice of reason. I've never seen you angry. You were almost human." Sabrina released a breath. "I need you on my side, Michael, not as an impartial android. I'm so scared I feel ready to jump out of my skin. I need you to be with me emotionally because no one else understands what I'm going through."

Anger evaporated from his expression. He strode over to her, seized her hands in his. "Trust me, Brie. To fight Ambrosis, you have to work past the fear, past the animalistic instinct to run and hide from danger. You have to take all your love and all your rage at the idea of him hurting your loved ones and bring it up, and give him all you've got. It's the only way to survive this."

"Love isn't a weapon."

"It's the best one you have."

His obvious concern loaned her strength. She squeezed his hands. "I won't forget."

"I'll be with you all the way, as much as I'm permitted, Brie. That's a promise. I won't abandon you. No matter what."

Judging from his solemn look, she knew it was a promise he would keep.

Tree frogs cheeped from the ghostly sentinels of pine and cypress. The dank smell of muck and water mixed with the fresh scent of rain riding the wind. Hugging her knees, Sabrina sat in a small clearing on a tree island.

Floating on the nearby water, water ferns sheltered a shy turtle. Silvery light from the nearly full moon dappled the foliage. In the shadows, she sensed Michael nearby.

He could not help her. She had to do it on her own.

She lifted her gaze to the black sky, judging the time from the moon's position. Almost midnight. Her stomach flip-flopped.

Had to do this. Never again would another life be lost because she failed. Sabrina touched a protruding root. Tears burned her eyes as she remembered her mother and father laughing, her brothers and sisters bounding through the forest eager to explore. Their voices forever gone.

I'll never see them again. But at least I can make sure Ambrosis never again hurts someone I love.

She stood, brushing off pine needles from her jeans. Her hands trembled as she lifted them skyward. Summoning a demon was easy.

Dealing with him afterward was the tough part.

Her hands fell to her side as she remembered the Hellfire demon tearing into her family, the screams and the horror. Sabrina's ears buzzed as her stomach turned.

Nausea took over. She turned and clutched the sturdy tree as her knees buckled.

You can do this.

Michael's voice spoke in a reassuring tone inside her mind. Startled, she swiped at the air as if batting cobwebs.

Sabrina lifted clammy palms to call forth the demon.

Again, they fell to her side.

Please don't ask this of me, I can't take this, I can't...

Images surfaced; her grandparents, alone and scared, their faces etched with terror. They did not deserve Ambrosis's wrath.

All she had to do was summon the demon. She was clever and could hide, unlike last time.

You will not hide. You have the strength to defeat him, Brie.

Michael was communicating telepathically. He was a Guardian with such powers. Still, this thought was more like a soothing brush against her mind. As if he melded his strength and spirit with hers, bonding with her metaphysically.

She went still as an impossible thought surfaced. There was only one way to tell if it was true.

"Michael," she called out softly into the darkness. "Please, come here a minute."

He materialized before her. Silvery blue eyes glowed in the night.

Sabrina grabbed him by the lapels of his leather jacket, pulled him forward and kissed him.

Electrical shock zinged through her. They gasped at the powerful contact. Then Michael wove his fingers through her hair and tilted her head back.

He deepened the kiss. Sabrina moaned beneath the subtle movement of his mouth. He thrust his tongue past her parted lips. She drank in his taste, his scent. Awareness, sorrow and joy filled her as her ears buzzed.

Oh Michael...

Sabrina's throat closed with tears as he released her.

"Did you feel it?" She hugged him, needing his touch, needing him. "Don't you know what's happening between us? Can't you feel what we are to each other, feel it in your heart? Why didn't you tell me we share this special connection?"

A frown dented his brow as he eased out of her grip. "There's nothing happening between us. I'm forbidden from physical contact with you. You shouldn't have done that."

She searched his confused expression, the immortal Phoenix looking flustered for the first time since she'd known him. Hope died in her heart.

A lump lodged in her throat. Even now, he couldn't feel the same for her as she felt for him.

It didn't matter. She had to summon all her energy for Ambrosis. Sabrina's resolve returned.

A warm thought brushed against her mind. *I'll always be with you, Brie. Always. I wish I could offer you more...*

The thought trailed off, but she felt a desperate longing beneath it, as if he struggled to say what she had felt.

Then the Phoenix vanished. Sabrina steeled her spine. *I can do this.*

Sabrina raised her hands and spoke in a trembling voice, "Ambrosis, I summon you forth!"

Nothing.

She tried again, this time motioning with her hands. "Ambrosis, Hellfire demon whom I challenged one year ago, I summon you forth!"

Tree frogs continued their noisy song. Sabrina stared at

her surroundings in frank astonishment. A heavy silence draped the swamp.

She did her part. But Ambrosis had failed to show himself. Did it mean Nathan and Martha were safe? But Michael said only her actions could save them. She had to summon the demon. Yet he refused to show his face.

Maybe that was part of Ambrosis' plan. The loophole in the demon summoning thing. Anger began to build up as she imagined her cheerful grandparents facing the demon, unable to fight back. It wasn't fair. Sabrina fisted her hands and yelled.

"Sheesh, Ambrosis, you must be deaf. I mean, how loud do I have to speak and how much hand-waving is involved here? If there's an Official Demon Request form I failed to fill out in triplicate, then tell me. Or do you want me to deliver it on a silver platter, then forget it because I don't touch silver and I think you're just an ugly gray, hairy…"

A loud roar reverberated through the stillness. It sent icy shivers down her spine.

"Wuss," she finished on a whisper.

Rising from the murky water surrounding the tree island was a fleshy shape. The shape took form.

From a crouching position, the demon raised himself up on spindly legs. The backbone was a protrusion of knobby bone. Mottled gray flesh covered his sunken frame. Twisted pale green lips sneered at her, displaying rows of jagged, pointed teeth. Two gray membranous wings crawling with spiders grew from his back, fanning the air with the stench of burning sulfur. Yellow phlegm dripped from his eyes.

Ambrosis.

Filled with false bravado, she faced her nightmare. "Didn't recognize you at first, but I sure smelled you coming. You look pretty stressed. The year's sure aged you, demon. All those wrinkles…maybe you should consider Botox or a day at the spa?"

Michael's amused chuckle echoed in her mind.

Encouraged, she faced the demon. "Like the wings, but the accessories, hate to tell you, they need to go. Arachnids are so last year."

The demon snarled at her. Shock immobilized her as his body began to shimmer. He shifted into a much more familiar, endearing form.

"Dad?" she whispered.

"Hello, daughter. Why did you let me die?"

Laughter screamed through the swamp as the demon with her father's mouth, her father's face, her father's damn white Oxford shirt, advanced toward her.

She could not move, think or speak. Tears wet her cheeks. She forced herself to analyze the situation.

Think, think, look at the hands, remember demons can't fully mimic others, they have to retain some part of their physical selves.

She glanced downward. Instead of her father's fingers, she saw silver claws the size of a grizzly bear's. Ambrosis hissed and raised a hand.

Sabrina screamed. She wanted to shift into the more powerful wolf, but couldn't remember the process. It was as if someone immobilized her powers. Fogged her brain.

She turned and ran, and tripped over an exposed root.

Sabrina rolled over to see Ambrosis in demon form. Small blue horns on the front and back of his head turned into rotating razor blades. He grinned, exposing a set of whirling, pointed teeth.

Her heart hammered violently, her ears clogged. She barely comprehended the buzz saw headed for her.

Forcing her canines to emerge while still in human form, Sabrina dove for the ground and bit the demon's ankle. Spiders from its wings cascaded over her, sinking fangs into her exposed neck. Sabrina ignored the pain and held onto Ambrosis. Using her Draicon strength, she twisted his ankle hard and heard a snapping sound.

He roared with obvious outrage and limped away.

"Broke it, huh, you ugly bastard," she said, panting. "How does it feel to have someone hurt you for a change?"

Ambrosis flew forward and slashed her chest with his silver, grizzly-like claws.

Agony burned through her. She felt her magick begin to drain, her body fill with poison.

She was going to die.

Chapter Six

Ambrosis seemed too powerful to defeat. Memories accosted her. Her parents, brothers and sisters, screaming for someone to help them…

Anger fed her strength. She remembered what Michael told her and let all her love rush to the surface. Sabrina rolled away, kicking soft muck into the demon's eyes.

As he batted at his face, she grabbed a sturdy stick and jabbed it into his right eye. The demon screamed. Good, she thought, staggering to her feet. She ignored the burning pain, concentrated on her surroundings.

As wolf she could defeat him. But her powers were rapidly draining. She couldn't shift. Now she regretted not having the courage to face him as a wolf.

Blood poured through her fingers as she held them against her chest. The white-hot agony was almost too terrible to bear. She wanted to give in to the grayness pushing at the sides of her vision. Surrender.

Then she saw Michael. The silvery blue brilliance of his eyes faded, leaving them an ordinary brown. Shock filled her. Michael was forbidden from helping her. Now, because he did, his powers vanished.

He faced a Hellfire demon as an ordinary mortal, without even Draicon magick.

"No, Michael, don't," she screamed.

With a loud, furious yell, he charged the demon. Ambrosis whirled, laughed and lashed at Michael.

Blood gushed from Michael's chest. He staggered back.

"You bastard," she snarled.

Sabrina gathered all her strength. She head-butted the demon. Ambrosis sailed backward, recovered and glared. He advanced toward Michael.

She suddenly knew what it thought. She was a prize, but the now mortal Michael was the brass ring.

Not on her watch. Michael had already suffered enough for her sake.

"You will not hurt him. Take me instead." Sabrina summoned the last of her Draicon magick and waved her hands. A steel dagger appeared in one palm.

She ran forward, protecting the one she loved. Ambrosis screamed and rushed forward, his claws extended for a killing blow.

Sabrina did a dive roll, sprang up and sank the dagger into the demon's soft underbelly. A shriek like nails on chalkboard echoed through the swamp.

Ambrosis raked his claws across her stomach. Agony

burned through her. Sabrina gasped and fell backward onto the soft mud.

With the last bit of her strength, she whispered, "I surrender my life so he can live. Now go to hell."

Ambrosis roared. Sparks flew from his eyes. There was a brilliant yellow flash and a loud pop. The demon vanished.

She whimpered as warmth gushed between her fingers. Beneath the pulsing burn was a feeling as if everything grew hazy. Distant.

She was dying.

Michael took her into his arms. Gone was the terrible wound on his chest. She sensed the return of his powers, saw it in his blazing silver blue eyes.

"Did I do it?" she whispered. "Is he back in hell?"

"For a long time. You sent him there because you sacrificed yourself to save me." He brushed away the hair from her face.

She hated his anguished look. A memory, buried and forgotten, flashed to the surface. She lifted her hand to touch his neck where the mark of the Phoenix had been burned into him when he was reborn. Had there been a wound there, too terrible to heal?

"Ambrosis hurt you."

"I can't die. I'm immortal. My powers only deserted me. He couldn't kill me," he said fiercely.

"Couldn't bear to see you hurt." She frowned. It was getting difficult to think. "Not like before. Had to save you."

Michael let out a hiss. He placed his palms over her

wounds. A blazing warmth spread through her body. She cried out in shock and relief.

The agony slowed and then slowly dissipated. As her strength returned, she glanced down.

"You healed me. But you're not permitted to interfere."

He muttered a curse word that made her eyes go wide. Michael rocked her in his arms.

"It's all right now, Brie," he soothed. "I only bought you a little time and kept the pain at bay. That's the extent of my powers. I can't do anything else. At dawn, it will all vanish."

"I don't understand."

Torment flashed in his eyes. "I can't change your destiny now any more than I could a year ago, sweetheart. A year ago when you last fought Ambrosis and you died. You have until morning, Brie. And then you will die again."

Chapter Seven

Sabrina closed her eyes, unwilling to comprehend the horrible truth. Air brushed past her shivering body. Sabrina no longer scented damp earth. She smelled the salt of Michael's tears.

Opening her eyes, she saw they were in his penthouse condominium on a leather sofa on Florida's west coast. Never had she seen him look more despondent.

"I returned your grandparents and their pack to their hotel room, and erased their memories to ease their distress." Michael shoved a hand through his hair.

"I can't have died. I'm here, breathing and talking."

Sorrow etched his expression. "You were given a year's lease on life. You died in my arms, sweetheart. You died trying to save your family, just as I died trying to save you."

Shock made her speechless. It all made sense now. The

constant chill she felt, the taste of her favorite foods being all wrong. The feeling of doom hovering over her.

Sabrina forced herself to speak as he gathered her into his arms and laid his head atop hers. "Tell me how you died, Michael. Remind me and maybe then I can understand what happened to me."

"I had a family I loved as much as you loved yours. When I lost them, I moved to the country, next to your parents' farm. They accepted me, even though I was alone. But you were the one who coaxed me out of misery."

"I was ten when we met," she remembered.

"A stubborn, independent, courageous child who insisted on my joining her family each night for dinner, who wouldn't leave me alone and made me laugh. Your spirit kept me from sliding into despair. But you worried me because you had the same strength that had caused demons to kill my family."

His voice broke. Sabrina placed her arms around his neck, leaning into him, loaning him her inner strength. She felt him tremble beneath the soothing strokes of her palms.

"I've always been able to sense demons, but was too inexperienced to save my family," he continued. "I made a promise to myself to never let demons get you or your family, but your strong spirit attracted the demon Icktys. When you were eighteen, I scented him in your house one night. He'd materialized to steal your strength and kill you. I fought the demon, made the Demon Challenge. I had a full year to live and summon Icktys and then I died and was reborn."

His voice dropped. "When you give your life to save

someone, you have the choice to move onto the next plane of existence, or become an immortal to watch over them. I made my decision so I could always be there to protect you."

A bolt of pain speared her heart. "You've done so much for me, and I did nothing for you."

"You have. All those years you lived was solace to me, Brie. Your spirit was still alive and no demon could break it. It gave me a purpose I'd lost after my family was gone."

Michael's gaze was brilliant as he raised his head. "As your mentor, I must inform you it's your time to make the decision. When dawn breaks your time is up. You can either pass on to the next Realm, or remain on earth and be reborn as a Justice Guardian. But you cannot go on living as you had."

"And if I choose to be a Guardian?"

"The way is not easy. You will never live in a pack again or know deep and lasting familial ties. You will always rove the earth, never to settle, never to raise a family." His voice grew strained. "You will always work alone, for a Phoenix never teams with another. You will always face adversity, for that is what we do. We see the exposed underbelly of life. You will never be blissfully innocent again of the cruelties others can impose."

"If I pass on, my family will be waiting," she mused.

"Yes. You will be reunited with them." He cupped her cheek, his expression filled with anguish. "The decision must be yours. I cannot impose my will on you."

"I suppose you can't change my destiny."

Michael's gaze was steady. "I already did, Brie. You see,

the full year had passed by already. You needed convincing to gather your courage to summon Ambrosis. I knew you'd get it if you saw your grandparents again. So I delayed Ambrosis' release by twenty-four hours, giving you a day with them. All you needed was a reminder of how strong and powerful love can be."

Overcome, she stared at him. "You did that all for me? They let you?"

His jaw tightened. "No, they didn't. There will be... consequences."

When she asked what kind, he gave a dismissive hand wave.

She hugged her stomach, remembering Ambrosis hurting her the first time when she'd died to save her family. "I need space," she whispered.

He let her go. She fled into the bathroom, turned on the shower and stripped out of her mud-soaked clothing. Beneath the hot spray, she scrubbed at her body. The sobs came out in choking gasps.

After regaining her lost composure, she stepped out of the shower and wrapped a towel around herself.

She had tonight. Wasting it was stupid.

Michael waited for her in the living room, standing against one of the potted palms. His gaze uncertain, he studied her approach.

"I have until morning. I'm not wasting a minute more of my life. And since you've already broken the rules, I figure you can stand to break one more," she told him.

Sabrina kissed him.

Chapter Eight

They kissed each other with fervent hunger, tongues tangling, their moans mingling as they held each other tight.

When Michael let her go, he looked dangerous as his gaze became brilliant with passion. His jaw was clenched tight as if it were made of stone.

"I have to get inside you. Now," he said thickly.

Sabrina felt wet and aching, swollen with need. Shivering with anticipation, she kissed him again, wrapping her arms around his neck. He was hard, steely muscle as he kissed her back in a desperation equaling her own. Michael reached beneath the towel, skimming the soft flesh of her thigh. She cried out in shock as he delved between her wet folds. He slid a long finger back and forth, creating more dampness. She opened her thighs wide, feeling vulnerable and shaky with need. With his other hand, he ripped off the towel, and then backed her up against the wall.

His hands cupped her naked breasts, thumbing the hardening nipples. Michael took one into his mouth, his tongue flicking over the cresting bud. As he suckled her, she threw back her head on a moan.

He dropped his hand to the zipper on his jeans, the rasping of metal mingling with his panting breath.

His palms were warm and calloused as he cupped her bare bottom, lifted her against the cold, hard wall. She felt the thickness of his cock push at her wet, swollen center. Shocked by the unaccustomed pressure of him stretching her, Sabrina whimpered. Michael grunted and adjusted himself and began working himself inside her.

With a determined relentlessness, he thrust, penetrating her fully.

They went still for a moment. Sabrina trembled, struck mute, feeling impaled by male hardness and strength. He nuzzled her neck, murmuring soothing reassurances.

She could do nothing but wrap her arms around his neck and writhe against him in an attempt to draw even closer. Michael shoved into her, hard and fast and urgent. Sabrina lifted her legs and locked her trembling thighs around his pumping hips.

Grunting, he thrust higher and deeper. She moaned as his thick penis pushed into her with relentless urgency. Her back slammed against the wall, erotic pleasure building where they were intimately joined. The whisper of a climax danced outside of reach. Sobbing, she dug her nails into the thick muscles of his shoulders. Needing this, needing his closeness, feeling the bonding of their flesh.

This was what she'd waited for her entire life.

Michael muttered as he adjusted his position. His hand dropped down, touching her at where they were joined. She exploded into a violent, screaming orgasm.

He threw back his head, the veins and cords on his neck straining. With a loud shout of her name, he released himself into her. For a moment they clung to each other, the sound of their ragged breaths echoing in the still room. Michael dropped his head on her shoulder, kissed her neck as he slowly pulled out.

Dazed by sensual pleasure, she slid down the wall as he feathered light kisses over her cheeks and jaw.

He led her to the bedroom, turned to regard her in the brilliant moonlight.

"And now," he murmured, "we take it slow."

His lean body had the strength of a predatory animal. Sabrina watched in hungry silence as Michael undressed. Muscles rippled beneath the tanned skin of his flat belly. His legs were long and dusted with dark hair.

His penis stood erect once more. She placed her hands on his firm chest, feeling the steady and slow beat of an immortal heart.

She'd had sex with a few partners. Always something felt lacking. Not with Michael.

Emotion overwhelmed her as she placed her mouth on his collarbone, tasting the salty tang of his skin. Michael cupped her chin, lifted it to his face.

"Why the tears?" He gently kissed them away.

She smiled through them. "You mean everything to me. I wish I'd have done this sooner."

"You are so beautiful." His voice was husky as he drew her over to the bed and they lay down.

His skin was hot to the touch as she stroked his broad shoulders and neck. She placed her lips against the mark of the Phoenix, feeling him quiver beneath her mouth. He slid a palm over her healed belly, circling it in soothing strokes.

Then he kissed his way down her torso. She felt him smile against her stomach. Then he flicked his tongue around her belly button. Sabrina cried out with pleasure as his hand reached between her thighs.

They explored each other's bodies, taking their time, discovering pleasure points and laughing with abandon.

Michael's gaze was blue fire as he mounted her. He held himself up on his hands as he settled between her opened legs.

"Love me, Michael," she told him. "Pretend nothing can ever separate us, not even death."

He pushed into her. The thickness of him filled her completely. She closed her eyes and tilted her hips up as he began to thrust.

His deep chest slid over her, the silky hairs from his legs whispered against her as she wrapped her limbs around his. They were entwined together like snakes.

Sabrina fisted her hands into his hair and kissed him hard. He moaned into her mouth and thrust harder and faster, the pleasure pushing her higher. She arched beneath him and cried out his name as she let go.

Rigid muscles locked as he stiffened above her and shouted her name. She felt the wet warmth of semen that would never father her baby.

She touched his cheek as he rolled off and he buried his damp face into her shoulder.

Her heart broke at the thought of never seeing him again, after searching for him for so long....

They'd made love once more, Sabrina atop him, riding him slowly. Michael smelled the salt from the tears trickling down her face.

Afterwards, she'd excused herself to get some fresh air.

Wrapped in one of his shirts, she now stood at the balcony and stared out into the moon-splashed sand. Michael's heart squeezed. His voice dropped to a bare whisper.

"Why do you tug at my heart so, little Sabrina? What is it about you that I could not bear to let you go?"

He could not love her. Yet the intense feelings washing through him, the idea of losing her left a hollow ache in his chest. As if he had fallen in love with Brie.

"I care about you. I always have. It isn't love," he muttered. "I don't remember how to love anymore."

Had not, not since the day his family died.

Enough reflection, Michael decided. Little time was left. He could not waste a moment more.

"The water looks so peaceful," she called out softly. "I wish I could go swimming one last time." And then she headed inside to change.

When she returned, he lifted her into his arms and carried her outside. His powers cloaked them from curious eyes.

Humid air washed over them as he carried her to the

shoreline. Michael set her gently down on her feet, stripped off her shirt and then took her hand.

Together, they waded into the warm water. A dolphin splashed nearby.

They swam out a long distance until the water reached her chest. She wrapped her long legs around his hips, her center positioned directly over his erection. Adjusting their positions, he pushed inside her.

They both gasped at the contact. Sabrina began to cry again.

"Shhhh," he murmured, rocking her back and forth. She slid up, down, the water gently lapping around them. Her arms wrapped about his neck.

In the moonlight, she studied him with a tender look. Sensations pummeled him, the tight, warm feel of her flesh surrounding him, the tangy scent of her, the delicious emotions filling every pore. He couldn't get close enough to her.

He wanted the moment to last forever.

When her core squeezed him tight and she cried out her release, he surrendered. Michael threw back his head and groaned, shaking from the power of his orgasm.

A while later, after they'd showered and made love again, he lay with her in his bed. Knowing the minutes were slipping away, Michael held her tight.

"Did you make your decision?" he asked thickly.

She nodded.

He did not ask what she decided. He didn't want to know. It hurt too much to think about losing her.

Emotional involvement distracts you from the job,

Tristan always said. "Go have sex, ease your physical needs, but nothing more. Because you're always on the move and you can't take her with you."

Too late, Michael thought.

He needed no sleep, but when she slept, he closed his eyes. He wrapped her in his arms, feeling her soft body mold against his.

In the morning when he opened his eyes, his arms were empty.

She was gone.

Chapter Nine

Hands cuffed in golden spiked links behind his back, Michael knelt naked on a large mirrored floor in a room filled with brilliant light. The light hurt his eyes, as it was intended to do. The hard surface cut into his knees, the bracelets felt like razor wire on his skin.

He'd lost track of how long Tristan had punished him. The day Sabrina vanished, Michael had turned himself over to his mentor for discipline. The punishment was for giving Sabrina an extra day to gather her courage and summon the demon. When Michael had asked in a defiant tone about the other rules he'd broken, such as making love to his charge, Tristan only shrugged.

The memory of their lovemaking was a balm that soothed the punishment's subsequent humiliation. Michael took a deep breath, muted the pain with exact concentration.

The cell door opened. He stared at the scuffed biker boots before him.

"You know why you broke the rules?" Tristan asked.

Michael lifted his head. Despite the burning in his watering eyes, he forced himself to lock gazes. With his shoulder-length hair, piercing eyes and arrogant chin, Tristan looked the same age as Michael. In reality, he was a thousand years older, and a Guardian elder.

"I bought her an extra day to stir her memories. My only concern was keeping her safe," Michael said.

"You sound like a pompous ass. Admit the truth. What is Sabrina to you?"

"She is my closest friend. She made me want to live again after my family died."

"You keep telling yourself that. Haven't figured it out yet, have you?" Tristan shook his head. "Love must be blind, as well as deaf and dumb."

His immortal heart pounded hard. Michael felt white-hot pain in his chest as the realization slammed into him like a sledgehammer.

"No," he whispered.

"Yes." Tristan sat cross-legged before him. "You blinded yourself to the truth, thus the mirror of truth. And you're still as blind as ever. You love her. She's your destined mate, or was, since you're not Draicon anymore."

Michael closed his eyes, the burning in them too much to bear. Moisture seeped from the closed lids and fell like crystals onto the mirrored floor.

"I can't love her."

"The memories of losing her family were too painful for

Sabrina, but the thought of not being able to have her was equally crushing for you. You blocked everything out. Your feelings. That little gut instinct telling you who she really was when she turned eighteen and you became aware she was a woman. You were debating how to tell her your suspicions when the demon targeted Sabrina. That's why you were so furious, Michael. You weren't mad about being cheated out of finding your destined mate, but because you had already found her."

A long, low moan escaped him at the painful realization. Michael hung his head, and opened his eyes. He could only see Sabrina's face, her eyes reflecting his love.

He had ignored it before because it hurt too much to lose her, just as he'd lost everyone in his family.

In the mirror, he saw Tristan loom over him. "You only knew you wanted Sabrina close by. I will ask this only once, Phoenix. Why did you lie to her? The crap about not imposing your will on her was pure B.S. You could have swayed her decision with a mental push and she'd have chosen to become a Guardian and be with you instead of her family."

He raised his head to regard his mentor. "And I'd have been wrong, because she needed to make the best decision for herself. It would have been selfish."

"What if she chose the other realm with her family? You won't see her again for centuries until your tour of duty is up. "

Michael grit his teeth. "I knew I'd survive, like I have."

"Admit it. You did it because you wanted to make her happy, even if you were miserable," Tristan said softly.

"Damn you." Michael felt his pain cease. "Yes."

All his memories he'd suppressed rushed to the surface. He remembered the night he died to keep her safe. The burning pain, and Sabrina's hysterical sobs as she tried to slow the blood streaming from his body. He remembered the vow he'd made to challenge the demon so she'd never again be attacked by Icktys. The year he'd spent trying to control his anger at being cheated of his destined mate and why he'd chosen to be reborn as a Phoenix.

It was so he could watch over her, always, even if they could never be together.

"All those times you wanted to kiss her, you didn't. Why?" Tristan asked.

"I didn't want her to get hurt," he admitted. "I remember now. Something inside me warned me that she would realize what we were to each other and it would be agony for her. My immortal powers prohibit her from bonding with me."

"You tried to protect her. Very noble. You want to ask me something," Tristan pointed out.

It wasn't permitted. He asked anyway.

"Is Sabrina all right? What did she decide?"

Pain speared his temples as if someone thrust an ice pick into them. He breathed through it.

"She's happy. That's all you need to know."

The heavy handcuffs fell from his wrists. Michael felt a weight lift. His muscles screamed in agony as he struggled to his feet. Rubbing his wrists, he shot Tristan a puzzled look.

"You're free now, my friend. I think you've suffered

enough. I want you patrolling territory in the western United States far from me. If you don't stay out of my sight—or any other Guardian's sight—I'll haul your ass back here in chains for much longer than a month."

"Can I at least see Sabrina's grandparents?"

Tristan grunted. "Next year, at their anniversary, and not before. I'll grant you that much. And stay out of trouble, Phoenix."

Chapter Ten

Time dragged by for Michael. He kept to his duties, careful to avoid contact with any other Guardians. The loneliness was more honed and piercing now that he remembered in sharp detail exactly what he'd lost.

He'd almost gotten used to it. Almost, Michael thought as he trudged toward the Florida hotel where Sabrina's grandparents were once again celebrating their anniversary. The year had finally passed.

Dread filled him. He wanted to see Nathan and Martha again. Wanted to hug them, feel contact with those Sabrina loved so much. But seeing them would be hell, because they were a reminder of all he'd lost.

Michael turned a corner and walked into the hotel parking lot. His gait slowed as he heard riotous laughter from the Tiki Bar. For a moment he wanted to turn away and leave, and never look back.

I can't do this.

I must do this.

Michael swallowed hard and slowed his pace as he neared the bar. Could he ever learn to laugh again, enjoy all he'd been given as a Phoenix, without Sabrina?

Doubtful. Yet he had to try. This was a good place to start.

Nathan and Martha had their backs to him as he approached. Michael set down his backpack. He gathered his courage and forced a smile.

Delighted cries filled the air as they turned and saw him. The pack converged on him. He found himself engulfed by bear hugs from Draicon wolves much older than himself.

When they stepped back, Nathan and Martha gave each other delighted looks.

"About time you showed up, Michael. You sure took your sweet time getting here," Nathan said.

Martha squeezed his arms. "There's a friend of yours here. Nice man."

Michael stiffened as the crowd parted to show Tristan standing by one of the tables. With him was a dark-haired woman, who had her back turned as she gazed out into the green Gulf waters.

"He's no friend," Michael grated out. "I should leave."

Before he could make a move toward his backpack, Tristan flashed to his side. "Ah, no you don't. Before you run away, there's someone you need to meet first. I'm requiring you to take on a new trainee."

Michael's voice dropped to a deep growl. "I work alone."

"Not anymore. Part of your continuing discipline, champ. You'll be paired with her for a long time."

His guts clenched as anger surfaced. He forced it down, assumed an impartial expression. "Whatever."

"Come here." Tristan crooked a finger at the woman with her back turned to him.

When she turned and came forward, Michael forgot to breathe. He could only stare in rapt wonder.

"It's not possible," he said thickly.

Then all words failed him as Sabrina flung herself into his arms. He felt the wetness on her cheeks and realized she, too, was crying.

"She needed constant mentoring for a year, like all new Guardians." Tristan sounded amused. "But I'm tired of teaching her. She needs a new mentor, someone to stick around and work with her. Two Guardians can be more effective than one these days. More demons to fight, more shifters being targeted."

"For how long?" His voice was a bare whisper.

"A while. Say, five hundred years or longer." Amusement danced in Tristan's voice. "You know the rules. Nothing in the books about two Guardians having a close physical relationship...or being in love."

Michael's throat clogged as Sabrina held him tight. He stroked her hair, and squeezed his eyes shut. Afraid she was a vision and she'd vanish again.

He opened his eyes. Joy shone on her face as she leaned forward and pressed her soft mouth against his trembling lips.

Her kiss was urgent and filled with passion. He breathed

in her scent, wrapped his arms around her and deepened the kiss. He heard the murmurs die away, felt their surroundings shift.

When they ceased kissing, they were in a hotel room. Michael blinked.

"I see you've learned a lot in a year," he told her.

"Teleporting and cloaking the action from humans was the first skill I asked Tristan to teach me. I've had this in mind ever since I made the decision to be reborn as a Phoenix." She touched his wet, warm mouth.

"Why, Brie?" He cupped her head, running his fingers through the silk of her black hair. "You missed your family, you could have been reunited with them."

"I missed you more," she said, kissing the corner of his mouth. "All those years you sacrificed your life for me, it was time I did something for you. Because I love you, and I'd do anything for love." Her voice cracked. "Even if you didn't think you loved me."

He brushed back a strand of her hair. "I was a fool who forgot how to love, because it hurt too much."

"It won't ever hurt again, Michael. I promise you this, just as you made a promise to keep me safe all those years ago."

His voice deepened as he cupped her face in his hands. "And I make a new promise to you now. I love you, Brie, and I will never again deny you my feelings."

Her green gaze, now as brilliant as his own, regarded him. "Your mind forgot you loved, but your heart never did. That's why you let me choose my destiny instead of asking me to be with you as a reborn Phoenix. You set me free. So I made you my choice and came back."

Stunned, he stood in mute wonder at her perception. Sabrina flashed a grin and snapped her fingers. Air brushed against his bare skin. He glanced down.

He was naked.

Michael smiled. "I see you've learned to put those new powers to good use. But if you don't mind, I prefer the old-fashioned method of undressing you."

They made love with a fierce intensity, clinging to each other as if afraid to let go. When it was over and they lay in breathless exhaustion in each other's arms, he gently stroked her cheek. Sabrina gave him a solemn look.

"There's only one thing I've wondered about. Do you think our lives would have been different had you not died that night protecting me and we were still Draicon destined mates?"

He kissed her, savoring the feel of her soft mouth beneath the subtle pressure of his. "It doesn't matter, Brie. Because deep inside, I'm still a wolf pining for his mate. And this wolf doesn't mate for life. He mates for an eternity."

* * * * *

HER WICKED WOLF
KENDRA LEIGH CASTLE

Kendra Leigh Castle was born and raised in the far and frozen reaches of northern New York, where there was plenty of time to cultivate her love of reading, thanks to the six-month-long winters. Sneaking off with selections from her mother's vast collection of romance novels came naturally and fairly early, and a lifelong love of the Happily Ever After was born. After graduating from SUNY Oswego (where it also snowed a lot) with a teaching degree, Kendra ran off with a handsome young Navy fighter pilot and has somehow accumulated three children, two high-maintenance dogs and one enormous cat during their many moves.

Her enduring love of all things both spooky and steamy means she's always got another paranormal romance in the works.

Kendra currently resides wherever the Navy thinks she ought to, which is Maryland at present. She also has a home on the web at www.kendraleighcastle.com and loves to hear from her readers! She can usually be found curled up with her laptop and yet another cup of coffee at kendraleighcastle@yahoo.com.

Chapter One

She needed to quit daydreaming about the guy downstairs.

Brienne Fox dropped her pen onto the table, barely hearing it roll off the edge and clatter onto the linoleum. The half-finished grocery list in front of her vanished from her thoughts like so much smoke. All she could hear was the key in the door, the footsteps…and the murmur of that dark, silken voice as he greeted what she assumed must be his cat. Not that she'd spent too much time thinking about what might or might not be in his apartment. Or what he did while he was in there.

Or anything.

Brie closed her eyes and dug her hands into her hair, resting her elbows on the table and slumping a little as she castigated herself. Every day was the same. She was a perfectly normal, well-functioning human being until that car pulled into the driveway they shared. But as soon as she heard the steady hum of his sleek little sedan's engine, all of her functioning brain cells dropped whatever they were doing to focus on one thing, and one thing only.

Him. Or more specifically, him naked and in one of a wide variety of compromising positions, all of which involved her.

It wasn't exactly productive, since Alistair Locke had barely given her the time of day the few times she'd managed to bump into him. When speaking was almost out of the question, a torrid affair didn't seem all that likely.

Brie pushed back her chair, got up and wandered over to the window to look out at the fresh tire tracks in the snow-dusted driveway. Alistair's car would be parked by her sand-and—salt spattered SUV, as it always was, in the old carriage house that had been converted into a garage. Just as she had boxes of stuff next to his in the upper level of the garage. Unfortunately, her possessions got more time with him than she did. There was plenty of space for two people here—almost too much.

She hadn't been sure about renting an apartment in such an old house, no matter how beautiful it was. She'd had visions of lousy heat, electrical and plumbing issues, and of course, a resident ghost that would doubtless terrorize her into leaving anyway. But the place had sucked her in, from the high ceilings and gleaming wood floors to the big window that looked out on the wide street lined with old trees and stately old Victorians much like this one.

The upstairs was hers, apparently ghost-free, and she loved it. It was the perfect hiding place for somebody like her, a working writer who thrived on a certain amount of quiet and personal space. Of course, having Alistair downstairs had provided a little *too* much fodder for what was already an overactive imagination.

If she hadn't been so boringly normal in every other way, she might have been really concerned about herself instead of just uneasy. She'd liked guys before. She'd lusted after plenty of them. But this didn't feel quite...*normal.*

Brie's eyes rose to the sky, and she found herself momentarily diverted. The snow clouds that had hung heavily on the horizon all day had darkened to an ominous slate-gray, and they seemed to be moving in swiftly. They were predicting that the massive nor'easter would start hitting by early evening. She'd promised herself she'd get to the grocery store before the snow started falling, just in case. With luck, the power would stay on. Without luck...well, she'd cross that bridge when she came to it.

And of course, Alistair had the only working fireplace in the house in his apartment....

Brie squared her shoulders and headed back to the table to grab the grocery list. Food first. She'd just figure the rest of it out as she went. And along the way, it would be nice if her mind could focus its energy on something actually productive, instead of creating scenarios with her neighbor that involved firelight and a soundtrack loaded with songs by Enigma.

Minutes later she was headed out the door and down the stairs, cozy in bulky boots and a heavy coat. She purposely avoided looking at the door to Alistair's apartment. He never came out when she was around, and he wasn't going to—

Oh God, there he is.

The door opened, and well over six feet of dark, shaggy, antisocial male walked out. Brie stopped short three steps from the bottom, so startled she could do nothing but stare. She rarely got this close to him...which was a shame, because up close, he was even more delicious than he was from a distance.

Then again, considering the sudden pounding heart and lightheadedness, a little distance might be the healthier thing. She just wanted to climb him like a tree, wrap her legs around him, and bite.

Brie's eyes widened in horror at the images that flickered, unbidden, though her mind. *Biting*? What the hell?

Alistair froze for a moment when he realized he wasn't alone, and they stared at each other in the silence. Brie drank him in, unable to help herself. He was wearing all blacks and grays, which seemed to be a habit of his—black peacoat, gray-and-black scarf, black pants, all covering a long, lithe form that moved with sensual, effortless grace. His hair was black as a raven's wing, and seemed less to be cut in an actual style than simply overlong. It waved slightly, falling around a face that was a study in hawkish beauty. His cheekbones were high and sharp, a perfect match for his blade of a nose. Handsome was probably the wrong word for him, Brie thought. Compelling was probably a better one.

Alistair's lips pressed into a thin, hard line as he watched her. His eyes—big, thickly lashed, and the blue of the deepest ocean—seemed to exert a gravitational pull that she had to struggle to resist. And she would keep struggling, Brie thought as she collected herself as best she could. Because she was reasonably certain that Alistair was not thinking "Please, hurl yourself at me right this instant," no matter what his eyes looked like..

"Miss Fox," he said, his deep, cultured voice making a formal address sound more like a lover's endearment.

"Mr. Locke," she replied, her lips curving up into a small smile despite herself. He couldn't be much older than she was, early thirties maybe, but he'd never addressed her by her first name. The combination of his British accent and his old-fashioned manners fascinated her. It was like meeting a character from a Jane Austen novel right outside her door.

She'd certainly pictured him in breeches enough times.

Alistair inclined his head and hesitated. Brie imagined he was trying to decide whether to continue outside and risk actual conversation with her, or simply slink back into his apartment and wait for her to leave. Her smile faded in the face of the usual hurt and confusion. She wasn't some troll, and as far as she knew her conversational skills were just fine. So what was his problem? For about the millionth time, Brie wished she could take this ridiculous attraction, light it on fire, kick the ashes away and move on with her Alistair-free existence. He was probably like this with everyone, she told herself. The man never had company that she'd seen. And some people simply didn't like other people. But it got harder all the time not to take his repeated snubs personally. They were neighbors. She was low-key, neat, didn't throw wild parties, never blocked the driveway, and had never reacted to his presence by turning into a slobbering idiot. Despite all that, all she generally had to do was say hello to get him to bolt.

So she found herself shocked when Alistair shut the door behind him, locked it and continued speaking to her of his own volition.

"And where are you off to before the storm, Miss Fox? Somewhere safer, I hope."

Chapter Two

Alistair had promised himself he wouldn't get this close to her, but surely a walk to the garage was safe enough.

Though of course, nowhere with Brienne Fox would be completely safe, he thought. At least, not where he was concerned. The woman had no idea how appealing she was. How much he wanted to explore every inch of that curvy little body with his lips, his tongue.

His teeth.

That last impulse was the most worrisome. It had been a long time since a woman had stirred his senses this way—if one ever had. No matter what he tried to tell himself to rationalize it all away, some deep, dark part of himself kept quietly insisting that Brienne was different. Singular. Which would explain why he was compelled to spend an unreasonable portion of every evening simply breathing in her scent, which seemed to permeate every nook and cranny of the house, and wishing he could just…roll around in it. Preferably with her.

Frustrated, Alistair forced the unwanted thoughts away. He had good reasons for staying a solitary wolf, and he had no intention of endangering anyone…no matter how mouthwatering she might be.

"I'm just headed to the grocery store, actually," Brienne said, blissfully unaware of the heated images cascading through his thoughts. "You?"

"I have a few last-minute things to pick up. Nothing more," he replied. Such a casual way to put it, Alistair thought, smirking at the dark humor in the moment. Brienne was talking about buying milk and bread to weather a storm. He was talking about making final preparations to take on an enemy that had been snapping at his heels for years.

It wouldn't be long now. He could scent trouble on the wind, pressing in all around him. Owain was close by, searching. This time, he would allow his brother to find him…and somehow, he knew that the end of their long battle would come during this storm. It didn't just provide convenient cover to avoid human attention, it was dramatic in a way that would suit Owain—howling wind, blinding snow, and a bloody crescendo.

Alistair often wished his brother had decided to channel his impulses differently and just become an actor instead of a psychopath. In the meantime, he would rather not give Owain another weapon to use against him. Enough people had been punished for earning his affection.

Alistair drew in a deep breath and opened the front

door for Brienne, catching the scent that had slowly been driving him mad for months now—vanilla and apricot, a breath of summer on a blustery winter day.

"Thanks," Brienne said, the look she gave him bemused. It would be, he supposed. Chivalry was basically dead these days, but old habits died hard. And his were very old indeed. Old enough to terrify a beautiful young thing like her.

"Of course," Alistair said, hoping his voice sounded steadier than he felt as he stepped out after her.

"My first real nor'easter," Brienne said, her tone as warm as it always was when she tried to speak to him. "I'm not sure whether to be excited or worried."

She seemed to be both, which didn't surprise him. Their longest encounter to date, shortly after she'd moved in, had involved Brienne chattering happily about the "adventure" of moving to this small Northern town from the sunny Florida coast where she'd been raised. She seemed to carry that sunlight with her, he thought. The woman was so damnably *inviting*. What puzzled Alistair was why she continued to try and initiate contact with him when he was anything but. He was an unsociable creature who'd spent too long focused on honor, duty, and nothing else. He was under no illusions about his meager appeal to someone like her. Most women seemed to sense his *otherness* and steered clear.

And yet here she was again.

Fascinated despite himself, Alistair fell into step beside her, letting his eyes rake her from head to toe when she looked away. Brienne's beauty was striking each time he saw her. She'd twisted up the loose curls of her honey-blond hair into a bun, though a few obstinate tendrils had already escaped to frame the perfect oval of her face. Alistair's gaze lingered on the pretty pink rosebud lips, the pert little nose, and the eyes, wide and an arresting shade of forest-green that quickly returned to him. He already knew the body that was hidden beneath her winter coat was perfect, small-waisted and amply curved in all the right places. He'd admired it often enough from afar.

Not to mention imagined it enough in his unoccupied moments.

Alistair didn't realize he hadn't responded to her until she tried again, her voice taking on a nervous edge that he knew he'd caused. *Good*, he thought. She ought to be nervous around him.

"So do you think it'll be bad? The storm, I mean? The weather people seem to think we're going to get dumped on, but they're wrong at least half the time."

"I think they're right this time," Alistair said. He could feel the approach of the storm deep in his bones, could smell it on the cold breeze. They would indeed get hit. One storm among hundreds he'd experienced, and one more he would spend without the warmth of his pack to surround him. He let himself wonder, just for a moment, how they were before pushing the thoughts aside. They were safe, according to his last conversation with Edwin. His nephew was doing a good job acting as Alpha in his stead, but lately, he'd begun pressing Alistair to come back. Edwin was increasingly insistent that with Alistair now healed, they could fight off whatever army Owain could muster.

He was almost tempted…until he looked at his scars. And remembered the bodies—the friends—they'd had to burn.

Alistair's guess had been right—his brother hated him even more than he wanted control of the pack. As long as that stayed true, he would stay in this self-imposed exile and keep this the way it always should have stayed.

Between the two of them.

"Well, hopefully the power will stay on," Brienne said, drawing his attention back to her. "I'm not sure the land-lord has a generator to lug over, even if he could."

He frowned. "One never knows. Surely you have friends locally who've done this before."

She shrugged, flushing a little. "I've had some pretty tight deadlines since I've been here. And, you know, it's kind of harder to make good friends when you don't work outside your house. Not that I don't have friends," she added hurriedly. "They're just mostly not, you know, *here*."

It hadn't occurred to him until that moment that the woman wouldn't have a backup plan that involved leaving. Or that she wouldn't have dozens of friends lined up waiting to help her, even though he'd never actually seen any of them. It was a shock to realize they had something in common.

"But you seem so"—*delicious, beautiful, irresistibly lickable*—"friendly," Alistair finally managed, nearly choking on the word.

Now she looked amused. "Oh. Well…thanks?"

"You may want to think about visiting your family Miss Fox, or at least getting out of town if you don't want to go that far. There's still time to pack a few things and start driving. It's likely to get very bad. Have you looked at the news? This is nothing like the hurricanes I expect you've seen. When the storm moves out, we could be snowed in for days." *And I'd hate to see you caught up in anything that might happen*, he silently added. Surely Brienne had safer places to go, places she wouldn't be alone without heat or light. Places where she wouldn't be compelled to ask to share an unfriendly werewolf's fireplace.

One look in those intelligent green eyes and he knew that was exactly what she expected to do. That, and perhaps more. There was no ignoring the desire he saw simmering just beneath the surface...though the gods knew he'd been trying for months now. This would be so much easier if everything in him didn't want to respond to her need by revealing his own. Alistair swallowed hard.

"Please call me Brie," she said. "And thanks for the advice, but I'm sure I'll manage. You're staying put too, right? If things get sticky, I'm sure we can figure something out."

It was spoken innocently enough, but Alistair found himself suddenly inundated with visions of how it might be if he drizzled honey all over her body and licked it off. Sticky, indeed. He fought back a shudder, glad he was wearing a coat that covered the hard, throbbing evidence of his thoughts about her. It was time to end this before he did something foolish. Fortunately, they'd arrived at the garage. Alistair opened the side door for her, and she stepped inside. He followed, but she startled him by stopping short and turning to look at him, a determined look on her face.

He only narrowly avoided crashing into her. As it was, they were less than an inch from being pressed up against each other—and Brienne stood her ground. Pride had him standing his own. Surely he could manage to be so close just this once without tucking his tail between his legs and running.

He'd always been supremely self-controlled. And yet with Brienne, and her alone, things had gotten infinitely more difficult all at once.

She tipped her head back to look up at him in the dim light, the steam from her breath mingling with his. Alistair could feel her warmth, enticing him to get even closer.

She knows I want her, damn it. She must. I should have stayed away.

"Is there something wrong, Miss Fox?" he asked softly, and then, when her brows drew together, remembered what she had just instructed him to call her. "Brie?"

The intimacy of being asked to use her nickname affected him more than he'd expected. Much like the woman herself.

"No," she said, still frowning a little, as though he were a puzzle she was attempting to work out. "I just…I wondered…if you might want to get dinner sometime."

"Did you," he murmured, enchanted as much by the way her eyes went soft and hazy as he was by the innocence of the question itself. Before Alistair could think better of it, he'd lifted his hand, tracing the contour of her cheek with the back of his knuckles. She sighed, turning into his touch as he marveled at how very soft her skin was. Alistair's breath caught in his throat. It was just a simple touch. But from the way it affected him, she might as well have pressed her entire body against his.

He brushed his fingertips along the path he'd just traced, then across the temptation of her lips, which parted at his touch. Alistair gave a strangled moan when her tongue darted out to flick over his finger before she sucked it into her mouth, hot, wet, impossibly sweet. Her eyes slipped shut on a soft, breathy sound of pleasure. He hadn't expected it, and the light suction on his sensitive fingertip nearly buckled his legs beneath him. The rush of desire carried with it visions of her using that mouth on him in ways he'd only dreamed of.

Licking. Sucking. *Biting.* Every instinct roared to life, sending heat racing over his skin. The scent of her, each delicate pull of her lips around his oversensitive flesh, was suddenly overwhelming. The ancient beast that slumbered within him was awakened all at once, and when he groaned again, it sounded like the guttural growl of a wolf. A snippet of a rhyme from his youth drifted through his mind, just an ominous whisper.

The mating bond, when true and real, is soft as velvet, strong as steel.

Alistair didn't know how he found the strength to pull away from her. As it was, it was a clumsy, frightened stumble, but there was nothing to be done for it. He could barely breathe. All he could do was feel, one sensation crashing into another until every inch of his body vibrated with need. All for her.

Even in the shadows, he could see Brie's furious blush, bright pink on peaches and cream. She didn't understand. And he didn't have time to explain.

"I...I'm sorry," she stammered, sounding as shaken as he felt.

"No, that's...I have to go," Alistair said, hoping his rough voice sounded more human than he thought it did. He fumbled his way into his car, hitting the garage door opener with such force he was worried he'd broken it. A claw, long and black and only halfway retracted, punctured his visor as he pulled his hand away. He backed out too quickly, unable to get his breathing under control...or his arousal, which coursed through his blood like wildfire. His final glance at the garage before he sped off showed Brie bracing herself against the side of her car, head down.

Alistair tried to regret touching her. How could he not have realized what she was, when he'd barely been able to get her out of his head all this time? But some part of him had known. It was why Brie kept trying to engage him, why he'd stayed here much longer than any other place he'd hidden in the past five years. He needed to stay safe, stay alone. But as he left Brie standing there, all he could think of was the release he knew he would find buried deep within her, tangled in her arms. Because no need on earth was stronger than that of a wolf for his mate.

Chapter Three

By the time Brie got home, the snow was falling.

By dinnertime, the wind was howling, and the homes across the street had vanished behind an impenetrable curtain of white.

Brie huddled in her overstuffed armchair by the window, watching it come down. She had her knees tucked into her chest, comfortable in baggy jeans, a thick cable-knit sweater, and slipper socks. A cup of hot cider cooled on the end table beside her.

She was brooding. And mentally kicking herself, repeatedly and very, very hard.

Alistair's car had been back when she'd gotten home. She wasn't exactly sure how she was ever going to see him again without running in the other direction. Asking him out had been a brief instant of bravery, or maybe just insanity. That would have been embarrassing on its own, but she would have managed to get over it after his inevitable rejection. Things had gotten weird fast, though. He'd seemed so sweet and concerned and actually kind of...shy, almost. So she'd decided to take the plunge and get it over with, *carpe diem* and all that. In the garage, though, with him so close to her, her body had overridden her brain in a way she hadn't realized was possible. Had she really sucked on his finger? *Really*?

Brie closed her eyes and made a soft, strangled sound. Yes. Yes she had.

Maybe she needed therapy. Or medication. Or more of a life. She'd been pretty happy with her life, though, until discovering that she was turning into some kind of nympho stalker.

Brie sighed and sipped at the cider. She'd given up working for the rest of the day. It wouldn't cost her much...she was a couple months away from her deadline. She just wished she could figure out a way to rationalize behavior that had been completely unlike her and accept the fact that her hot neighbor must be horrified that he was living in the same house with a creepy finger-sucking sex fiend.

A gust of wind slammed into the house, making it creak and groan. The lights flickered, and Brie held her breath, waiting to see whether the power would stay on. It held just long enough for her to exhale, relieved.

Then the lights went out.

"Damn it," she muttered as the apartment was plunged into darkness. The mug in her hands still steamed, everything around her cozy and warm. It wouldn't be for long, though, if the power stayed out...and she knew it likely would until the storm had passed and the crews could get out to work on the downed lines. She hadn't been completely honest with Alistair. There were a handful of people she'd be reasonably comfortable begging a bed from. There was, however, the problem of getting to their houses. Tonight was going to be out of the question. Good thing she had a lot of blankets.

Brie groaned softly. She'd moved to Vermont because she'd loved the scenery and wanted an adventure, along with some fresh inspiration. She'd even wanted the snow. This, however, might end up being a little more than she'd bargained for. Especially now that she'd hit the self-destruct button on her little fireplace fantasy.

She finished the cider, tapped her fingers against the mug, and then got up to light some candles. Maybe she'd get lucky and the power wouldn't be out long.

The thundering crash below her startled her so badly she nearly knocked the last candle off the counter. It was followed by a furious bellow that sounded—

No, that was stupid, Brie decided as something glass shattered downstairs and another gust of wind blasted the side of the house. That had either been Alistair, his cat or a movie. Which he was somehow watching without electricity. Laptop, maybe? Except that had been awfully loud. Like, surround-sound loud. Another thud below her had the walls shaking.

Her throat went as dry as the desert. Something was wrong down there.

He's in trouble.

That single thought was more powerful than a lifetime

of accumulated common sense. Brie hurried into the darkened kitchen, grabbed the big knife she'd splurged on one of the times she'd pretended she was going to learn to cook gourmet food, and left the apartment in her sock feet. Years of sneaking up on her older brother had made her an expert at moving silently, and she made no sound on the stairs as the blade of the knife glinted dully in the darkness.

Doubt tried to creep in, even as her feet kept moving. Did she seriously think she was going to stab someone with this? Brienne Fox, the girl who spent more time catching and releasing bugs that got into her apartment than squishing them?

A low, pained moan drifted up from somewhere behind Alistair's door, and she tightened her grip on the knife. Fear vanished in the face of fury. If she had to use it, Brie thought grimly, she would.

The doorknob turned easily in her hand, and the door swung inward. Directly in front of her, a cheery fire crackled and snapped in the fireplace. And there in the middle of the floor, sprawled out facedown on a heavy Oriental rug, was a man. He was big, blond…and definitely not Alistair. Brie sucked in a breath, looked to her left and right, and saw nothing. The apartment was quiet apart from the fire. There was no sign of struggle, or of blood.

There was also no sign of Alistair. But there was something…a feeling, pulsing through her, pulling her step by step into the apartment. He was here. She knew he was. And the need to find him was overwhelming, even as her common sense screamed at her to turn around and run out into the storm, to find someplace warm and safe that was *not* here.

Brie kept putting one foot in front of the other, unable to shake the image of Alistair lying somewhere nearby, hurt and bleeding.

Then the door behind her shut with a neat little *snick*.

Brie froze, and a voice behind her, gravelly and yet somehow familiar, spoke.

"Don't. Move."

There wasn't even time to panic. The blond stranger was on his feet and rushing at her so quickly that Brie saw nothing but a blur of movement. Then she was flying, shoved out of the way with such force that she landed hard on her backside several feet away. Her knife spun away beneath the couch, out of reach. She gave a sharp, pained yelp that was immediately drowned out by vicious snarling that filled the entire room. Her eyes widened as she saw Alistair hurl the blond man to the floor, then leap at him. The blond rolled out of the way, incredibly fast for the blow he'd just taken.

And then somehow, there were no more men, only an enormous pair of wolves, one silver, one jet-black, destroying furniture as they clashed in a huge, snarling, snapping mass. Brie was too terrified to doubt what she was seeing. Whether or not her mind had snapped, she knew she needed to get as far away as she could. She'd only just begun to propel herself backward, away from the fight, when the silver wolf twisted away from the black and lunged at her again. She screamed, trying to arch away as it snapped its massive jaws shut on the loose fabric of her sweater, then shook its head as if it had just caught a particularly choice bit of prey. There was a terrible ripping sound, a sharp, high-pitched yelp, and the attacking wolf was gone again, leaving a gaping hole in her favorite sweater.

Brie felt as though she was watching a film in slow motion as she looked up from her ruined clothing. It was surreal, seeing the big black wolf, at least twice the size of a normal wolf, tear the throat out of the one that had tried to hurt her. She tried to breathe in, but only managed a shallow little sip of air. Then another. The urge to run was all but gone, replaced by a hazy disbelief that any of this could actually be happening. Her body tingled from adrenaline, but her mind, her emotions, were numb.

When the black wolf raised its head, jaws wet and red, it looked right at her. It took a step toward her, then another, padding slowly across the room, head lowered. It watched her through eyes that glowed faintly, a deep, true blue that was vaguely familiar. But in her shock, she couldn't quite gather her thoughts enough to know why.

"No," was the only word Brie managed to say, and it came out as a quiet, pitiful moan that was barely a word at all. When the wolf continued to approach, the only thing she could do was put her arms up, trying to shield herself. She closed her eyes, beginning to shake, and wondered whether it would kill her quickly. Whether it would hurt.

She jerked when hands curved around her wrists, gentle but firm, and pulled them away from her face. Then there was only Alistair, crouching down beside her. His blue eyes shimmered faintly with light, not all of it a reflection from the fire. But at least he looked human. And very, very concerned. Brie stared up at him, still rigid with fear.

His eyes. He was the wolf. But…that was impossible.

"Here, now," Alistair said softly. "It's only me." His deep voice held the sort of warmth she'd wanted to hear since the first time she'd set eyes on him. Not like this, though. Not when she could still see how red his lips were from—

Brie swallowed hard as her stomach gave a roll. Despite herself, she looked past Alistair to the limp body sprawled out in the middle of the room. It had become a man again too. A very dead man.

"Oh my God." Her voice shook just like the rest of her. "I…oh my God."

"Brienne. Brie. Look at me."

She obeyed him, mainly because she didn't want to look at the dead body anymore. Panic hovered just out of reach, but closing in. Her breathing quickened.

"You killed him."

"He didn't give me much of a choice." Alistair was so steady, so calm. He might have been discussing the weather. It was the only thing that kept her from screaming.

"But—"

"He was sent here to kill me. He would have been perfectly happy to spill your blood as part of the bargain. But we're safe now…for the moment." He sighed then. "What possessed you to come downstairs with—" He stopped himself abruptly, jaw flexing. "You should have stayed up where it was safe, Brie."

"But…you were a wolf, and he was a wolf—" It sounded insane to say it out loud, despite what she knew she'd seen.

Her obsession with Alistair notwithstanding, she'd always been firmly grounded in reality. If she were going to decide to hallucinate something, it wouldn't have been like this.

"Yes, we were," Alistair interrupted her, his tone firm. "I was born a werewolf, a very long time ago. But that doesn't mean I'm not also a man, Brie. And I would sooner have my own throat torn out than have you hurt." The sentiment, graphic though it was, managed to cut through some of her panic. Alistair's hands were warm against her skin, still curved around her wrists. His voice, deep and soothing, didn't hold the slightest hint of fear. Her racing heartbeat slowed, her breathing evening out.

The warmth where their skin touched spread, rippling through her. With it came a measure of calm, and sanity. Whatever this was, she didn't want to question it. She needed to be able to think clearly.

"But," Brie protested again, but it was softer this time. She couldn't seem to finish the sentence…there were too many things she didn't understand. How was she supposed to know where to begin?

Alistair looked at her, then at the body, and then at something over her shoulder while he appeared to sort through the situation. Finally, he seemed to come to a decision.

"Come on and sit on the couch," Alistair instructed her. "You'll feel better."

Brie stared at him, incredulous. "I…seriously doubt that."

He surprised her with a smile, the first genuine one she'd ever seen from him. It turned his dark, somber face into something beautiful. It was an unexpectedly lovely surprise in the middle of a nightmare.

"There you are," he said softly. "Come on. Up you go."

She allowed Alistair to help her to her feet, and found she was reasonably steady—as long as she kept her eyes off the dead man.

I'm not going to sit in here with a dead body. I'm not, she thought.

His grip on her hands tightened all at once. "Hell. Brie? Close your eyes."

She frowned, tilting her head quizzically an instant before he dragged her against his chest and held her tight. There was a roar from somewhere behind him, then a series of cracks and hisses. Brie jerked away, certain that some other terrible thing had entered the apartment and was about to destroy them. Instead, she looked beyond Alistair and saw, the last few flickering white flames where the corpse had been, leaving nothing that she could see. The remaining ash evaporated before her eyes. Even the rug was intact, not even singed. The scent in the air, faint and rapidly vanishing, was like a blown-out match.

"Oh," was the only word she seemed able to manage. It was more a breath than a word, too.

"Don't panic," Alistair said quietly. "That's how my kind ends, is all. It's one of the ways we've stayed hidden. Better that than being trapped in the snow with his carcass."

Brie nodded slowly, wondering if she really *had* snapped. Werewolves, burning bodies, nearly being eaten... Alistair's eyes searched her face, and then he sighed.

"Tea, I think," he said.

For a moment she wondered if she'd heard him wrong. "Tea?"

"Mmm. Get comfortable on the couch. I've got the fire, and you're safe here for now. I was expecting my brother, but all I got was a scout. Wherever Owain is, he isn't close by, or I would know. So I'll make tea, and...explain. If you're in the mood to hear it." He paused, watching her carefully. She could guess what he saw.

"I'm not going to hurt you, Brie. You're in no danger from me. You have my word."

Brie watched him warily. "How am I supposed to believe that? Even if you're telling the truth, you just said there's another—"

"Owain," Alistair interrupted. "My brother. It's true, he's anything but safe. All I can tell you is that when he's nearby, I can...feel it. All his hatred. Wolves of the same pack are like that with one another, especially family members. Sensing one another's emotions. It's uncanny, I know. But useful. If you want, though, you can walk upstairs and try to pretend this didn't happen." His voice dropped, softening. "I won't come after you, Brie. I swear it. You might be better off that way, really."

She considered it, or tried to. But the invisible bonds that seemed to pull her to him every time she was anywhere near him only seemed to tighten. He looked so impossibly sad, all the chilly distance he normally maintained gone. And her heart ached for him, in a way that shouldn't have been possible given how little she knew him.

"How long have you been running?" she asked. She

could see his surprise at the question, but Alistair didn't hesitate.

"Five years," he said. "I was badly wounded. Until I healed, running was all I could do. It's kept him busy. And my pack safe."

Slowly, Brie nodded, her decision made. Though she supposed it had been made long before she'd run down here clutching a kitchen knife.

"I'll stay for tea," she said. And then maybe she'd walk upstairs and shut the door. Or not.

"Good," he said solemnly, and held out his hand. She looked at it, suddenly sure that accepting such a simple gesture was actually a very important choice. Then Brie slipped her hands into his, feeling the bright snap of connection between them like a shock. Alistair gave no indication that he'd felt anything, but the echoes of it left her palm tingling.

She allowed herself to be led to the large, overstuffed couch. Alistair took care to skirt her around the section of rug where the other werewolf body had been, and Brie was grateful for it. It would be a long time before she got those images out of her head.

He could have been killed. Someone had come here and tried to kill him. The fact was slowly sinking in, just like her realization that she'd nearly gotten herself killed with her crazy need to protect him. He hadn't seemed to need the help, and she'd probably done more harm than good in interfering. But because he was Alistair, he hadn't said a word about it. Nor, she expected, would he. Shaken, confused, and unable to deny the overwhelming need to stay close to him now that she was here, Brie accepted the fact that she wasn't going anywhere. It was nonsensical, but she wanted to find out exactly what was going on with her neighbor.

The werewolf.

She stopped in her tracks right in front of the couch, her hand still in his. Unlike earlier, he stopped as well, managing to keep a small amount of distance between them instead of nearly crashing into her.

"Alistair?"

The sudden wariness in his expression surprised her. After all this, what could she possibly do to him? All it did was drive home the fact that they didn't know one another. She knew him even less than she'd thought, and that was saying something. Maybe he'd been lying about who the dead wolf was. Maybe Alistair was the cold-blooded killer.

Except the second she thought it, Brie knew that wasn't true. He might be a lot of things, but not that. Her certainty about it was so strong that it was actually unsettling. She was just a writer, not a psychic.

"Yes?" he asked when she said nothing.

Brie hesitated, trying to find the right words, hoping not to get tongue-tied around him the way she occasionally did. Finally, she said, "Look, I appreciate the…tea…but I'm the one who came storming in here. You've obviously been keeping to yourself for a reason. If you want me out of here, don't worry about saying so. You don't even know me, and I…I mean, especially after earlier…"

God, she hadn't meant to bring that up. She was supposed to be an artist with words. She should have at least managed to say something like, "*Look, I know I've been completely creepy with you, and that the finger incident coupled with the botched heroic act probably make your skin crawl when you see me. In short, I should go.*"

He didn't need her in his life any more than she really needed a hunted werewolf in hers. "Earlier," he repeated, and then understanding dawned. Brie wanted to sink through the

floor. Incredibly, a light flush stained his cheeks. Even Alistair Locke, it seemed, could blush. "Ah. Earlier."

"I have no idea what happened," she rushed out while she still had the nerve. "I'm not like that. I mean, I don't find random attractive men and..." Flustered, she tried a different angle. "And then tonight, I've never chased after anyone with a knife before. I don't know what came over me." She looked at him beseechingly. "Please understand that I'm not a freak, is what I'm trying to say. I'm not a freak, and I'm sorry your brother is trying to kill you, and don't feel like you have to make me tea." She closed her eyes, wincing. "Yeah. Look, I should go."

Alistair was completely silent, just for a moment. Then she heard his voice, beautiful and soft.

"No. Stay."

Brie opened her eyes to look at him and saw that he was, as always, deadly serious. But there was more there, emotion she could only guess at. It gave her the courage to ask the question that encompassed everything she'd longed for and worried about since the first time she'd seen him. Everything she didn't understand and desperately wanted anyway.

"Why?"

Alistair said nothing for a long moment, watching her with eyes that began to glow faintly again. Brie made no move to back away, determined to get some kind of answer. But he said nothing, instead stepping closer to her, leaving their fingers entwined. Brie drew in a soft, shallow breath. Even now, the hunger she saw in his eyes didn't frighten her.

Werewolf. She forced herself to think the word, willing herself to feel the right kind of fear, some modicum of terror. Instead, Brie felt safe when there was no reason she should have.

Their eyes locked. He didn't touch her, but she could feel his nearness like a caress, every inch of her body thrumming with it. Waiting for his touch.

"Brie," he said, a soft sigh filled with so much longing. Then Brie was rising up, melting into him as Alistair lowered his mouth to hers. And all she could think was: *Yes.*

Chapter Four

The first brush of his lips against hers was feather light.

The second pressed just a bit more firmly, though it was just as fleeting.

But when his mouth met hers a third time, Alistair sank into the kiss with a soft sound of yearning that Brie thought was the most sensual thing she'd ever heard. Her eyes slipped shut and, with the first tentative sweep of his tongue, she opened for him on a broken sigh. Brie curved herself around him, lifting her mouth into his as he began to taste her.

Some part of her expected the rough, wild kiss of a man who was part wolf. Instead, even now, Brie found herself more aware of how much Alistair was holding back rather than what he'd chosen to give. It left her with the kind of want that had her quivering, almost afraid to move for fear that he'd pull away altogether. One of Alistair's hands slid into her hair while the other skimmed down to the small of her back, fitting her to him with the barest hint of pressure.

It was the sweetest kiss Brie had ever had, though it was excruciatingly gentle, as though he worried she might break—and as Alistair continued his lazy torment of her lips, it was Brie who found herself struggling with the urge to sink her nails into his back and drag him to the floor. She moved against him restlessly, wanting to get closer, to feel more of him against her. Tension pooled at the apex of her thighs until all she could feel was the hot, insistent pulse of her growing need to have him inside her. And still, he held her as though she were fragile, kissing her softly, thoroughly.

"Please," she finally managed to gasp between kisses, pressing her fingertips into his back, urging him closer. When that produced little change, she dragged his lower lip through her teeth, not hard enough to draw blood but plenty hard enough to get his attention.

Through heavy-lidded eyes, she caught a flash of glowing blue. His voice, when he spoke, had dropped to a sexy growl. The sound of it had her breath catching in her throat.

"Careful," he warned her.

"I want you," she whispered, most of her inhibition already stripped away. "All of you."

For whatever reason, those were the words that spurred him to action, though not exactly the kind she so desperately wanted. In a flurry of movement, Brie found herself backed against the wall, her wrists pinned at either side of her head. Alistair's face was only inches from her own, and she was stunned to see how haunted he looked, like some tormented prince of darkness. His breathing was uneven, his eyes dark and glittering. And she wanted nothing more than to have him against her again.

"This is madness," Alistair said roughly, and she could hear the wolf in his voice. It stirred desires in her that she hadn't even known existed. "You have no idea what you're asking for, Brie. What it would mean. I can't do this."

"If I don't know, then tell me," Brie replied, her jaw tight with frustration. Was he really going to walk away again? *Now*? "What am I asking for that you can't do?"

"This," Alistair groaned, and he crushed his mouth against hers. It was an entirely different kiss than his last one, hard and hot. The rough thrusts of his tongue kept time with his hips, which ground rhythmically into her. He kept her hands pinned to the wall, and Brie's fingers flexed helplessly as Alistair switched from sweet seduction to raw possession in the blink of an eye.

She whimpered softly, widening her legs and sliding one of them up to hook around his hip. Words deserted her, along with rational thought. All she had left was a flood of desire so potent she didn't know quite what to do. The friction between them, even through their clothes, drove her quickly to the edge of orgasm. She'd waited too long, wanted him far too much to be able to hold back. The hard ridge of his cock pulsed over and over again between her thighs, until finally Brie surged against him with a harsh cry. Her body bowed with the force of her climax, back arching while her hands stayed pinned against the wall. There was something intensely erotic about being at his mercy this way, and the shock waves washed over her for longer than she would have imagined, until she could only barely stay upright.

Alistair's body quivered, strung tight as a bow, against her as he went still. He closed his eyes, touched his forehead to hers.

"That...wasn't quite the lesson I'd hoped for," he breathed. It would have been funny, but for the torment etched onto his face.

"You could try again, " Brie suggested. She was barely upright from what he'd just done to her, and still she knew they'd only just scratched the surface of what it could be like together. "I'm game."

Alistair chuckled, but there wasn't much humor in it. He sounded pained.

"You have no idea what I want to do to you, Brie. And we should probably leave it at that before you get a lot more than you bargained for. I'm not human."

"If that bothered me, I wouldn't still be here."

"It ought to bother you."

He backed away, releasing her, and the few steps he put between them might as well have been miles. He seemed to be struggling to collect himself. It was small consolation when it was all she could do not to melt into a puddle on the floor.

Brie let her hands slowly drop back to her sides, and without Alistair's warmth the room seemed chilled despite the fire. Brie wrapped her arms around herself, to ward off both the cooler air and the distance she felt Alistair trying to put between them. After that intense blast of heat, she hated to see him retreat back behind his shield. Though a single glance at the straining fabric between his legs told her that it was costing him.

He looked away and shook his head as though he was trying to clear it, his shaggy black hair gleaming in the firelight. His smile was as sharp as the blade of a knife, and the bitterness it held surprised her.

"Tea," he said. "It's safer. Though if you prefer to get as far away from me as possible, believe me, I understand."

Then, with a flicker of graceful movement, he vanished from the room. Brie leaned back against the wall, trying to catch her breath and figure out what had just happened. After a moment, she managed the few steps back to the couch and sank down onto the comfortable cushions. If she'd wanted confirmation that he was just as affected by her as she was by him, she'd just had confirmation, Brie thought. But his reaction to it, to her, to everything tonight just raised more questions than it answered. He wasn't just running from the wolf—his brother—hunting him. He was still running from her.

And she still wanted to know why.

Chapter Five

Alistair ached for her, and it was no one's fault but his.

Pointless, he told himself furiously, remembering how she'd writhed against him, asking without words—and then with words—to have his hands all over her. Knowing that he could be taking her against the living room wall right now instead of brewing this blasted tea. She'd come for him so quickly, so sweetly. He could only imagine how much better it would be for both of them if he brought her to that peak moving inside of her.

Alistair groaned, curling his hand into a fist and resting it on the counter. He felt like putting it through a wall. He was harder than he thought he'd been in his entire life. And still, here he was, forcing distance between himself and what he wanted. What, in some twisted joke the gods had played on him, was *meant* to be his. His destined mate.

And of course, he'd figured it out just as he was finally

going to let Owain catch up with him. If he lived through it, which he intended to, then he could start thinking about Brie. Would she want the kind of life he lived? How would she feel about being uprooted and joining a pack? Would she even want to be turned?

He breathed deeply, tried to focus. He couldn't deal with any of that until Owain had been dealt with. He couldn't sense his brother, couldn't feel him near at all. But given the scout, it wouldn't be long. Days, at most. This was what he'd chosen, what he had wanted. Now he knew he'd made a mistake in his decision, staying here to be close to his mate without allowing himself to acknowledge the reason. And of course she was just as drawn to him. He'd put her in danger. That was unacceptable.

Until the day he was free to return to his pack, he refused to inflict his life on anyone else. But…God, he wanted her.

Soon, he told himself. *I'll leave here as soon as the sun rises, meet Owain head-on somewhere else. Gods willing, I'll be back before long and we can do this properly. Whatever "properly" is.*

Alistair tried to collect himself as he stood in the small galley kitchen, lighting the gas burner with a lighter to heat the water. The process was often soothing to him, the length of the steeping, the scent of the tea leaves. Not tonight, though. Though the wind howled and the electric lights stayed dark, he was almost certain he'd walk back out to find her gone, and the better for both of them if she was…but Brie was very quietly waiting for him on his couch when he emerged. Just the sight of her, those honeyed curls tumbling around her shoulders, lips still swollen from his kisses, left Alistair with an ache deep in his chest. The part of him that still possessed any rationality where she was concerned was uneasy about having insisted she stay, even for a little while. He was both man and wolf. And he was very familiar with what sorts of things happened when the wolf decided it really wanted something, whether or not it was the best idea.

Mine, he thought, a fierce snarl from within. It had him moving to one of his wing chairs once he set the tray before her on the heavy chest that served as a coffee table. Alistair picked up his cup and settled into the chair as he watched Brie, who looked slightly dazed as she doctored her tea with milk and honey. She stirred it contemplatively before looking at him, her expressive eyes guarded. The air, however, still smelled of her desire. His jaw tightened.

"So," she finally said. "Who exactly are you, Alistair?"

She had no idea how different her willingness to listen made her. But then, he already knew she was different than most. Alistair considered carefully how to begin.

"I'm a werewolf. And I'm very old," he said.

Brie tipped her chin down. "Old. Are we talking fifty years? A hundred? Vampire old?"

That made him laugh, a soft chuckle that helped a little with the tension that hung heavy in the air, sexual and otherwise.

"There are no vampires, only the werewolves. The legends seemed to have gotten muddled together over the years, though. My kind lives for centuries, sometimes even longer. It's hard to know, with so many of the older ones having died in battle before their time."

"And...you're an older one."

Alistair frowned. "I think I'm more middle aged, honestly. I was born in England in the year 1509," he said, "during the reign of Henry VIII. We were on the lower rungs of the nobility, but...isolated out of necessity. You see, my family is one of a handful ever to have produced hereditary werewolves. Not in every generation, but often enough that life at court would have been impossible. My father was not a werewolf, but he seems to have been a strong carrier of the genes required to create them. All four of my brothers, and three sisters, manifested the trait. My parents were...we'll say *disappointed*...but they made do." He smirked, remembering. "And our woods were known to have some of the best hunting in the kingdom. Remarkably free of predators."

Brie looked fascinated. "So you were actually born this way. Your whole family."

He shrugged, unused to discussing it. It felt odd to remember the earliest years of his life. "Yes, but we weren't immune from the shortened life expectancy of the time. Three brothers and two sisters never made it out of the 16th century. Most were killed hunting, and one, Mary, turned out to be susceptible to the English Sweat, a plague of the time. Catherine, Owain and I survived. The wolf pack we founded remains one of the most respected in the world. I've worked hard to build that."

"So you went from being human nobility to wolf nobility."

Alistair smirked. "Yes. Though we're better at being wolves than we ever were at being nobles. My situation is unique, even for a werewolf. I've been able to personally oversee generations of wolves brought in, the first either turned by or descended from Catherine and Owain."

"But not you." It wasn't a question. Somehow she knew. Sensed it, the way only a woman so compatible with him would.

"No." He knew it sounded odd. "As the eldest, I took on most of the responsibility. I didn't have time to go hunting for a mate. Even if I had, I'm not sure I would have stumbled upon one." At Brie's quizzical look, tried to explain, worried that he would give too much away. "Wolves mate for life. Werewolves are no different. The problem is that true wolf mates are rarer and more...I'll say combustible. It takes a certain chemistry, one that has to be just so. When it's right, we know it. When it isn't, we tend not to bother, not for long, anyway."

"Oh." There was a wealth of meaning in that one word. He raised an eyebrow.

"I didn't say we stayed celibate, Brie." Her blush amused him. It seemed to be her standard reaction to him.

"I assumed that," she said, sounding as flustered as she looked.

Alistair felt his lips curving into an unfamiliar smile, relaxing into the comfort of conversation with her. It was nice to find he enjoyed talking to Brie, though perhaps not quite as much as he enjoyed kissing her.

Thinking about it provoked a fair amount of heat in his

own cheeks, and he tried to get his story back on track before they moved further into dangerous territory.

"In any case, I've been busy dealing with Owain for most of my life," Alistair said quickly. "He and I are like night and day. It hasn't been pleasant. Roughly a century ago things got far less pleasant. Five years ago what I thought was a meeting to finally make our peace nearly resulted in my death. Which brings us to tonight."

"I don't understand why your brother would want to kill you. That's awful," Brie said quietly.

Alistair shifted in his seat, trying to remember a time when he'd thought of it as anything but normal. "Werewolves aren't paragons of virtue any more than humans are. Owain always struggled with the violence in his nature. It didn't take him long to focus on me as the source of all his ills. My death won't get him what he wants, but that won't stop him from trying. It never has. He's got a substantial body count to attest to that."

"What does he want? The pack? You're still the leader, right?"

"Alpha-in-exile, right now. He does want the pack. He wants the legitimacy he feels like he never had as the youngest son. He wants the power he thinks I've squandered by showing restraint."

Brie looked confused as she took a sip of tea. When she looked up again, she said, "I don't get it. He's nuts, right? It's not like he can just kill you, waltz on in and take over. Is it?"

"No. He wouldn't waltz. He'd attack with his group of bloodthirsty mongrel drifters until there was no one left in charge and then demand submission. If he proves strong enough to do that, they won't fight him. He's a Black. Heredity matters in our world, probably more than it should. Heredity and strength. It can be a vicious existence when things are unstable."

"What about your sister?"

Alistair thought of her, eternally young and beautiful, and let himself miss her laughter and mischievous nature, just for an instant. "Catherine is mated to the Alpha wolf of another large pack. The two of them have their hands full even on a good day. One of her sons, Edwin, acts as Alpha in my stead. My nephew is a good wolf, but this isn't something he wants as a permanent job." He blew out a breath. "I've been gone five years. Not so long by some measures, ages by others. My pack is safe, with allies on either side of our land. But they're getting restless. Now that I've healed, they want me back. And I need to find a way to do that, soon, before that restlessness turns into challenges to Edwin's authority."

He wished she didn't look quite so crestfallen. It would make this easier. He didn't want her to worry over him... in case.

"You left so that Owain would chase you instead of focusing on your pack," Brie said. She shook her head. "You've been running for five years? What did he do to you?"

"He gave me wounds so deep that they would have killed a human man a hundred times over," Alistair said, setting his teacup down. "We'll just...leave it at that." he remembered that night too well—the relief that his brother finally wanted peace, the regret in Owain's eyes, so sincere...his brother's jaws fastening on his throat, claws in his chest, looking to tear out his heart.

Brie was silent for a moment, staring into the fire. When she looked at him again, he saw she understood...possibly more than he wanted her to.

"You're going to fight him. Here. He just sent that scout first to feel you out."

He hesitated. "That was the plan." He didn't see any reason to tell her that he'd decided that the plan had changed. But perhaps, before she discovered he was gone, he could give her something that would help her understand. "Over the years, the pack has lost good wolves to his madness. Eventually, everyone I called friend became a target. Since I've been gone, not a one has been lost. My pack is a force to be reckoned with, and they would gladly fight for me, but my injuries were so severe that I couldn't have stood with them. No good Alpha lets his people die for him while he simply *lays* there, weak as a pup. My absence has kept them safe. My brother is my problem. I have to take care of him on my own."

She paled. "You're ready for this...this fight to the death?" She looked out the window nervously, where sheets of white shifted and blew as the wind howled. "Is this happening tonight?"

Alistair tilted his head, closed his eyes, and reached out into the darkness with his mind, looking for a connection. He found nothing, only night and storm.

"I don't think so," Alistair said, opening his eyes again. "But after tonight, you need to stay upstairs. Or elsewhere." He managed a small curve of his lips. "Not that your kitchen knife wasn't appreciated."

Brie shook her head gently. "And here I was, all this time, thinking you just didn't like me."

The admission startled him, and guilt twisted in his gut. "It should be obvious by now that I *like* you quite a lot. More than I ought to."

"More than you want to," Brie said, looking into her tea as though it might hold some of the answers she was still looking for.

"What I want has been irrelevant for years now. I do what I need to, until this is done." His eyes drifted over her, curled innocently on his couch with her tea. Possessiveness made a hard, hot knot in his chest. He couldn't deny it—Brie was exactly where he wanted her.

The prospect of leaving here tomorrow left him with a sick, sinking feeling. He had no choice, once again. Owain knew him far too well. If he discovered Brie, he would quickly mark her as a valuable prize...and Owain liked to play with his prey. This was a misstep he hadn't intended to make, Alistair thought. If he didn't act quickly, it would be the downfall of him. Too much was at stake to let that happen.

Brie was looking at him in the oddest way. It unsettled him, until Alistair finally said, "Don't pity me, Brie. I get by well enough, and it isn't forever."

"It's not pity."

"Then what?"

"I just have to wonder...you've sacrificed a lot for your pack. To take care of them."

Alistair shrugged uncomfortably, not wanting her to lionize him. He was just a man, at the heart of it. One who took his responsibilities seriously. That didn't make him a hero. It often made him tired.

"They're an unruly lot. Someone has to."

"I'm sure," she said. "But that doesn't tell me what I want to know."

"Which is?"

She didn't move a muscle, but her voice was as warm and smooth as any caress could be.

"Who takes care of you?"

Chapter Six

Alistair's shocked, slightly panicked expression told Brie that she'd hit on the one thing he really didn't want to talk about. Unfortunately, it was the thing she found she most wanted to know. Five years completely alone, she thought, and he'd spent much longer than that isolating himself to protect his pack. "I don't need anyone to take care of me," Alistair finally stammered. "I'm a five hundred year old werewolf!"

Brie looked back at him skeptically. "You're living in an apartment in a little Vermont town, and you never talk to anyone. Except…"She looked around with a frown, suddenly remembering. "Don't you have a cat? I always hear you talk when you, ah, come home." She flushed, realizing that she'd just made it sound like she listened for him. Which she did. Brie hunched her shoulders, aware that she probably looked fairly pathetic.

Alistair burst into unexpected laughter. It was the first time she'd heard the sound, and it was richer, and sweeter, than she could have expected.

"No," he said as he subsided into chuckling. "Cats don't like me, for obvious reasons. I have a fish."

"A…fish?" It was so normal that after all he'd told her, it actually seemed a little bizarre.

"A betta," he said. "Galahad. He's lovely. No, don't look at me like it's sad, I know it is. I'd rather have a dog, but I'd worry too much about it, considering."

"You talk to your fish." Brie considered this. "That's actually kind of sweet."

Alistair snorted, looking mildly embarrassed. "I'm not *sweet*. Gods, I'm glad none of my pack is around to hear that. I've got a reputation to uphold, you know."

Brie watched him with a soft smile. She'd bet his pack found him intimidating. And grouchy. It was amazing how different the man underneath that image was. Alistair veered between formal and charmingly awkward now that he wasn't trying so hard to get away from her. But she'd seen the other side of him when she'd seen the huge black wolf he'd become. It would be a mistake to forget that part of him, and of his life. Her smile faded.

Brie looked over his shoulder, out at the darkness full of wind and snow beyond his partially drawn curtains. He might say they were safe tonight, but morning would come eventually. And given everything he'd told her, she could only come to one conclusion.

"You'll leave as soon as you can, I guess. Tomorrow?"

She saw his surprise. And she saw the truth.

"I haven't got much choice, Brie."

Her mouth tightened, but she nodded. Protecting his pack, now protecting her. That seemed to be Alistair's mission in life, making sure no one got hurt but him. It was ridiculous, the despair she felt at the idea of him not being here. But that didn't make it any less real. Something he'd said earlier played on a loop in the back of her mind, refusing to let her be. That true wolf mates had a chemistry that was combustible. Like a wildfire, she thought. Or an explosion. The kind of thing that would have a normally nice and polite woman sucking on a complete stranger's finger in a dark garage. Or have a mind-bending orgasm from little more than a passionate kiss.

The truth landed on her like a ton of bricks. *No wonder he bolts every time he sees me.* Alistair knew. And he had too much honor to act on it and drag her into this.

His unguarded expression was haunted as he looked into the fire, and Brie found watching it almost painful. He'd been alone for far too long. She couldn't stop him from leaving, and she wasn't foolish enough to think she could take on a werewolf in battle.

But she could be his, even if it was only for a little while. Even if it was only for tonight. It was what she'd wanted since the first time she'd laid eyes on him, Brie thought. It would be a relief to finally give in to all those wild impulses. And now that she finally understood them, she had to think that Alistair would feel the same.

She hoped, anyway. But there was only one way to find out. All her nerves kicked in at once, unleashing a torrent of butterflies in her stomach. Alistair was the definition of nobility on the surface. She would have to get through to the wicked wolf underneath.

It took every ounce of Brie's confidence to get to her feet and approach him. The wary look Alistair gave her was no surprise, but she didn't miss the way he drank her in from head to toe, or the way his eyes began to glow again in the darkness.

"Careful," he said. "I bite."

"What a coincidence," Brie said, trying to keep her voice light even as her heart started to pound. This was important. She knew it on a level so deep it was impossible to question. "So do I."

His deep chuckle was more of a groan as she braced her hands on either side of his head, gripping the chair, and leaned down, only inches from his face. She had never played the seductress, always too self-conscious. But with him, it felt right. She felt…powerful. *More.*

"What do you want of me?" he asked, and it sounded more like a plea for mercy. Brie couldn't find any. So close to him, every inch of her body was vibrating with need. If she walked away now, she could very well burst into flames.

"Wrong question," Brie said softly. "What do you want from *me*?"

He shuddered, his eyes beginning to burn like blue flames. "You'd run if you knew what the answer was."

She shook her head slowly. "No. Actually, I don't seem to be able to get close enough to you. I have some theories on why that is, and since there's just you, me and a warm fire, I don't see any reason not to test them."

Alistair licked his lips, and she saw a flicker of the hungry wolf within. "Brie, try to understand. I'm warning you. That might prove to be…"

She leaned closer, breathing in the woodsy, slightly exotic scent of him, and spoke with her lips only a breath away from his.

"Combustible," she finished for him. "Did you think I wouldn't figure it out?"

His sharply handsome face flooded with understanding, regret, and terrible need. Before he could say another word, she brushed her lips against his, and a tremor ran through him that told her all she needed to know.

"Alistair. Let go, just for tonight. You know what I am, and so do I. I'm yours."

He groaned, and in it she heard his surrender. His hands dug into her hips, and then she was being lifted, carried in a rush of air. Before she'd even had time to make a sound the plush rug was against her back, the fireplace warm and crackling to her left. Alistair loomed over her, his breathing harsh, hands at either side of her head. She could see the animal in him now, in the tense way he crouched over her, in the way the light glinted off his incisors, which seemed much sharper than before.

It shocked her, how hot it made her.

Alistair seemed to know, curling his lip and growling in a way that sounded utterly inhuman. "This is what letting go looks like. Are you sure that's what you want?"

In response, she lifted her hands and slid them into his hair, gently pushing the heavy silk of it away from his face, then again, stroking. Seeing how even that simple touch affected him had her breath stilling in her throat. Alistair's eyes rolled back, then shut as he groaned softly. He leaned into her touch, urging her to continue. There was nothing explicitly sexual about it, and yet it was one of the most sensual experiences Brie had ever had.

She hated to think of how long it must have been since he was touched…though she couldn't wish the pleasure of it on anyone but her.

Lost in sensation, Alistair's face cleared of worry. He still looked somber—she doubted there were many in-stances when he didn't—but his expression was softer, seductive. When he opened his eyes again to look down at her through impossibly long lashes, she could feel that something had shifted between them. He'd stopped fight-ing, at least for now.

She'd take it.

"Brie," he said. She worried, just for a moment, that he would start to protest again. But all he did was repeat her name, more softly this time. "Brie."

He lowered his head, touching his nose to hers. Her lips parted when his breath teased them, but Alistair held back, looking in her eyes once more. He seemed to be searching for something, though she couldn't imagine what. Then, before she knew what was happening, his mouth was on hers.

It was exactly what she'd wanted, and far better than she could have imagined. Where his earlier kisses had tugged at her heart, this kiss was all about raw possession. Alistair's mouth was hard on hers, his tongue sweeping into her mouth to taste her. She felt the scrape of his teeth against her lips as he deepened the kiss, stoking the slow-burning fire in her until she couldn't hold a single thought. There was only feeling.

She dragged her nails down his back, over the soft material of his sweater, and then slid her hands beneath to find taut muscle, heated skin. She flattened her hands against his back, trying to pull him down to her, but he didn't seem inclined to obey. Instead, he pushed back onto his feet, rose and looked down at her as he pulled the sweater off. The look on his face as he threw it aside was deadly serious.

"Be sure," he said. And when she saw the scars, she understood. They were long and white, crisscrossing his chest and torso. Some were thin, some so wide that she knew the wounds had originally gaped open. He'd been savaged, she saw. Even his throat bore marks that bespoke sharp teeth.

His brother, she thought sadly. He was warning her. Maybe he thought the truth would repulse her, or frighten her. Instead, she got to her feet, placed her hands gently on his chest, and leaned down to press a soft kiss to scar after scar, lingering on the ones over his heart.

"I want you naked," he said, his voice rough, his hands far gentler than his voice as he wound them in her hair and urged her to stand upright again. She straightened, and he skimmed his fingers down her jaw before letting them drop to his sides and stepping even closer, eyes burning down into his.

"Now," he said in a whisper that brooked no refusal.

Brie swallowed hard at the command, so different from the perfect manners he usually showed her. But this was what she'd asked for—the wolf. And there was indeed something predatory about the way he looked at her.

The firelight played over the hard, lean muscles of his bare torso, and Brie gave herself a moment to enjoy the sight before she did as she was told. Scarred or not, he was beautiful. Slowly, she lifted her own sweater over her head, leaving her in nothing but her simple black bra. She shivered in spite of the warmth coming from the fire, then reached behind her back to unhook the clasp.

The focus in his glowing eyes as she pulled away the fabric to bare her breasts was like nothing she'd been subject to before. Her nipples pebbled in the cooler air, and her breasts felt full, heavy, aching to be touched. She shook her hair back over her shoulders. Undressing for him this way felt wicked, erotic.

She heard his sharp breath, watched, fascinated, as he stepped back and his hand dropped to unbutton his pants. One button, then the zipper...and then a pause, an arched brow.

Brie knew what he wanted. He'd already made it perfectly clear. And it seemed this was going to be a give-and-take. She slid out of her jeans quickly, stripping off her socks afterward. Then she was left in nothing but her underwear, simple bikini briefs that matched the discarded bra. That was where she hesitated.

"Everything off," Alistair said. "No turning back now."

No, there certainly wasn't. Nor did she want there to be. Brie slid the scrap of fabric down her hips to the floor, then stepped away from them.

Alistair's gaze as it raked over her body burned hotter

than the fire. She heard his shuddering intake of breath, saw the preternatural flash of his eyes.

"So beautiful," he growled.

"Now you," Brie said, but he shook his head. She frowned, not understanding. Unbuttoned and unzipped, his pants hung open just enough so that she could see the thin, enticing trail of hair that vanished beneath. When she raised her eyes to his again, what she saw there gave her pause.

He looked…hungry. It wasn't until that moment that she realized how much he was still holding back. And how close he was to snapping that tether.

"I want to take a good look," he rasped, "before I'm on you. In you. *Mine.*"

She swallowed hard, her heart pounding.

"Show me," Brie said, barely getting out the words. She could hardly breathe.

"My bed. Or maybe the floor." His lengthened, dagger-sharp incisors flashed when he smiled at her. The reserved man she'd known was gone. This was the wolf. "Run."

She spun and heard the rustle of fabric as his pants came off. Brie sprinted away, almost giddy with a potent mixture of desire and fear. Not fear of Alistair, but the primal fear that being pursued always inspired, the impulse to get away, knowing that a predator was right at your heels. She knew she'd be caught—she wanted to be caught—but that didn't stop the adrenaline from bursting through her veins as she sprang through a doorway and down a short hall. She could feel him, could hear his breathy snarl as he closed in on her.

Brie only made it two steps into the bedroom before she was seized around the waist. She made a single, sharp sound of surprise as she was tossed into the middle of a massive four-poster bed. She caught only a glimpse of blazing eyes in the dark before he leaped at her, covering her body with his and entering her with a single hard thrust.

Then Brie cried out for an entirely different reason. To be against him, skin to skin, had every nerve ending alight with pleasure at once. And he was filling her, the hot length of him stretching her so that she fit him like a glove. She was already slick with need, and Alistair gave a guttural groan as he began to thrust into her, the bed rocking from the force. Brie clung to him, pulsing around him more tightly with every stroke. She reached around to grip his ass, to feel the rhythmic flex of his muscles. At the apex of each thrust was a frisson of sensation that had her tightening, arching into him, wanting more.

Alistair pulled out without warning, flipping her onto her belly. Brie clenched her fists in the comforter as he trailed his tongue down her spine, then back up.

"Like this," he growled, pulling her hips so that her knees were tucked beneath her. She rose up on her hands, struggling to make her limbs move the way they were supposed to, and found herself pulled back against him. He was also on his knees, and he spread her legs so that she straddled him, just facing away. She could feel his cock against her lower back, and she pressed back against it as Alistair began kissing her neck, running his hands up her waist to cup and knead her breasts.

"Please," she managed to say as he rolled the hard

buds of her nipples between his fingers. She arched into his touch, letting him fill his hands with her. One hand dropped between her legs and began to play with her, circling and stroking, while the other hand drew her hair away from her neck. He began to torment her, nipping and sucking at the sensitive skin where her neck and shoulder met, all while teasing the sensitive nub that pulsed with every flick of his clever fingers.

Brie whimpered, straining back against him as everything inside her began to tighten at once, quivering.

"Please what?" he whispered in her ear, then dragged the lobe through his teeth. The words began to fall from her lips, all the things she wanted him to do to her, soft, gasping words as her hips rocked against his hand. Every dark fantasy she'd had about him, the things she'd wanted him to do with his mouth, his cock, while she'd been in bed alone at night, was revealed in the heated darkness of his bedroom. As she told him, his hands moved back to her hips, his own beginning to pulse against her again. The sexy little noises he was making in the back of his throat at the apex of every pulse nearly undid her—as it was, Brie was teetering on the edge of a shattering climax. She would need so little to push her over the edge…but she wanted him to come with her.

It was the last thing she said before he pushed her back down before him, grabbed her hips, and thrust into her from behind. The different position, coupled with the deeper penetration, had Brie clenching around him immediately. She came hard, in an explosion of pleasure that blinded her with its intensity. And still he rode her, pushing her higher even as the first waves of her climax subsided. Brie realized she could feel the prick of his claws against the bare flesh of her hips, could hear the wolf's growl in every shallow exhalation.

She felt herself pressing back into him, wordlessly asking for more. She didn't know what the *more* was, only that it hovered there, teasing, just out of reach. Brie could feel Alistair tensing as his thrusts grew wild, more rapid as he neared his own release. When she acted, it was on instinct she hadn't known she possessed. Just when he began to gasp and shudder, she reared back, jerking her hair aside and baring her neck to Alistair.

He reacted like a wild thing, giving a snarl before sinking his teeth deep into the tender flesh. The bright burst of pain was almost immediately followed by a wave of pleasure so intense that Brie screamed with it, a climax that took everything she had left to ride out. Alistair slammed into her twice more, holding her tight as he came, pouring himself into her with his teeth still in her neck.

Light flashed in front of her eyes, and for a single, perfect moment, Brie felt the connection she had with Alistair strengthen, pulling tight, until she wasn't sure where she ended and he began. They fused, sparked. Combusted.

Then he pulled his mouth away, gasping for air as the tremors began to subside for both of them. The light vanished, but the feeling of intense connection lingered like the echo of a blissful dream. Brie collapsed to the bed, feeling boneless, weightless. Thoughts tried to gel, but broke apart. She could barely move, so sated that her entire body felt as though it was buzzing.

Brie made a soft sound, the only one she could muster, as Alistair fell to the bed beside her and dragged her back against him. He pulled the covers over both of them and then buried his face in her hair. Within seconds his breathing had gone deep and even. Brie's eyes drifted shut, and she wondered, just for a passing moment, what on earth she had just done, what it had changed.

Everything. The word was there and then gone, fluttering away from her in the face of the onrushing dark.

Then, exhausted, Brie joined Alistair in sleep.

Chapter Seven

Brie knew something was wrong when she woke up alone.

She blinked slowly, surfacing in the cold dark. Her body felt strangely heavy, every movement taking longer than it ought to. The tender flesh between her shoulder and her neck ached miserably. It wasn't until she'd pushed herself to a sitting position that she remembered why.

He hadn't just let go. He'd bitten her. She'd wanted it, Brie thought. Wanted all of him. The connection between the two of them had been too strong to resist taking that final leap.

And now here she was. And Alistair was...wait...

Brie shivered when she threw the covers off, getting to her feet in her own cold, dark apartment. The night could almost have been a dream, apart from her throbbing shoulder and the fact that she wasn't wearing anything in a house that still had no power. Her clothes would still be on the floor downstairs, she guessed, before seeing them stacked in a neatly folded pile on a chair in the corner of her bedroom.

She could see them, Brie realized, eyes taking in the confines of her familiar room. She looked quickly to the window, where the cold gray light of early morning was filtering in. the wind still moaned, but not as fiercely. Her stomach sank..

Somehow, she knew he was gone.

Brie hurried to her dresser, digging out a pair of old flannel pants and a sweatshirt, a thick pair of socks, and dragging them on as quickly as she could. She didn't bother with her hair, instead rushing past her dresser and out into the darkened chill of her apartment. Brie didn't shut the door, leaving it open as she hurried silently down the stairs, hoping to catch Alistair unaware before he vanished.

It wouldn't be for good, she told herself. He said—

Well, he hadn't exactly said he would be back. He'd just said he had no choice. What if he put off facing Owain again? What if she never saw him again? What if he *died*? What if…

A litany of questions played over and over in her head as the knob of his apartment turned easily in her hand. Brie rushed in, knowing what she would fine, knowing she had let herself in for this. Still, it felt like a punch to the gut to see the cold, dark fireplace. She walked in slowly. The furniture was still here.

Alistair was gone.

She didn't know how she knew, only that she felt his absence. Was that what Alistair had meant about being able to sense Owain? She'd thrived on Alistair's presence for a long time now, Brie realized, even though they hadn't been speaking. The house was empty without him.

You wanted this, she told herself. Yes, she had. She seemed to have found the pinnacle of bad relationship decisions—sleeping with a five-hundred-year-old werewolf with issues. *Mating* with him, she reminded herself. Now all she could do was deal with the fallout.

She just wished it didn't hurt so much. He could have left a note. He could have left *something*.

Numb, Brie wandered through his apartment, wondering if she'd missed something. She paused by the bed, which was neatly made, and wondered what had been going through his head

As he'd straightened up, packed his things. He couldn't have packed much.

"Damn it," she muttered, angrier at herself than anything. Alistair had been honest about his situation. And she knew she would only be a target. Still, being left so abruptly wasn't what she'd expected.

She trudged back out to the living area and stood in front of the fireplace, staring into it as though she might find some sort of answer in the ashes. All at once there was a prickling warmth behind her, coursing up her back and making the hairs at her neck prickle. Brie turned, her heart leaping at the thought that he'd come back for her. And for a brief instant, she thought the burning blue eyes watching her from the doorway belonged to Alistair. But almost as quickly, she realized her mistake.

"*Well*," said a raspy voice that held an eerie echo of Alistair's velvet tones just the same. "So this is why he went running off into the snow so quickly. I wondered what he was hiding. I could feel his happiness…and my brother is *never* happy. He's too busy with honor and duty for things like feelings."

Owain stepped into the light filtering in through the window, and Brie stayed frozen in place, unable to do anything but watch him move towards her. There was no question that he was Alistair's brother. They had the same coloring, similar features. But there was a cruelty in the set of Owain's mouth that she had never seen in Alistair, and his eyes, a blue so deep it was almost black, were flat and without pity. A jagged scar slashed across his mouth, even whiter than his pale skin. There was no honor in this wolf, Brie thought. This one was a killer. And though Alistair wasn't here, he seemed to have found just what he was looking for.

This was what Alistair had feared, Brie knew. And suddenly, his rapid departure made sense. He'd been trying to save her. But this time, no diversion was going to keep Owain from getting his hands on something that could hurt his brother without laying a finger on him.

Desperate, and wondering whether Alistair had realized that Owain had come here instead of following, she tried to stammer out some sort of believable lie.

"I'm sorry…I don't know who you are, but I just live upstairs. I…I heard a sound, and wanted to check on—"

Owain snorted and waved his hand as though he were batting her words away. "Please. Don't bother. I can smell him all over you." He breathed in deeply, eyes flickering like candles. "This is an unexpected surprise. I'd started to think my brother was simply incapable of making love to a woman. Turns out he just hadn't found the right one. So particular." He grinned, and it was terrible. "Should I bother checking for his bite? I can smell your blood, pretty little bitch. Oh, I *am* glad I decided not to follow him. He'll be so sad when he realizes he can't always keep me away from what he loves." He stepped closer, and Brie finally found it in her to take a step back. But the fireplace was right there, and after watching Alistair fight the scout last night, she knew there would be no outrunning Owain regardless.

His grin widened, and he laughed, a sound like nails on a chalkboard. "Yes, run. Please. I could use a little sport before I make you smell like *me*."

Brie stumbled back and off to the side, unable to catch her breath, or to really make a sound. She was on her own, she realized. Desperate, she tried to do what Alistair had described when he'd talked about knowing when his brother was near. She tried to catch some sense of another wolf, her wolf, out in the snow. But she felt nothing, and Owain laughed again. Mocking her.

"No, we're alone, pretty. And by the time he gets back, you're going to know exactly why they used to write stories about the big bad wolf."

That was when she felt him, all the heat and joy and passion and need singing through her blood, rushing towards her out of nowhere. A furious howl echoed through the house so loudlyit hurt Brie's ears, but it was still the most beautiful sound she'd ever heard.

"No!" Owain screamed, and as he lunged at her, she saw his eyes blaze like twin suns, his human form bunching and shifting into that of an enormous black wolf with a slashing scar across its muzzle.

Brie screamed just as another huge wolf—Alistair— slammed into Owain, knocking him into the fireplace with a grunt that was half roar.

The two wolves tangled together before Owain kicked Alistair off. Brie darted across the room toward the door as Owain turned his attention on her, tongue lolling out of a wolfish grin. He jumped at her, and she dove out of the way just as Alistair leaped, sinking his fangs into Owain's hide to take him down again. They rolled in a snarling, biting mass across the floor, smashing into furniture as each tried to get the upper hand. Her passage to the door was effectively blocked by the fighting werewolves. She looked around desperately for an escape route.

Owain lunged at her again, far more nimble and graceful than the scout he'd sent last night. This time Alistair barely managed to drag him back, and Owain's jaws snapped shut mere inches from her face.

He would kill her. And from the look in Alistair's eyes when they caught hers, if Owain managed to do that, he would have killed them both. Alistair hadn't left her. He'd only been trying to get Owain away from here. From his mate.

If they managed to get out of this alive, Brie thought, she would love him until there was no breath left in her

body. He already mattered to her. He was meant to matter
to her. She had no doubt it would be no time at all before
she gave him her heart. That was, if she had the chance.

She hit the floor behind a chair and tried to clear her
head, to force herself to think of a way she could help
Alistair gain the upper hand. She was no wolf, or she'd
have been at Owain's throat already. Maybe that part of the
legend was true and it would come in time, but not yet. She
was still available help, though, despite being only human.

A glint caught her eye then, coming from beneath the
couch. She frowned at first, then blew out a shaky breath
as she realized what it was: her kitchen knife. This was
where it had landed when she'd walked in and Alistair
had tossed her out of the other wolf's path. She started to
inch forward, hoping Owain would be too busy to notice
what she was doing.

A high-pitched howl of pain made her wince, and she
looked to see Alistair staggering around the side of Owain,
who was bleeding from a huge gash in his side. Alistair
didn't look much better, though…blood dripped steadily
from his underbelly onto the floor, and she didn't like the
way he was struggling to keep his feet beneath him. As
she watched, Owain knocked him off-balance, then began
trying to fasten his jaws on Alistair's throat.

Brie nearly sobbed with relief when her fingers closed
around the hilt of the knife. She drew it out quickly and
tucked it behind her, then turned her head just in time to
see Owain looming over a panting Alistair, ready to go in
for the kill.

I can do this, she thought. Alistair had gotten some of

those wounds protecting her. She had no problem repaying it. They were in this together now. And they deserved to be able to make a fresh start.

"Owain!" she shouted.

He looked up, and there was a terrible joy in his eyes the instant before he jumped. Everything seemed to slow down in that instant, and Brie saw Alistair's mad scramble to regain his footing. She lifted the knife just before Owain made impact, and saw the instant he realized what she had. His roar was deafening, full of pain and fury, and she felt the first press of his flesh and fur just before he was yanked roughly back again, crashing to the ground where Alistair finished the chase that had begun so long ago. Blood hung in the air like crimson rain as Owain thrashed, then was still..

When Alistair finally staggered over to her, still a wounded wolf, Brie had no misgivings. She wrapped her arms around his neck and buried her face in thick fur. She felt the burst of heat when Owain's body self-immolated, but she didn't bother to look. It was over. She and Alistair would get their chance.

They'd earned it together.

Chapter Eight

Alistair awakened with a smile on his face, the first time in memory such a thing had happened.

He inhaled deeply, his thoughts still pleasantly groggy, and was treated to the warm scents of vanilla and apricot, sweet as sunshine. Slowly, he became aware of the woman he was curled around, the warm skin pressed against his, the peaceful sound of a woman's breathing.

His woman. Brie.

And now she was his in every way she could be, save one. There were words he needed from her. It was odd, to be the one needing reassurance after all that had happened. But he couldn't have done what needed to be done without her. It was strange, to depend on another person so quickly after all this time relying on himself.

Strange. But in this case, it felt right. He'd been so determined to stand for everyone else that he hadn't imagined anyone might stand for him. He owed Brie his life. But for now, he thought his heart would suffice.

That would please her, he thought. He hoped to find many more things that would please her, as long as she promised to stay by his side. The terror he'd felt when he'd sensed Owain's approach near sunrise was a thing he'd never forget. He never wanted to lose her. Not when he had only just had a taste of all he'd been missing in his life.

Alistair lifted up on one elbow to look down at Brie's sleeping form. His heart ached at the sight. She was so beautiful, an endlessly fascinating mix of innocence and experience. He remembered the way she'd stood before him last night, like some moonlit goddess without a stitch on, and felt his cock stirring immediately. He didn't think he'd ever get his fill of her. But then, that was what happened when you found your mate.

Especially, Alistair thought with a smile, if it was at the most inopportune time imaginable. It was a good thing Brie had decided to take matters into her own hands, or they might still be dancing around one another, looking and not touching.

And gods, did he like touching.

Brie stretched against him with a sexy little sigh, then opened one green eye to peek sleepily up at him.

"You're awake," she said, punctuating her sentence with a yawn.

"Finally."

Werewolves could heal from all manner of wounds if given the time and rest, and from the look of the sky just visible beyond his curtains, they'd slept all day. It was what he'd needed, what they'd both needed after Brie had done her best to tend his wounds and they'd collapsed on his bed. Neither of them had spoken much. They hadn't needed to.

At that point, it had been enough just to quietly bask in their relief.

Now, though, he was awake, and feeling better than he had in a good long time.

"How do you f—*oh...*"

He answered her question before she could even finish it, entering her in a single, swift stroke and finding her wonderfully ready for him. He stilled, looking down at his woman as they lay together, joined. *Mine*, he thought, and savored the heat in Brie's eyes that told him she was thinking just the same.

"I owe you my life," Alistair said gruffly.

"I already owed you mine," Brie said, then gasped when he teased her with a pulse of his hips, nudging even deeper inside of her.

"I need you, Brienne Fox. You've got the heart of a wolf already. You fought for me."

"Well...you're worth it."

He felt as though every last ounce of the weight he'd carried with him all these years had been lifted from him. Finally, he felt as though he could go home...and he realized he could have done it long ago. That he was never truly alone in this battle. But then, fate would never have brought him to Brie. He would trade none of it.

"Come home with me," Alistair said softly. "I want a partner, a mate. I want a chance with you."

The emotion he saw in her eyes humbled him, and when

she nodded, he knew they would have lifetimes together. She came here looking for an adventure, and she'd found him. He would do everything in his power to make sure the one they'd have together would surpass anything she might have imagined.

When she spoke, she echoed the words she'd said to him before they'd made love. This time, they were even sweeter for all the meaning behind them.

"I'm yours," Brie told him, reaching up to cup his face.

"And I am yours," he told her before claiming her lips with a kiss that promised her everything he'd waited so long to give…his life, his loyalty.

And most of all, his heart.

* * * * *

ONE NIGHT WITH THE WOLF

ANNA HACKETT

Mining engineer by day, writer by night, Australian-born **Anna Hackett** grew up a reader, without dreams of being a writer. "I wasn't one of those kids who was always writing stories," Anna notes. "I was too busy reading." But in 2006, on a work trip to a gold mine, something changed. "I figured, I'd read so many romances, how hard could it be to write one? Little did I know!"

She bought some how-to books, joined some writers groups and started writing. "As a teen, I raided my mother's romances and my father's shelves of action adventure books," she remembers. "So no surprise I love writing action-adventure stories with a strong dose of romance." Add in a lifetime love of ancient history and mythology (she's been to Egypt twice) and it became apparent that paranormal romance was a perfect fit.

Anna learned the importance of grabbing every opportunity that presents itself.

After three years in beautiful Denver, Colorado, Anna and her English-American husband currently live in an isolated mining town in northern Australia. When she's not wearing her boots and hard hat, Anna is at her computer, working on her paranormal romances.

Chapter One

She needed a man.

Jade Thorne stared out the window at the party going on in the crisp Montana darkness. A huge bonfire roared, flames reaching high into the night sky. Around it her wolf pack celebrated with their visitors.

Teenagers flirted, enforcers talked business and the elders sat together smiling as they watched the young pups—some in wolf form—tumble and play. Near the fire, a group strummed guitars. Jade watched a couple close to her age dance to the beat. Their bodies sliding against each other, hands moving over tanned skin.

Jade's gaze ran over the woman's upturned face, saw the way her eyes drifted closed, a smile tugging at her lips. Jade's stomach tightened and switched to look at the man.

Like most shifter men, he was big, broad and radiated animal power. Well-worn denim hugged a firm ass and long legs. His big hands slid down the woman's sides, molding her to him as he settled a strong thigh between her legs.

Heat rushed over Jade's skin. Air caught hard in her lungs, her gaze glued to the mating dance. One of the man's hands tangled in the woman's hair, pushing it aside. Then he leaned down and pressed his lips to her neck. To that sensitive spot every wolf possessed. The woman's head dropped back, her eyes turned to the starry sky, her lips open.

What did it feel like? Jade swallowed, the sound of her rapid heartbeat loud in her ears. How hot was the man's hand? Was his touch rough and needy or heated and sensual?

The man pulled the woman farther into the protective circle of his arms, turned his head and pressed his cheek to the woman's hair.

Jade touched a hand to the glass. By Luna, she wanted. A knot tangled in her belly, tight and hot. She wanted what all those people out there had—laughter, desire and love. She wanted a young, firm body sliding against her, into hers.

She wanted a man who loved her.

A cool shiver swept over her skin. Her hand dropped to her side. She would never have what her people shared. She wrapped her arms around her middle. In order for them to have it all, she denied what she most desired.

She straightened her shoulders. She was the alpha of this pack now. It was up to her to preserve their way of life. Her duty to keep them safe.

Her husband was dead and now the neighboring packs—stronger and wilder than her own—were sniffing the edges of her territory, lured by her pack's mineral-rich lands and lucrative mine. They were searching for any sign of weakness.

Her fingers curled and she stared hard at the flames. She'd do what needed to be done, what any alpha would do—put pack first.

She wasn't strong enough to fight their battles alone. Female alphas did exist, but they were surrounded by a strong team of enforcers. Jade didn't have that asset. All she had to protect her pack was herself.

Tomorrow she'd pledge herself in marriage to yet another aging alpha.

All the surrounding packs were congregating on Thorne land for the Courting gathering. She would marry the dominant alpha in attendance and ensure her pack's survival.

Jade bit down on her lip, her eyes closing. Again she would go to a wolf too old to show his bride the pleasure of the marriage bed. Shifters aged well, lived forty to fifty years longer than humans, but they still grew old and tired.

Just once—just for one night—she wanted to feel firm skin against hers. Her eyes opened and she once again stared at the party beyond her windows. She wanted to know the pleasure of a man's hands on her body, wanted a strong, muscled male between her legs and she wanted the raging passion of a wolf in his prime.

Her gaze alighted on a familiar face in the crowd. Her husband's second-in-command—now her second—Chris-

tian Tallant. In the months since she'd been widowed, he'd
helped her assure the pack she'd look after them.

He stood a head taller than the shifters surrounding
him, his legs longer, shoulders wider. Most shifter males
wore their hair long, but Christian's dark hair was shaved
short. While the others laughed and gestured, he was still,
his face impassive.

In the year since he'd joined the Thorne Pack, he'd
served her husband and now her with dedication. They
knew nothing about him or where he'd come from. She
wasn't sure of the dark, hard look she sometimes saw in
his golden eyes. He'd arrived on their land bloody and
wounded...exiled from his pack.

Jade had no idea what he'd done to deserve the cruelest
punishment a pack could mete out, but he was an excellent
enforcer, brilliant strategist and had been a skilled second
the last six months.

And he was a muscled, hot-blooded man.

A vicious wave of desire twisted her insides. Her skin
felt too tight, hot, itching with need. As though he felt her
stare, Christian turned his head and looked up at the house.
Jade stumbled back from the window.

Christian Tallant wasn't for her. He left her edgy, uncomfortable. And the wolf in her knew he was too much
for her to handle.

He was a wolf who'd demand her submission in every
way. Jade couldn't afford for her pack—or their enemies—
to see her as anything but dominant.

No, tonight she needed an easily controlled man who'd

show her pleasure and leave her heart untouched. Because tomorrow she needed to marry a stranger.

Tossing her caramel curls over her shoulder, Jade headed outside. Moving down the flagstone path leading to the bonfire, she vowed that just for one night she'd take something for herself.

Her gaze moved upward to the brilliant full moon hanging above the trees. Thankfully her species had evolved past being ruled by its pull. But it still affected them—quickened tempers, heightened desires.

Nearing the group, she smoothed her hands down her hipster jeans. She knew the dark denim hugged her hips and her azure-colored shirt complimented her golden skin and matched the shade of her eyes. She breathed deep and forced a smile onto her face. She nodded at those who greeted her, accepted their nods of deference.

"Good evening, Jade."

"Hi, Jade."

Members of her pack surrounded her. She kissed cheeks, stroked hair and offered them the reassuring touch and scent of their alpha. It was a need buried deep in their wolf blood. The need to belong and be protected.

A big, male body stepped in front of her.

"Jade? Everything okay?"

Christian's deep voice rumbled through her. She looked up into his golden eyes. Somehow he always knew when she was upset or troubled. He could read her easier than a used paperback.

"I need to talk to you," she said.

One of his hands circled her upper arm. He leaned close

and she caught his scent. Her stomach clenched tight. Luna, he smelled good. A potent combination of man and wolf, forest and heat.

"What's wrong?" he demanded.

His power swirled around her. Dominance oozed from his pores. If he'd been born to the right family, if he wasn't an exile, she had no doubt he'd be alpha.

She glanced around them, saw strange wolves studying her. On the other side of the fire she noted one of the alphas who'd arrived early for the Courting. He watched her with flat, dead eyes that made her skin crawl. She looked away and noted a small group of women watching Christian with speculation in their eyes.

Jade's wolf scraped her insides, eager to bare claws. "Not here."

His head tilted, his golden eyes searching her face. Without a word, he pulled her toward the trees.

They didn't go far, just enough to block the prying eyes. The music still echoed around them.

"Tell me what's wrong."

She turned away from him, her mouth going dry.

"Jade?" His tone softened.

She swallowed. The way he said her name made her want to believe he cared about her. More than just as his alpha.

Foolishness. She couldn't afford to dream. Life had taught her harsh practicalities. For just this night, she wanted something real. Something that could never be taken from her.

"I need a man."

Christian moved up beside her, a dark frown creasing his forehead. "I know. That's why we called the Courting." His tone was biting.

She shook her head. "I'm not talking about that."

Silence.

Christian's face showed no emotion, but she sensed the tensing of his muscles. The silence grew until Jade's nerves itched like a bad rash.

"What *are* you talking about?" The words were a low growl.

She lifted her chin, met his gaze. "I want a lover. Just for one night."

Chapter Two

*F*orbidden.

Christian's hands compressed, his claws threatening to burst from his skin. He stared down at Jade—the woman he'd wanted since he'd dragged his broken, beaten body onto the Thorne Ranch.

As he had that spring day, he fought not to notice her face, her crystal blue eyes, her lush lips.

She wasn't beautiful. *How many times had he repeated that to himself?* She was pretty at best. But there was something else that drew him.

There was a deceptive strength in that appealing face. In the last few months, he'd seen her steel core, her sense of duty and her unfailing dedication to her pack.

But unlike the others who depended on her, he also saw the woman beneath the alpha. He saw the reflection of loneliness in her eyes, the yearning on her face when she thought no one was watching.

She's forbidden to you. He forced his wolf to relax and uncurled his hands. Jade Thorne was as unattainable to him now as she was when her husband was alive.

She needed to marry an alpha to keep the Thorne Pack from being torn apart. There was no room in her life for an exiled wolf with no belongings, no connections, no power.

A year ago his life had been ripped apart and he had nothing left to offer anyone. He had no idea who he was anymore. He was nothing.

But she could be yours for one night.

The words echoed in his ears, tormenting, taunting. He gritted his teeth. He knew his wolf wouldn't tolerate having this woman for only one night.

It would demand everything from her—body, mind *and* soul. He'd dominate her. Own her.

One night would never be enough.

"Christian?" She pushed a strand of honey-brown hair back behind her ear. "Say something."

"What the hell do you want me to say?" He hadn't intended to bark the words.

Her eyes narrowed. "I was hoping you'd help me."

He studied her face. Her skin was a golden shade that begged a man to touch. He knew there were numerous wolves in attendance who'd leap at the chance to take this woman to bed.

"Why?" He had to know.

Her big, blue eyes dominated her face. "Do you know how old I was when I married?" She didn't wait for him to answer. "Sixteen. My parents led a small pack and we were under attack by a larger group that surrounded our land. My parents offered me to Marius in return for his protection."

Luna, sixteen. Heat welled in Christian's chest. Not even an adult.

"He was kind. He was in his eighties and had no heir, so he needed to marry." She pulled in a long breath. "He'd lost his mate a few years before."

Air hissed through Christian's teeth. Wolves mated for life but few actually found their mates. Once they'd left the forests, abandoned the wild ways and started to blend with humans, they'd started to marry those they liked rather than waiting for the rare lightning bolt of mating.

He'd heard the loss of a mate was near debilitating and killed a wolf's naturally high sex drive. The only way to know your mate was at the height of making love, that moment when two people were so close their souls brushed.

If a wolf lost their mate, well, there wasn't much point in needing sex anymore. Despite having an attractive young wife, Christian doubted Marius would've cherished Jade.

"Marius waited until I was older until he…consummated our marriage." She spun away, like she couldn't face Christian, her arms wrapping around her middle. "He was a kind man, a good alpha and he taught me so much about leading a pack." She turned back. "But I want…" Her arms fell to her sides, pressing against denim. "I want someone to show me passion. I want strong hands on my body. I want to know what it feels like to be held."

Her words were a kick to his gut. The look in her eyes slashed him open.

She reached out, her fingers gripping his arm, burning into his skin. "Tomorrow I'm going to marry another alpha. You've seen the list, you know the ones who are coming are Marius's contemporaries."

Christian had seen the list. There wasn't an alpha under seventy on there. And some he wouldn't let near her. They were too hard, too cruel.

Thank Luna the Bane pack hadn't learned of the Courting. He'd deliberately avoided inviting them. They were powerful, covering much of Canada, but he knew from personal experience their alpha was beyond vicious.

"I want one night for *me*." Jade's fingers tightened. "Please help me, Christian."

The plea in her eyes was something he couldn't fight. His jaw tightened until it burned. He doubted he could deny this woman anything.

"I trust you to find someone…suitable," she whispered.

His wolf clawed at his belly. It begged him not to let another touch her, it begged for a taste of her.

In that moment, he knew he'd give the power to shift to be the one to show this woman desire, to watch pleasure explode in her eyes and hear her cry out his name.

But this was about her needs, not his.

His stomach twisted, hard and vicious. He stared down at his scarred hands and opened his palms. She deserved better than the tough calluses of an exile on her skin.

He knew himself well enough to know his raging, carnal urges would dominate her, demand her submission. It would be rough, hot and violent.

No, he'd find her a nameless, faceless wolf to serve her needs. One who'd walk away tomorrow and never utter a word.

"Go wait in the clearing by the stream. I'll send someone." He forced the words past his stiff lips.

Her teeth dug into her lip. "Thank you."

Christian's hand flexed closed, his knuckles turning white. Yeah, he'd find her a man, then he'd find a bottle of the highest proof whiskey and get roaring drunk.

Jade stood in the moon-drenched shadows beside the stream and warred with the butterflies winging in her belly.

She was far from the party now, could no longer hear the music or laughter. It was just her, the quiet hush of the water and her nerves.

Christian had been so mad. She'd read it in the hard lines of his body. She gripped her hands together. For a breathtaking second, she'd been sure he was going to offer himself.

Then the shutters had come down.

For the best. Deep down she feared he'd dominate her and give her a breathless taste of desires she didn't even know she wanted. Desires she could never have.

At least he'd offered to help her.

She started to pace. She was doing the right thing. The pleasure of this night would help her get through the Courting. It would help her survive another marriage she didn't want.

Conjuring up a faceless man, she imagined big hands on her skin, stroking, caressing. She wanted to explore a muscled chest, a ridged abdomen, a thick, curving... *Luna*. She imagined the man's groans and her cries echoing through the trees.

She imagined golden eyes boring into hers.

No. She pulled in the cool night air. She realized that none of her fantasies held a faceless man—they all had Christian's face.

Suddenly the thought of a stranger touching her turned her stomach. She pressed a palm to the vicious churning and took a backward step. She couldn't do this.

A twig snapped nearby. Jade froze.

She sensed a man closing in on her. He was downwind, so she couldn't scent him.

Run? Stay?

He came up behind and she couldn't turn, couldn't move. Her hands went cold. A contrast to the heat she felt pumping off him.

When a hand brushed her shoulder, her muscles tensed so hard she thought she'd shatter.

"Shh," he whispered, his hands brushing her hair to one side. Giving him access to her neck.

Clever fingers skimmed across her skin, over the rapid pounding of her pulse, and made her shiver. He traced the shell of her ear, and she felt the small touch all the way through her.

When he tugged her back against his big body, she gasped. He was solid muscle. Strength and heat.

His fingers slid lower and flicked open the top button of her shirt. "Are you sure you want this?"

His words were a muted whisper. She trembled, her throat dust dry. When he flicked open another button, his callused fingers brushed the top of her breasts, she closed her eyes. She couldn't form the words to answer him.

Against her buttocks she felt the hardening length of him. Her hips moved on instinct. Pressing against him. Seeking.

He growled in her ear. "Tell me what you want."

She stared blindly at the moon partly hidden by the tree-tops. Her lips parted. What did she want? She wasn't sure anymore. Not with this man's hands on her.

His fingers toyed with the next button but didn't open it. "Say it."

"Pleasure," she choked out.

He undid another button. The night air was cool on her skin.

"What else?"

"Desire." She rubbed against him. "Heat."

"What do you really want?"

A sob caught in her throat. "You."

With a muttered curse, his hand slashed down and ripped the remaining buttons from her shirt. He spun her, yanking her hard against his chest.

Rough hands tangled in her hair, angling her face up to his.

Her gaze clashed with liquid golden eyes.

Christian called himself all kinds of names and fool wasn't the worst of them. He would damn himself tonight, but at least for one night, Jade would be his.

"Christian—"

"Don't talk. You want pleasure, I'll give it to you."

She shuddered. Indecision warred on her face. They both knew they shouldn't do this.

Then her hands ran across his shoulders. "Show me."

He crushed his lips to hers, thrusting his tongue into the warm welcome of her mouth. He plundered, he tasted and her head dropped back from the onslaught.

Too rough. He reined in his raging desire. He gentled the kiss, made it an exploration. Her tongue mated with his, strokes that made the blood rush to his groin.

Breaking off the kiss, he let his mouth slide down her neck. She smelled so good and the taste of her skin was mind-blowing. Her hands moved to the back of his head, scraping over his short hair.

How many times had he imagined this? Her is his arms, surrendering to his desire? His mouth met lace. She wore a wispy bra the same color as her eyes. He nudged the fabric out of his way and closed his mouth over her nipple.

She cried out, arching her back, pushing more of that beautiful mound against his face. He sensed the desire strumming inside. Waiting to be unleashed.

He'd be the one to show her what true passion was like. He'd be the one she'd remember in the dark hours of the night.

He scraped his teeth over that small nub, then moved to the other. Her leg wrapped around his hip and she made contact with the hard heat of him. He couldn't control his growl.

Damn. He had to slow down. Had to stop her touching him so he could pleasure her.

He sank to his knees with her in his arms and laid her back on the soft grass. With a vicious tug, he yanked his shirt over his head. Her palms pressed against his skin before he could stop her. The touch was electric. Lost, he closed his eyes and let her roam.

"So strong. All these muscles." Her nails scraped his nipple. "I've watched you a lot when you've had your shirt off training with the other enforcers."

The thought of her watching him made him harden more.

With barely leashed hunger, he pushed her down, unbuttoned her jeans and pulled the denim off her. Inch by inch he uncovered skin that even in the pale moonlight gleamed like gold. He wanted to lap at her, bite her.

Lifting one slim leg, he started at her delicate ankles—small nips of his teeth soothed by the kiss of his lips. She twisted, husky cries caught in her throat. He worked upward, paid special attention to the sensitive area behind her knees.

He wanted to sink his teeth into the smooth flesh of her inner thigh and make it sting, but he choked down the dark urge. She needed tenderness, not his feral hunger. When he nudged at her panties, she went taut.

"Relax, sweetheart." He pushed the lace away and wished they were in the light so he could see her sweet flesh. "Feel."

Leaning closer, he closed his mouth over her wet heat. She tried to rear up, but he held her down with a palm on her quivering belly. Her scent surrounded him, inflamed him. He licked, circling his tongue around the swollen nub. She tasted sweet, fresh and her moans drove him higher.

He'd never held himself back like this. For him, sex had always been hard, fast and sweaty. A release of tension. He'd always made sure his partner had been left satisfied, but he'd never focused solely on a woman's pleasure before.

This was torture, but watching Jade's pleasure—seeing it, scenting it—was also pleasure for him.

Her legs wrapped around him, her heels digging into his back. She lifted her hips rhythmically, her tensing muscles telling him she was close. He lapped at her harder, caught that nub between his teeth.

She screamed, her hands scratching at his shoulders so hard he knew she'd left marks. Satisfaction cascaded through him—at her pleasure and being marked by her.

He rested his face on her thigh, waiting while she caught her breath. He had much more planned for her tonight. It was all for her and he didn't plan to waste a minute of this night sleeping.

When she sat up, they stared at each other. She smiled. "That was… Well, I bet you know, so I'm not going to stroke your ego."

A smile tugged at his lips. "You can stroke anything you like, sweetheart."

Something sparked in her eyes. "That's a wonderful idea."

Her hands were on his chest again. Long, firm strokes tracing his muscles. He caught her wrist. "This is about your pleasure. Not mine. Why don't you—"

She gave a hard shake of her head, causing her curls to

slide over one bare shoulder. The sight of her hair brushing the curve of her breast distracted him.

She pulled her hand free. "My pleasure is to touch you. Explore you."

Those last words were drawn out in a way that made his stomach tighten. "Jade—"

"Stand up."

He heard the order in her tone. It was her alpha voice, the one he'd heard her use with unruly members of the pack. It rankled.

"Now, Christian."

He reminded himself this was her show. He stood, back stiff.

She rose to her knees. Something about seeing on her knees in front of him, her face level with his thighs, caused the temper to drain out of him. Hot, liquid desire replaced it.

When her fingers brushed over the bulge in his jeans, he jerked. When she unsnapped the top button, he sucked in a breath.

Her blue eyes glinted in the darkness. "Take off your pants."

Chapter Three

Christian was everything Jade had imagined. Big, hot and male. *Hers.*

She could hardly believe this was Christian in front of her, slowly sliding his jeans off. He'd just licked her to orgasm. She shivered. She was anxious for more.

But what about tomorrow when you have to walk away? Jade drowned out the voice. She wouldn't let tomorrow intrude. For her there was only tonight.

Only Christian.

He stood naked before her. His thighs were strong columns covered with a light dusting of dark hair. The hard muscles of his stomach looked carved by a master. His erection curved upward, thick and full.

Heat curled in her belly, storming through her veins. "Lie down."

She saw the flash in his eyes. He didn't like her commands. He was an excellent second and never questioned her orders in front of the pack, but she knew he was dominant and guessed that in the bedroom he was used to holding the reins.

Well, she only had this night and she wanted to experience everything she could. Right now she wanted to touch him. Taste him.

He dropped down beside her, at complete ease with his nakedness. Most wolves were. They stripped off to shift and more than one pack member came back from a run naked.

She explored that chest again. Gave the dark hair there a light tug. Her wolf liked that. She scratched her nails over his skin. He was so hard, solid. He'd hold his mate with that strength and keep her safe from the world. She'd never have to fear. She'd always be treasured.

Jade hated the faceless woman.

She ran fingers over his navel, his hipbones. Then she closed a fist around his length. He bucked beneath her, and then went still. She took her time, stroked the heated steel of him. Mesmerized, she found a rhythm, then leaned down and tasted him.

He growled, a long, deep sound that shivered through her. She savored every sound he made, every buck of his hips, the hard grip of his hand in her hair. She tucked away every memory in a deep place in her mind. A place she'd visit again when she wanted to remember.

"Jade—" he tugged at her hair gently "—let me love you."

Tears pricked her eyes. No one had ever said that to her

before. She swirled her tongue over the head of him and almost smiled at his curse. She wanted to finish this discovery first. She wanted to love him.

She closed her mouth around him. Reading the movements of his body, his guttural sounds, she slid him deep into her throat. When he couldn't hold back his release any longer, she reveled in the taste of him.

Then she collapsed on his heaving chest. His hands slid over her back, his fingers tracing up her spine.

"I'm pretty sure Marius didn't teach you that," Christian said in a lazy voice.

Heat filled her cheeks and she was glad he couldn't see her face. "No. Let's just say I've had plenty of time to imagine."

Sitting up, he scooped his arms around her. Then he stood, bringing her with him in a display of shifter strength. She wrapped an arm around his neck.

Closing her eyes, she fantasized what it would be like to belong to him. To have him carry her to their bed.

"Let's wash off in the stream." He carried her down the gentle bank and walked into the water.

"It'll be freezing," she protested. When the cold water lapped at her bottom, she squeaked.

"It's stimulating." With a laugh, he ducked under the water.

She came up spluttering. "We'll freeze to death."

"Then how about a run to warm us up?"

Christian knew other ways to warm her up, but right now he needed to do something to shore up his control.

She'd just shattered him with that clever mouth of hers and if he was going to make it through the night without attacking her and rutting on her like an animal, he needed that naked body hidden for a while.

He watched her shift, that pleasurable sensation of skin to fur, human to beast. It wasn't the ripping and popping of bones like in the movies. It was a glide from one form to another and it felt impossibly good.

She was a gorgeous wolf. Small and sleek in all shades of gray. Her ears were rimmed in black, but the color of her eyes stayed the same. That stunning azure-blue contrasting with her fur.

He'd thought with the naked skin gone, he'd feel better. But she was still too damned tempting.

He called on his animal and stepped into the change. Muscles stretched and tingled. Pleasure washed over him and his wolf rejoiced.

Moments later he stood beside her. He was much bigger, towering over her. His fur was white on his legs and belly, bleeding to tan at his middle and black along his spine.

Jade rubbed up against him and he smelled her scent. Earth and forest, but under it she still smelled like Jade. Like flowers and vanilla.

He nudged her with his muzzle. She spun and launched into a run.

He followed her through the trees, admiring the way she ran, the graceful movements of her body.

The pull of the moon was strong tonight, tempting him to let his human instincts recede behind his wolf. It was always a balance, the relationship between man and wolf. They weren't entirely human or entirely animal.

He leaped a fallen log and gave Jade a hard nudge. She spun and tried to nip his shoulder. Then she pranced away. She cast him a look over her shoulder, and he saw the challenge in her eyes. This time she melted into the trees so fast he almost didn't see her move.

Christian took chase.

He was bigger and faster, but he didn't want the game to end too soon. She was enjoying herself. It was rare to see her without the mantle of responsibility weighing her down. She looked free and easy, like any other woman her age.

They ran through the moonlight, sometimes stopping to explore smells that lured them or to investigate a rustle of leaves that caught their ears.

Heading back toward the clearing, Christian sensed the prickle of someone watching them. He didn't say anything to Jade, just prowled around, sniffing for a scent.

Nothing. The prickle faded away, but his nerves stayed taut. Could just be an animal.

Then Jade danced around him and ran ahead into the clearing. Shaking off the feeling, not wanting to waste any of their time together, he raced after her and pounced. He came down on top of her.

She shifted to human form, laughing as she ran her hands through his thick fur. "You're a handsome wolf." She ran hand down his flank in a long stroke. "All honey and black."

Content to stay in wolf form, he pressed his muzzle between her breasts.

"One track mind, no matter what the form." She curled against him. "That run was wonderful. I haven't let my wolf out for so long. Too long."

Since Marius's death. Christian knew she'd been too busy. And over the last month she'd been nervous preparing for the Courting, reassuring her pack she'd protect them.

The reminder of what tomorrow held had the happiness in Christian leaking away. He tried to move away, but she held firm.

"Not yet," she whispered.

Unable to deny her, he relaxed against her.

"I remember when you came to my pack, Christian." Her words were a murmur. "I remember every detail. You were so beaten, bruised, but your gold eyes were aflame."

He tensed under her hands. There was a gaping hole inside him when he thought of his pack. Being exiled was like losing a limb, losing the heart of what made him wolf.

Jade made him yearn for all the things he'd lost, made him wish things were different. But he could never go back.

Her slim hands slid up into the fur on his neck. "I've wondered where you came from. Who was stupid enough to let you go?"

Emotion churned inside him. He changed back to human form and ignored her slim legs tangling with his. "I come from nowhere. I'm an exile."

"But—"

His hands cupped her shoulders and he gave her a quick

shake. "No buts. I don't look back. Exile means I have no family, no pack, nothing to offer."

She sat up, eyes sparking. "Anyone with half a brain can see you have skills well beyond my enforcers. And you have a pack. You're a brilliant second, and Thorne is lucky to have you."

She was magnificent. Defending him against himself.

"As alpha, I have to wonder if someone will come looking for you one day."

Pain twisted his insides. He remembered the heated words, the slash of claws and the thud of fists that had led to his exile. "No one will come looking for me."

She wrapped her arms around him, her head tucked under his chin. "They can't have you anyway. You're Thorne now."

Her breasts rubbed against his chest, sparking his hunger again. He closed his eyes and drew in her sweet scent. What she didn't realize was that after tonight he couldn't be Thorne any longer.

He couldn't watch her marry another alpha. Couldn't see her every day knowing she belonged to another man.

The urge to howl choked him. He wanted his claws unsheathed, ready to challenge anyone who'd take her away from him.

Instead, he pushed to his feet. "How about you try and catch me this time?"

That was all the warning he gave her. He shifted and headed for the trees.

Christian ran hard and fast, hoping he could shed some

of the aggression pumping through his system. He didn't want to waste this night filled with fury.

He heard her behind him, fighting hard to keep up with his brutal pace. He wanted to smile. Jade was tough and hated losing. He didn't slow down. His dominant wolf admired her strength. A meek, submissive woman would never have touched him like this one. She'd be a mate a wolf could be proud of.

When he reached the stream, he slowed. Turning, he watched and waited.

Nothing. Something rustled high up in the trees, then the sound of wings taking flight. But no sleek, gray wolf bulleted from the trees.

His chest tightened. Had she fallen, hurt herself?

Or had whoever he'd sensed earlier returned?

His chest froze, then he broke into a run. He should've trusted his instincts earlier, not let her cloud his mind.

He picked up her trail and followed it. He saw other wolf prints join her smaller ones. Two large wolves were chasing her. Had members of the pack come looking for her?

A few feet later, he saw a trail of her blood on the ground. The stench of her growing fear mixed with her scent.

Christian felt a molten rush of fury. He charged forward, driven by the need to protect.

Chapter Four

Christian's paws pounded a hard rhythm through the darkness. The temptation to let his beast have free rein was great, but he held the leash on it with single-minded focus. He had to find Jade.

One huge gray had her pinned to the ground. She was still in wolf form, trying to bite her assailant as she twisted beneath him. Angry slashes bled on her tender belly, and the gray had matching gashes on his.

Courageous little fool. Another gray, taller and rangier, paced close by, tension in his body.

Christian didn't stop to plan or think. He attacked. A feral snarl erupted from his throat.

The rangier beast he took by surprise. With a slash of claws, he tossed the wolf into the solid trunk of a tree. There was a sharp crack of bone and the wolf slid to the ground, not moving.

The other wolf pressed his jaws around Jade's vulnerable throat, his dark eyes daring Christian to come closer.

Fighting back the bloodlust of his animal, Christian tried to think. Who the hell were these wolves? Rouges out for blood and females?

He didn't think so. Rogues never roamed in pairs. Then the scent of them worked into senses, past the red tide of his rage.

Bane.

Damn it. He'd wanted them nowhere near her.

But they'd come. Their bastard of an alpha no doubt wanted to see what he was missing out on. To see what part his exile played in Thorne. Christian cursed himself. He knew better than to underestimate Bane.

Christian shifted to human form. He flexed his hands, ready for a fight. "What do you want?"

The gray shifted as well and stayed crouched close to Jade, his fingers gripping the fur at her throat. The site of the naked male so close to her made the veins in Christian's neck throb.

"I want nothing from you, exile." The man's tone dripped disdain. "You're nothing."

Christian had heard it all before. He flicked a gaze at Jade and saw her watching him. A blend of fear and fury mixed in her eyes.

"You're on Thorne land uninvited. Let her go and leave." He lowered his voice to a lethal murmur. "Or I'll make you leave."

The man snorted. "Exiles can't give orders."

"But the Thorne second can."

Now the intruder's eyes widened. "She made you second? Must be a desperate little pack you joined."

Christian was well aware he'd never have become second if Thorne had more able-bodied young wolves. Jade's third was barely twenty-three years old. They were a small pack made up mostly of the elderly and pups.

They were also a peaceful pack who'd taken him in when so many had turned him away. Marius had accepted him, no questions asked. Christian had little to offer them but his fighting skills, and right now he'd use them to protect Jade.

"Last chance. Get off her and I might let you live."

The man growled and then sprang. He moved fast and shifted midair in a stunning display of shifter ability.

The big wolf crashed against Christian and drove him to the ground. He felt the sting of claws at his side. Using all his strength, he held the snapping jaws away from his throat.

The wolf was strong and his moves betrayed what he was—a well-trained enforcer. Christian shoved against the heavy body. He couldn't shift or the wolf would sink his teeth in. Muscles burned. Christian couldn't hold him off forever.

Out of the corner of his eye, he saw a flash of movement. He prayed Jade was getting away. She needed to get back to the security of pack.

But when he saw the other large wolf slink into view, favoring his right hind leg, Christian's jaw tightened.

It might be injured, but it looked riled enough to add its strength to the fight.

Christian couldn't take on two of them. Not in human form.

He had to keep these wolves busy long enough for Jade to make her escape. She was needed. He was a nobody. And deep inside, his wolf would give everything it had to see her safe.

Christian released a hand from the wolf's throat and punched his fist into the animal's flank. When the second wolf rushed in from the side, he kicked it hard.

Growls and snarls filled his ears. Then another body flew into the fray.

Luna, no! Jade sank her teeth into the rump of the wolf on Christian's chest. *Run, Jade, run.* He willed her to get far away.

The gray spun around, ready to attack her.

It gave Christian the opening he needed. Strength like he'd never felt roared through him. He launched to his feet and gripped the wolf around the neck with two hands. It bucked against his hold, desperate to get at Jade.

He saw her scuttle backward, her ears flat against her head.

"I won't let him hurt you. Never again." With a vicious twist, Christian snapped the animal's neck.

Then he turned on the second wolf.

It took one look at its fallen partner and loped into the trees. For a hot second, Christian thought about giving chase.

The wolf would return and whisper to Bane. Tell the alpha that the exile protected a woman. Bane loved knowing the weakness of his enemies.

Then Christian heard a small whimper.

He spun. Jade had shifted back and lay on the ground, her arms curled around her naked body. She was shivering.

"Jade." He raced to her side. Dropping down beside her, he pulled her into his arms, cradling her against his body. "I've got you."

She pressed against him, her face nestled against his throat. "I'm sorry. Just give me a minute."

"Don't be sorry." He tightened his hold. She wasn't used to these types of confrontations. Adrenaline was charging through her system, leaving her jittery.

He touched a gentle hand to the scratches on her belly. They were shallow. He closed his eyes.

"Who were they? They came out of nowhere and chased me down."

Christian cast a glance at the dead wolf. He wanted to hurt the bastard all over again. "Bane."

"What?" She lifted her head. "You said they weren't invited."

He heard the tremor in her voice. She was right to be afraid. "I guess they wanted to check things out. Don't worry, Jade. I won't let them or their alpha anywhere near the Courting."

At the mention of tomorrow's gathering, she seemed to shake off her shock. She pushed her hair back over her shoulder and cast a quick glance at the wolf's body. "Get me out of here. Please."

He stood with her in his arms and strode into the trees. She needed a hot shower and some rest. He'd take her back to the house.

A part of him filled with regret. They hadn't gotten the chance to have their night together. He'd wanted to know the tight, hot clasp of her body, wanted to watch her face as he claimed her.

When he reached the stream, he moved to their clothes and set her down. "Get dressed and we'll head back." He leaned down to grab his jeans.

She snatched them from him in a savage move and tossed them away. Slowly, Christian straightened, watching her carefully.

Her chin lifted. "You promised me the night." She stalked up to him. "I'm not letting *anything* stop me from having what I want."

"You've had a shock—"

"I'm not weak." Her tone held fire. "I'm not some little submissive you need to coddle. It *was* a shock. Now I'm over it." Alpha was in her voice.

When she shoved him hard in the chest, she caught him by surprise. He went down and she followed, straddling his thighs.

Luna, she was beautiful. All that honey-gold skin and full breasts playing peekaboo through her hair.

Her nails raked his chest. "I need you, Christian. I don't want to talk about the fight or tomorrow. I want you to touch me."

She wanted *him*. The thought made his blood shoot to boiling. She didn't care where he came from or that he was an exile. More than anything he wanted to make her his.

He reared up, catching her face in his hands. "Jade." His guttural growl was more wolf than man.

He kissed her, bit into her lower lip and swallowed her moan. She was so responsive. When he slid his mouth down her neck, she arched her back, offering him her breasts. He latched on to one nipple, nipped at it, left it red. Then he worked the other one.

Her cries were the sweetest sound he'd ever heard. He could spend the rest of his life listening to her find pleasure in his touch.

Desperate for more, he slid a hand between her thighs, pushed his fingers inside her. She arched back with a cry, drawing in uneven breaths. She was already wet for him. He stroked her, watched the need build in her eyes.

She pushed his hand away and leaned down to press a kiss to his lips. He felt the wetness of her brush his thighs and the scent of her arousal dug deeper into his senses. His wolf begged to push her to the ground, hold her down and thrust inside her, over and over until they were swallowed up in the raw, primal need.

Christian warred with the wildness inside him. He had to keep his wolf locked down enough to give her everything she wanted.

This first time was for her. Later he'd take her the way he—and his wolf—needed.

Her mouth trailed down his jaw, over this throat. She nipped at him, a little wild, lost in her pleasure. When she licked his nipples, he groaned. This was the most intense torture.

Enough. He grasped her waist, marveled that he could span it with his hands. Her hips were restless, moving to entice. *More than enough*. He had to have her. He moved her so his throbbing erection nudged at her damp entrance.

For one humming moment, they stared at each other. A wealth of emotion flickered in her eyes and he wondered what she saw in his.

She was *his*. For now. He'd make sure she'd never forget who she truly belonged to. His fingers dug hard into the skin over her hips. He thrust her down as he surged upward.

"Christian!"

He froze, lodged inside her, deep as he'd go. "Did I hurt you?"

"No, I—" Her voice trembled. "You're so big. It feels good."

Luna, she was tight and wet. Savage satisfaction rose in his chest. And she was *his*.

Jade moved her hips, drowning in the heated sensations crashing through her. Christian was big and hot inside her, stretching her in a pleasure-pain that was indescribable.

She started to move, rising and falling on him. She ran her nails over his strong, sweat-slicked shoulders, stroking the flexing muscles.

A strong man. A hard, protective wolf. He'd fought for her. He was everything she'd ever fantasized about.

Wanting this moment to last forever, she slowed her movements and dragged off him inch by inch. A growl caught in his throat, his big body tense beneath her. She smiled.

It was the most seductive pleasure to have a strong man holding back for her. To be focused on her pleasure.

She wanted to throw her head back and howl at the night. Her wolf pleasured in the fact fate had given her this man. She closed her eyes and moved her hips down in a slow, tortuous move. Sensitized nerves throbbed, and she ground herself against him. He growled again.

She loved that she could drive him crazy. She felt every inch the desirable woman, the hot-blooded wolf. She wanted to keep that slow tempo, make it last for hours and store up every moan, every move, every caress.

But as hot feelings flooded through her limbs, she couldn't keep up her torture. She picked up the pace. She found a hard rhythm that suited them both. One of his hands slipped between them, a finger finding her sensitive pearl of flesh.

She bucked under the intense flash of pleasure.

"You like that?" He didn't wait for an answer, just stroked and touched her in the way her body needed.

Her stomach tensed, pleasure growing higher, faster. What woman wouldn't want this? A man who could read her, knew her body. Knew her.

The sensations rushing in her made her quiver, her breath catching in her lungs. The promise of release shimmered.

She went taut. A part of her didn't want it to end. In this moment they were one, and no one could separate them.

"Shh." He took control, his hands sinking into the soft flesh of her bottom. He forced her to move again, harder,

faster. "We have all night, Jade. I'm nowhere near finished with you."

When he thrust his hips up, fire ripped through her,
color exploding across her vision. She heard his groan,
felt his hot release inside her.

Jade scratched her nails down his chest and heard her
scream echo through the trees.

She expected to collapse, spent, but just as the pleasure
started to ease, lightning shot though her system. Inside
she felt her wolf keening, crying out in pleasure.

Jade let out a cry, heard the rumble of surprise in Christian's throat. He reared up, his arms wrapping around her
in a possessive embrace.

Mate.

Oh, Luna, no. Jade's gaze collided with Christian's and
saw the terrifying knowledge reflected in the golden depths
of his eyes.

Powerful energy gathered around them, closing them
in and locking them together. Wolf lore said it was at this
moment two mates felt their souls brush. Two animals became one.

Then her thoughts were washed away as her body exploded.

Chapter Five

*M*ate.

Jade was his. Christian knew he shouldn't be surprised. He'd been drawn to her from the very beginning. His wolf had known long before him.

She shifted away, her silky skin sliding against him. Inside, his wolf snarled, not wanting any distance between them.

On her knees, she stared at him with wild eyes. "Christian—"

He sat up. "It's all right." He forced his voice to stay calm, despite the inner rage at the unfairness of it all ripping at his throat.

She shook her head. "No, it's not. We're…we're…"

"Mates," he finished.

She closed her eyes, her chin dropping to her chest. She looked so dejected. He wanted to take away her pain, but with his own beating at him, he wasn't sure he could touch her.

Then she looked up, her face shuttered. "This doesn't change anything. I'm still going through with the Courting."

He knew she was going to say it, but it was still a fierce punch to his gut. Being alpha was as much in the blood as being a mate. Jade would never shirk her duty to her people. It's what he admired most about her.

It meant she would never be his.

His wolf went crazy, clawing at his insides. Christian pulled the night air into his lungs. But it didn't help calm him. Raw anger pulsed in his veins.

Anger at himself for touching her. For the ruthless man who'd exiled him and destroyed his life. For the soul-tearing knowledge that he would never have his mate.

"Without the protection of another pack, we'll be torn apart. They'll break my people." There was a plea in Jade's tone. "If we mate, you'll be forced to fight every challenger." She shook her head. "I won't risk the pack and I won't risk you."

Christian wasn't afraid for himself. He'd fight every wolf on the planet to have Jade. But the lack of security, the tension and unrest would destroy the gentle pack she ruled. "I understand."

Tears welled in her blue eyes. "How can you?" Her voice was a shaky whisper. "How can you when I don't?"

Despite the tearing rage inside him, he surrendered to the need to soothe his woman's pain. He pulled her into his embrace. She pressed her face against his chest, her fingers gripping his arms.

Her hair was silky smooth under his cheek. "I've watched you the last year. I know how you feel about your wolves."

"Why can't I have what they have?"

He tightened his hold and wished with everything he was that he could keep her, protect her, love her. Give her everything she deserved.

"For the next few hours you can." She raised her head and he gripped her face between his hands, thumbs brushing at her tears. "I need to let my wolf taste his mate. If I don't…"

"There's a risk you'll go rogue." She swallowed, deep sorrow in her eyes. "I should never have asked for this night."

He gave her a light shake. "Don't say that."

He slid his fingers into her hair, massaged her scalp. She was right. A shifter denied his mate was ripe to let the wolf take over. The pain of never holding her, the longing to take her, would drive his human side back until only animal remained. Too many times Christian had seen the death and destruction rogue shifters left behind.

But one taste of her submission might hold him.

She nodded, her eyes glimmering in the moonlight. "I want to be yours."

Brutal hunger slammed through him. It mixed with his anger until he couldn't separate them. The only way he might survive this was for him to purge his fury at life in the hot embrace of his mate.

For the next few hours, she was his to do with what he wanted. His hands shook with the force of his need. He released her and helped her to her feet.

With her standing and him kneeling, he had the perfect view of her naked body. So slim and shapely. Her breasts weren't too big or small, just perfect for his hands. Her belly was flat but still feminine. Between her thighs, her sex was covered with soft caramel curls that begged him to touch.

"Run," he growled.

Shock skittered over her face. "What?"

"I want you to run. Stay in human form." He rose to his feet. "And know that when I catch you, I won't be gentle."

Her chest hitched and she stood frozen.

"Run," he snapped again.

She did. Opening into a full stride, she headed for the cover of the forest.

Christian's chest heaved. He waited a few seconds, struggling with his wolf. Then he released his control.

Embracing the wild predatory need to claim his mate, he followed her.

Harsh breaths sawed in and out of Jade's chest. She ran faster and harder than she ever had before.

She heard him coming. The crash of a big body through the undergrowth. She sensed his powerful presence drawing closer. Hunting her.

She was afraid. She was excited.

Her wolf, ever the predator, refused to give in easily. She embraced the wildness pounding inside her and pushed harder, steering between the trees. She'd make her mate work hard to catch her.

But he chased her down. His larger weight took her to the ground, pinning her under him. Jade fought for freedom, breathing hard and twisting, but he held her with ease. Awed her with his strength. Both the woman and the wolf loved his dominance.

His strong thigh slid between hers, his hard erection pressing against her buttocks. His hot breath brushed her cheek. "I'm going to take you hard. Make you remember my touch long after I'm gone."

Jade shivered, hot desire roaring through her. She wanted his possession. She wanted to watch him lose his control with her.

She wanted to forget that she had to give him up.

His weight lifted, rough hands gripped her hips and pulled her up to her hands and knees. His big, hot body crowded behind her.

A callused palm smoothed over her lower back, over one cheek, then dipped between her legs. He caressed her dampness, plunging a finger inside her. She moaned, moving back against him. She felt the energy pumping off him—rage, desire.

Then his hand was gone and she felt hair-roughened thighs against hers. He covered her, his fingers gripping her waist, then he paused.

She thrust back, desperate for him. "What's wrong?"

His big body quivered. "I don't...want to hurt you." His tone was low, tortured.

Her noble wolf, still protecting her, even when she wanted him rough and hard. "Do it, Christian."

He thrust forward, filling her in one plunge. Her cry echoed through the trees. He pulled out and thrust forward again. The rhythm he set was hard and fast, skin slapping against skin.

Jade drowned in the sensations. Her wolf reveled in being taken by her mate. It was everything she'd wanted— hot, animal passion. A man who needed her.

This time there was no finesse, no gentleness. He pushed her higher with ruthless precision. Her fingers curled into the ground. Her vision blurred, her senses condensed down to only him—his scent, his feel, his heat.

A hand tangled in her hair, pulled her head to the side. His hot mouth touched her shoulder, then he sank his teeth into the sensitive cord in her neck.

His claiming shoved her over the dark edge of pleasure, and she screamed. His pace increased and he followed her a second later, spilling his hot seed inside her.

They collapsed on the ground. With his weight on her, Jade could barely draw a breath. But she didn't want him to move. She wanted to stay like this—surrounded by him— forever.

But once he caught his breath, Christian moved onto his side, pulling her with him. He curled his big body around her, pulling her back against his chest with an arm snug around her waist.

They stayed there, listening to the gentle silence of the night.

Wrapped in his arms, she wanted no more secrets between them. "Why were you exiled?"

He stiffened, then slowly relaxed. "I disagreed with my alpha."

Not a crime with a good alpha who appreciated a trusted enforcer's advice. But a brutal alpha, who ruled by fear, would never accept it. Knowing him, he'd believed what he was doing was right.

"He wanted to punish some teenagers who were guilty of nothing more than being stupid kids."

Jade listened to Christian's steady breathing, glad he trusted her enough to tell her. She closed her eyes. How was she going to survive being married to someone else and seeing her mate every day? "And you stopped him?"

"No. I took their punishment instead."

She remembered the terrible wounds he'd carried when he arrived at Thorne. For the first night, their healer had been unsure if he'd survive. He was so protective of everyone weaker than himself, so she wasn't surprised at what he'd done.

"Then my alpha still punished the kids and exiled me."

His tone was blank, but under it she heard the pain and anger. Jade had always thought Christian cool and controlled, but so much seethed beneath his skin.

"One of the teens died."

She bit her lip and smoothed a hand down his side. She only hoped their time together helped soothe some of those wounds.

They held each other as the night slowly gave way to

morning. Each ray of sun sneaking through the trees cut into Jade, leaving her soul in shreds.

Their time was up.

"Christian?"

His lips pressed against her hair. "Yeah."

Tears slid silently down her cheeks. Inside, she felt like she was choking, like she would never take a deep breath of air again. She would marry another man today and forever yearn for the one who'd taken her heart.

"I don't want you to be there today."

His silence ate at her. He'd already suffered enough. He deserved his mate, a woman who'd make him happy.

It just wasn't going to be her.

"You can't be there—" *because I'm already dying without you* "—because if I see you, I won't be strong enough to go through with the Courting."

Chapter Six

Gravel crunched under Christian's feet. He walked down the long drive from the Thorne Ranch, leaving with what he'd brought with him. Nothing.

No. That wasn't true. He was leaving with even less because he'd left his heart behind.

The Courting was starting in a few minutes. Jade would be preparing herself, schooling herself to face the crowd of wolves gathered to watch her pledge herself to the most dominant alpha present.

Christian's hands curled, nails ripping into his palms. He hadn't told her he was leaving. Had decided it would be easier for both of them.

But it wasn't easy.

Inside, his gut churned, his chest was squeezing so hard he thought it would cave in. He wanted to howl out his sorrow to the sky and curse Luna for giving him a mate he couldn't have.

If only things had been different. *If only*. The words mocked him.

He'd thought one night would hold him. That memories of her would sustain him. But now he knew the terrible truth. They'd haunt him, twist him and give him years of torment.

He'd see her face in his dreams, hear her laughter on the breeze and know some other man was touching her, holding her.

Memories would haunt her as well. He stumbled to a stop. The thought sparked his fierce need to protect. As her mate, he was duty-bound to safeguard her, even from emotional pain. Maybe he could find a way for them to be together and to protect the pack.

Christian half turned, his gaze catching on the roof of the ranch house in the distance. Then he stopped.

No. He wouldn't make things more difficult for her.

With purposeful strides, he headed for the highway. He planned to hitch a ride out of state.

By the time Jade was the wife of another alpha, Christian would be long gone.

She'd never felt so alone.

Jade stood in front of the crowd, fighting hard to keep her features blank. She wanted to scream and cry. She wanted to tell them all to leave.

She wanted her mate.

But Christian had honored her request. He was nowhere nearby. She couldn't scent the faintest trace of him.

She held her memories of their night close to her heart. Hidden by her hair was his mark on her neck. And the soreness between her legs reminded her of his other possession.

Those marks would eventually fade, and she knew the day they healed, she'd cry.

She watched a few of the impatient alphas in the crowd. Men old enough to be her father or grandfather. She stiffened her spine and resisted the urge to run her hands down her tailored trousers. Nausea welled in her throat. She wanted to run.

A small hand tugged at the bottom of her shirt. Jade glanced down into the face of one of the pack's pups. She crouched down. "Hey, Ethan."

"You look sad."

Her breath hitched and she forced a smile. "Nope. I'd be better if I could have a hug, though."

With a crooked smile, the seven-year-old wrapped his arms around her neck, his little face burrowing against her. Jade breathed him in and savored the feel of him. She closed her eyes, her lips trembling. She was doing this for Ethan and the others depending on her.

She would do it. Even as her soul cried for another man.

A commotion in the crowd had her sending Ethan off with a tight smile. Jade stood, searching for the source of the grumbles and agitated chatter.

The crowd parted and a man strode forward. He was big with a head of salt-and-pepper hair and a wicked scar down the left side of his hard face. Behind him stood a man and a woman, both tall and lean, bodies coiled, ready for a fight.

His second and third. The older man was alpha.

"I'm here to claim my bride." The man came within feet of Jade, his amused gaze sliding over her. But his whiskey-colored eyes remained cold.

Who was he? She scanned the crowd, waiting for one of the other alphas to come forward, to dispute his claim.

But not one of them moved. In their eyes she saw fear. A chill slithered down her spine.

Swallowing, she put on her alpha face. "Who are you?"

His cruel lips twitched. "Harper. Alpha of the Bane pack."

Bane. Jade's stomach dropped away. She'd known in the back of her mind that there'd been more to the senseless attack in the woods the night before. This alpha was known as a cold-blooded killer. The most ruthless of shifters.

This couldn't be happening. She couldn't lose Christian and go to a man like this. She couldn't deliver her pack into the claws of the very thing she was trying to save them from.

But the Courting laws were ancient and revered. The only way she could avoid marriage to Harper was if a more dominant alpha stepped forward...or if she challenged him to death.

She was going to be sick. Jade wanted to press her hand to her stomach, but he watched her with his cold gaze, waiting for a sign of weakness.

She sensed her third at her shoulder. Cody was young for the job, but already showing signs of making a great leader.

"Jade, where's Christian?"

She shook her head, unable to say a word.

Cody moved closer. "He refused to let Bane join the Courting. He'd stop this."

Or die trying. A part of Jade was thankful he wasn't here.

"Let me challenge him," Cody whispered furiously.

"No." The boy would be dead in seconds despite his courage. She pressed a hand to the young man's shoulder. "Everything will be fine." Luna, what a lie.

Cody scowled, body vibrating with tension, but he stepped back.

"As Courting law requires, our seconds will witness the union." Harper gestured the dark man at his side forward. "Now where's your man? I want him to watch this."

Jade clenched her hands together. "My third will act as witness."

Harper tilted his head. "I demand your second come forward."

"He's not here."

A harsh laugh. "He always was a coward."

Jade tensed. This hard man knew Christian?

Harper stalked closer, crowding her. She made to step away, but he clenched her arms, putting his face in close to hers. "My spies told me he was sniffing around you. I decided to teach him a little lesson."

She gasped. This was all about Christian and nothing to do with her. What was this man to Christian? "Who are you?"

His voice dropped. "I'm the man who's going to have what that worthless pup can never have." He raised his voice to the crowd. "I invoke the ancient rite of *droit de seigneur.*"

The crowd gasped, and Jade's heart stuttered. No one had invoked the Alpha's Right in hundreds of years. It was an arcane law that allowed an alpha to bed any female he chose—whether she was married, mated or willing.

Jade wrenched away from him. "You can't be serious."

"Oh, very, my stubborn wife-to-be." He yanked her back to his side, pulling her close to his big body. "And if you fight me, I'll do it right here, in full view of your pack."

Frantically, she searched the crowd in the vain hope someone would stand up to this man. She wouldn't let Cody go to his death. She couldn't beat Harper herself. Her hysterical gaze collided with Harper's second.

She thought she saw a flash of regret in their vivid blue depths before he hid it. She saw Bane enforcers ringing the crowd, keeping them in check. Big, tough wolves who looked like they killed every day.

No one. The only person strong enough she'd sent away. As always, Jade was alone with no one to protect her but herself.

She struggled. While she knew she couldn't hope to match Harper's strength, she wouldn't go easily. She raked her nails down his face.

He growled and shook her, then bent one of her arms behind her back. Red-hot pain flared in her shoulder. She kicked out at him.

"Fight me, then. I like a little she-wolf in my bed." He ground his hips against her and she felt his growing erection. She wanted to vomit. "And the stories these people will tell should get all the way back to your gutless second."

Christian. Jade kept struggling, but her mind fought to protect itself from what she knew was coming. What she knew she wasn't strong enough to stop.

When Harper tore her shirt, baring her satin-covered breasts, Jade thought of her mate. She remembered his touch, his kisses. She remembered everything from their wild night together.

"Hey." Harper shook her hard, her head flipping back and forward. "Stay right here. I want you to remember everything I do to you."

A hint of scent caught Jade's senses. She tensed with hope and fear. Wildly, she looked over her shoulder, searching the crowd.

Then the fleeting scent was gone. Imagination. Her shoulders sagged.

"Now, pretty Jade, let's see what my worthless exile tasted."

He would sully the memories of her night with her mate. He would show her the worst of what a wolf could be.

"I suggest you let my mate go."

The dark voice skittered through Jade. Her head shot up. A familiar silhouette moved forward.

Hope warred with fear. Christian would fight the Bane alpha. She stared at him. Her lover was gone and in his place was the battle-hardened enforcer. A murderous look settled on his face, his lips in a flat line.

But she felt the strength and the animal power in Harper. He was older but more experienced. Her skin flashed from hot to deathly cold. It would be a bloody fight and Christian might not win.

Chapter Seven

"Finally, Christian Bane joins the fray," Harper drawled.

Christian fought to keep his wolf in check. It lunged and growled, wanting to slash at his father and yank Jade away.

He saw his true name register with Jade. Her confused eyes met his. He begged her to understand. Then he faced the ruthless man who'd sired him.

"I go by Christian Tallant now."

Harper snorted. "Your worthless mother's maiden name."

Christian's jaw locked. His mother had been beautiful enough to snare the eye of the Bane alpha, but too sweet for him. Harper had ground away at her until she'd given up living just to escape the horror of life with him.

There was no way he would watch Harper destroy Jade. Christian knew his father had sent his men the night before to search for yet another way to torment him. Somehow Harper had guessed Jade would be the one thing he could use to finally break his son.

Christian wasn't going to let his father touch her.

"I challenge you." His voice carried through the crowd. "I should've done this a long time ago."

Harper's smile was edged in vicious pleasure. Jade's eyes turned stricken.

Christian felt the calm before battle settle over him. This cruel man had shaped his life for far too long. He'd suffered the beatings, watched his mother fade away, watched Harper destroy so many others and turn the Bane pack into a ruthless, fear-filled group.

With the exile, he'd pulverized Christian into tiny little pieces until he had nothing to offer. Now, he was ready to fight. For himself and for the woman he loved. His mate.

"Let's fight then." Harper shoved Jade away. "Once again you'll feel my claws."

The crowd backed away, forming a large circle around them. Christian stripped off his shirt, leaving only his jeans. His gaze collided with his father's second, Seth. The man had once been his best friend. They stared at each other for a heated moment, then Seth nodded. Consent or luck? Christian wasn't sure.

"Christian, you can't do this." Jade's voice rang out.

She struggled against the Bane enforcer clutching her arms. Luna, she was beautiful. Had he really thought she wasn't? Now he decided he'd never seen a woman as gorgeous.

"I won't let him hurt you." *Even if I have to die.*

She made a choked noise. "No."

"This has been a long time coming." He needed her to understand. He needed to do this, not only for her, but for himself.

She gave a short nod, her blue eyes blazing with something he didn't dare name. He felt a rush of hope. He was fighting for something much more important than revenge.

Christian focused on his father. The older man was a brilliant fighter, skilled and cunning. He'd also stripped his shirt off, and despite his years, he was as hard and muscled as a wolf a third his age. Christian couldn't underestimate him for a second.

They circled each other, feet kicking up the dust.

Harper lunged with ferocious speed and Christian's dodge was a little late. The force of the punch was like a steel bar to the shoulder. Christian staggered.

His father had never gone easy on him. If anything, he'd treated Christian worse than the lowest members of their pack.

No more. He was done being Harper's punching bag. Christian struck out. His blow snapped his father's head back with vicious power.

Harper roared and charged. They traded more blows. Knuckles smashed into flesh. Christian shuddered under the impact of his father's fists.

He knew the damage they could do—had suffered them all his life. For a second, he was a boy again, wishing only to please the man who'd fathered him. Could he really escape this man's hold over him?

You already have. He pulled in a sharp breath and

smelled his mate's fresh scent. Chilling calm descended. He'd already escaped the day he'd left Bane and found Jade.

Christian looked for her. Tears glittered in her eyes. Fear was etched deep on her pale cheeks.

Harper, cunning as always, sensed his distraction. His brutal strike slammed into the side of Christian's head.

Christian's vision wavered, blood pouring down his face. He fell to his knees.

"You were always weak—" his father spewed the words "—no matter how hard I tried to make you stronger."

Christian spat the blood out of his mouth. "Is that what you were doing every time you beat me bloody?"

"Yes."

Christian shoved down the pain pounding in his body and pushed to his feet. "Liar. You did it because you were afraid of me."

Harper's harsh laugh was unconvincing.

And Christian finally knew the truth.

He'd always thought he wasn't good enough, strong enough or smart enough. But being with Thorne—with Jade—had allowed him to see his true worth.

"You were afraid I'd take the pack."

"Insolent son of a bitch." Harper moved forward, shifting into his wolf on the run. The giant black beast crashed into Christian, tackling him to the ground. They both went skidding across the dirt.

The wolf snarled, then thrust his claws deep into Christian's belly.

It was like the burn of acid. Christian coughed, tasted the hot metal of blood in his mouth.

Jade's scream echoed in his ears.

* * *

Luna, no. Jade struggled to get to Christian, but the enforcer held her back. He ignored her pleas and curses.

Her gaze stayed on Christian. *Get up. Get up.*

The scent of his blood stained the air. Harper's blow had gone deep. She willed Christian to rise. When the older man slashed his claws across Christian's face, Jade's stomach dropped away.

She clutched at the man holding her. "Let me go!" She had to stop this.

She'd marry Harper. She'd do anything to save the man she loved.

Like he'd heard her, Christian turned his head. She saw a feral glint flash in his eyes. He launched up, thrusting Harper off him and shifting in the next instant.

The two big wolves lunged at each other, meeting in a snarl of teeth and claws. But now Christian looked possessed, driven by something wild.

He drove the black wolf back. Each lunge Christian made, Harper tried to avoid. Some of Christian's strikes connected. The other blows slowly zapped the older wolf's energy.

They were both tiring. Jade bit the inside of her mouth. She saw their chests heaving, their paws dragging in the dirt.

Then with a final vicious lunge, Christian rammed into his father. He took the black wolf down, his jaws wrapped around Harper's throat.

The universal sign of domination for a wolf.

They shifted back, both naked, their jeans destroyed in

the change. Harper was flat on his back—bleeding and breathing hard. Christian towered over him, fists raised, chest heaving.

"It's over." Christian lowered his hands.

"Finish it, you coward," Harper rasped, his whiskey eyes molten hot. Blood ran down his chest.

Christian shook his head. "I won't kill you. I'm not like you. Death would be easier for you and I want you to suffer."

It was done. Air finally filled Jade's lungs. Harper was defeated and Christian was fine.

She broke from the enforcer's hold and raced toward Christian. He sensed her coming and turned to catch her.

"Christian…" She pressed her face against his chest, wrapping her arms tightly around him.

His hand tangled in her hair, his other arm banded around her middle, holding her so tight she couldn't breathe.

"You're okay?" She pulled back to study him. And realized she was covered in his blood. "Luna, you're hurt."

"I'm fine."

She gritted her teeth. "Don't go all macho on me now." She pressed a shaky hand to the deep lacerations on his stomach, then the claw marks on his face. "I need to treat these wounds."

He cupped her face. "Jade—"

Someone moved up beside them. Jade spun, standing in front of Christian, ready to protect him. Harper's second watched them with a steady gaze.

"As second of the Bane Pack, it's my duty to pronounce you alpha."

Alpha. Jade couldn't breathe. She hadn't even thought about the fact that Christian was next in line.

"I was exiled," Christian growled.

Seth gave them a small smile. "From this display, I don't think anyone's going to challenge you for Bane." Seth glanced at Jade. "Or for Ms. Thorne."

Lack of air made her dizzy. She was free to marry Christian, to claim her mate and secure a future for her pack.

She'd gone from despair and fear to such incredible relief and happiness, she couldn't quite trust it.

When her legs failed, Christian scooped her into his arms and held her against his chest.

"Welcome home, Christian," Seth said.

Christian nodded, then headed for the house.

"We need to hold the Joining ceremony," Seth added.

Oh, Luna, a wedding. Jade closed her eyes and clutched at Christian. Was this real or just a dream—a much wanted, yearned for dream?

"Tonight," Christian said over his shoulder. "My mate looks beautiful in the moonlight."

He carried her up to the house and straight into her bedroom. He set her on the bed, but she scrambled up. "I need to clean those wounds."

After staring at her for a few seconds, he nodded and sank onto the bed. Jade found supplies in her bathroom and knelt in front of him.

As she washed the blood away from his belly, she noted

the deep claw marks. There could be internal injuries, the risk of infection.

"They're already healing," he murmured.

She'd come so close to losing him, and not just from the fight—deep down she'd known he wouldn't stay after the Courting. Her hand trembled. "I'm sorry you were hurt."

His hands clasped hers. "You have nothing to be sorry for." He fingered a lock of her hair. "I'm sorry my father touched you."

She reached up and brushed her fingertips against one of the claw marks on his face. They'd leave a scar. A permanent reminder of everything he'd suffered.

"I need to make love to you, Jade. Here, in your bed, where I've imagined having you so many times before."

She realized he needed it more than he needed his wounds cleaned and bandaged. It was the way of mates to know what the other needed most. Maybe she needed it, too.

When he removed her torn shirt, she trembled. When he pressed her down into the big soft bed with his body, her blood fired.

He hovered above her, resting his weight on his elbows, his hands cupping her head. "Will you marry me? I have something to offer you now."

Hot anger tore through her. How dare he think she only wanted him because he now had a damn pack? She tried to push him off her, but he wouldn't let her budge.

"You had something to offer before…yourself. You may never have seen your true worth, but I did."

A smile moved over his lips. "I know. I didn't mean the Bane pack."

She stilled. "What did you mean?"

"Before you, I did think I was worthless. Exile ripped me open, left me doubting myself. But seeing the way you looked at me last night…." His smile was gone, replaced by an intense look. "You made me believe in myself again, Jade. And now I'm offering myself to you."

Her heart turned over. This proud alpha male was laying everything bare for her. "Christian—"

"I'll be a good alpha, although I'll probably need your help. Diplomacy isn't really one of my skills. I promise to do my best to be a good husband, mate and father."

The thought of children—of his dark-haired, golden-eyed babies—left her breathless. Mates were the most fertile union and usually produced twins and triplets. She'd never let herself dream of a family. It'd always been far beyond her reach.

Yet here he was, offering her a way to protect her pack, offering himself, children…a chance to have it all.

"But most of all, Jade, I'll give you the love you deserve. Every day for the rest of our lives."

Tears gathered in her eyes. Could you die from happiness? "I love you, Christian. I want you. I want your children and I know together we can merge Thorne and Bane and make it a good pack."

He lowered his head and kissed her. When they broke apart, she smiled through her tears.

"Now, didn't you say something about making love to me?" she murmured.

He growled, and the joy she saw on his face made her complete. He was hers. All she'd wanted was one night with her wolf and instead, she was getting a lifetime.

* * * * *

HER ALPHA PROTECTOR

GWEN KNIGHT

Born and raised in Canada, **Gwen Knight** grew up in Edmonton, Alberta. The arts were always in her blood. From a young age (like most Canadians), she took to the ice and for most of her childhood and adolescent years was a figure skater. Her favourite programmes were *Indiana Jones* and *The Mummy*, which seemed to have an effect later in her life.

Gwen began writing at age ten, and can still remember the first moment she picked up a pencil and started scribbling out what had to be the worst story ever. Like most children at that age, school had begun to bore her, and she sought solace in her own imagination. Thus began her obsession with the paranormal world and the many mysteries within.

When she wasn't on the ice, camping, attending concerts— or somewhere in all that, studying—she was reading and writing to her heart's content.

Her interests seem to change on a daily basis. This week it seems to be archery, boating, and zumba. Next week, who knows? It keeps her and everyone in her life on their toes. Gwen currently lives in Fort St John, British Columbia, with her high school sweetheart and husband, Shaun, and their three pets: Buddy, Galahad, and Merlin.

Chapter One

The moment Angel realized there was another of her kind in the restaurant, she should have run.

It was a simple solution. Running meant living to see another day, staying—well, that was the issue. She wasn't sure what would happen if she stayed, and she wasn't entirely willing to find out.

Her eyes lifted from a half-eaten plate, the scent of food drifting by unnoticed—an uncommon occurrence for a werewolf. She was surrounded by a sea of people, all swept away in their own little worlds, their stench pervaded by a musky scent of oak with a distinct hint of the wild. Her nose was usually better than this, but it was difficult to track a single scent with the abundance of aromas filling the dining area. This was when she should have run, just dropped the dishes and bolted. Her paltry possessions would take little more than an hour to gather, and she'd need even less time than that to hop on the next bus. But beneath all the different scents, something redolent held her in place, a familiar teasing fragrance she followed until a pair of dark eyes slammed into hers.

It was *him*.

Angel's heart stopped dead in her chest and an odd sensation uncoiled in her stomach. Those still had to be the sexiest eyes she'd ever seen on a man, a green so dark they were almost black. Eyes like that one didn't forget, not even after a decade of trying. In fact, they'd haunted her dreams practically every night.

She jerked to her full height when he straightened in his chair, studying her so intimately it felt as if they were the only two in the room. She knew this face, remembered the day they'd first met, not that he would. She'd been nothing more than a pup then. But Hunter had been—and likely still was—the alpha of the West Canadian Basin pack.

Oh, but so little had changed. He was still the same man who starred in all her fantasies, from his sharply angled face right down to the light stubble dusting his jaw. So often she'd imagined how his beard would feel grazing against her stomach or between her legs. But they'd been errant thoughts meant only to pass the time, and now her cheeks flushed with the unbidden memory, since he was sitting just across the room.

Those idle fancies meant nothing, though—it was doubtful he even remembered her. A decade, which was nothing to immortals like them, was still a stretch of time.

All that mattered was the fact that an alpha sat in her restaurant, and *oh, doggy*, he was watching *her*. She might have found the shocked look on his face comical if it weren't for the stark fear suddenly hollowing out her stomach. Her teeth pressed into her lower lip as trepidation rippled down her spine. Being that she was a lone wolf, this alpha was within his right to strike her dead for crossing onto his land without permission. The thought tasted like ash in her mouth—of all wolves, why did it have to be this one?

The same realization washed over his face and a storm flashed deep within those verdant depths. Alphas loved flexing their dominance and control, which meant every wolf in the vicinity was considered a member of the pack. Those that did not succumb were dealt with in methods she found unsavory. At first she'd feared the notion of striking out on her own; even in the wild, solitary wolves did not last long. But *anything* was better than submitting herself to a pack. It had taken her far too long to break free from the last one that had bound her, and when she finally had, she'd sworn never to go back. Her life might be chaotic, running from city to city whenever she was discovered by her former alpha, but it was still better than the alternative. She had her freedom, and what was more, she had her sanity.

Releasing an unsteady breath, she dared to meet Hunter's gaze again and her heart slammed against her ribs the moment his viridian eyes pinned her to the spot. The effect was just as powerful as the first time they'd met, and she doubted her poor knees would support her much longer. How could this be? Ten years had passed—surely the man couldn't still possess such a hold over her. Her struggle grew the moment her wolf awoke; she gnashed her teeth, now straining with the sudden desire to shed her skin and run—to *him*. Madness! She *couldn't*. What felt like an eternal moment passed as he held her gaze, his eyes brightening with those of his wolf. Her breath quickened and her palms grew clammy.

Finally, he severed the connection and gasping, Angel slumped, her dishes wavering in her trembling grasp. The plates slid from her arms, clattering noisily as they teetered over the table.

"Angel?" A soft voice lifted behind her.

She spun on her heel, coming face-to-face with her supervisor, Glory. "I—I have to go," she stuttered, fighting against the urge to glance back over her shoulder. He was watching her again—she could feel the heat of his stare burning through her shoulder blades.

"What?" Glory demanded under her breath.

Angel *did* glance back this time, her breath hitching in her chest. The way he watched her, as though he found her captivating—had he watched her that way when they'd first crossed paths? In her every fantasy, she pictured a similar look softening his face, *imagined* him pressing her into a wall or table as he ravished her. Surrounded by plenty of tables, her cheeks burned, along with something much lower. The last time she'd felt such heat between her legs, she'd been human. Suddenly she couldn't figure out what was real and what was the invention of her love-starved mind.

Whipping back around, she met her supervisor's wide eyes. "I—I'm sorry!" she whispered, afraid he could hear her.

"I don't understand, is something wrong?" Glory asked.

"Yes." She nodded.

Her fingers slid up her back and she plucked at the tight knot holding her apron together. She removed it and after piling it into Glory's hands, turned one last time, her heart leaping when she found him watching her again. How could she leave without knowing if he intended to hunt her? While she wanted him to pursue her for an entirely different reason, she couldn't forget that she was on his land. Werewolves did nothing in view of the human public, but that didn't mean she was safe. Her shoulders rounded and she drew in a long breath. Chaotic noise filled her ears and she resisted the urge to clap her hands over them. From all around came the thunderous assault of voices—conversation and laughter combined in a cacophony of chaos. Even the sounds of mastication were deafening and beneath all of that, someone was singing horribly off tune. The effort to sift through so much noise and focus on the party of two werewolves was difficult, but eventually their voices swept over her.

"Seth has been spotted in the city, Alpha." The voice of his companion rose above the endless prattle. "I am not the first to hear such whisperings. If he's come for her—"

"Enough," the sexy-eyed werewolf growled in a voice so deep it felt like liquid heat filling her veins. It awakened something she hadn't felt in years—something she hadn't even realized she missed.

Angel refused to focus on the sinful echo of his voice resonating in her head. Instead, her former alpha's name, *Seth*, replayed over and over, chasing after her scattered thoughts, mocking her. They couldn't be possibly talking about *her*, could they? She'd hoped for a little more time before Seth found her again.

"Angel!" Glory dragged her attention away from her dark thoughts with a heavy hand on her shoulder.

"I'm sorry," Angel whispered before wiping her hands down her thighs and leaving the restaurant, her jacket forgotten on the hook in the employees' lounge.

Chapter Two

"Did you hear what I said, Alpha?"

Hunter jerked his eyes back from the fleeing woman—no, not woman, *werewolf*, and not any werewolf, but *her*. He stared after her, unable to believe that *this* petite wolf had turned up in the same restaurant where he'd come to discuss her former alpha.

He'd known there was another nearby the moment he'd taken his seat, but never in his wildest dreams had he thought it would be *her*. Her scent was everywhere, though quite different from when he'd first laid eyes on her. When had that been? Ten years ago? Now it possessed a burghal presence, heavily imbued with toxins, chemicals and a pungent waft of pollution, very much the same smell as the surrounding city. His wolves all carried hints of the wooded areas they hunted, but this fragrance lacked those markers. It was smoky, but beneath it all was the faint taste of honey that he so vividly remembered—an odd aroma for a wolf, albeit…appetizing.

When he'd finally managed to track her scent, the last thing he'd expected to find was a sprite of a girl, barely large enough to fill the loose clothing she wore. But the moment those sharp sapphire eyes lifted, he was left breathless. Speared by such a look, he could hardly think, let alone register that it was *Angelica* gazing back at him. There she was, after so long searching. Her features were still delicate but with only a hint of the roundness he remembered. Sleek wheat-colored hair spilled around her shoulders, a thick fringe that hadn't been there before hiding her face. Oh, yes, he knew this one, and a surge of pleasure spread through his gut.

The wolf in him had surfaced immediately, his intrigue barely containable as a ghost of a memory arose. Time changed all, and while he could still pick out the young woman he'd known, she now looked infinitely different; a wraithlike shadow of the girl who had floored him the first moment they'd met. Not that it mattered, if his erratically beating heart was evident of anything.

The astonishing part was his wolf's response to the spritely woman the moment she'd glanced up. She'd been all but trembling in that oversized apron, and he'd wanted nothing more than to comfort, to protect her and oh, *so* much more, just as he had all those years ago. The realization staggered him—he hadn't felt anything of the like since the last time he'd seen her. So many years had passed since he'd felt this flicker of intrigue—she alone had been the only one to ever inspire it in him. Apparently that hadn't changed.

What he couldn't believe was that she was *here*. How long had she been hiding on his land? Years back, word had spread that Seth's mate had gone missing, and for years Hunter had searched for her, but he'd never caught a whiff of her location. How shocking that he'd *finally* found her, and on his own territory, no less.

Hunter lifted his eyes to his second, hardly hearing a word he said.

Brody's lips sealed, his gaze falling to the table. "Forgive me, Alpha, but this must be dealt with. You can't allow another alpha to wander your territory—it doesn't speak well of your control. If you ignore this, others will whisper of incompetence—"

A low growl leaked from his throat. "Careful, Brody."

His second winced and nodded. "My apologies."

Hunter might have laughed if Brody hadn't been so close to the truth. An alpha couldn't allow *anyone* to wander into his territory, and there were two wolves now on borrowed ground without permission, regardless of his personal emotions toward one.

"We're done here." Hunter spoke, his voice deep with authority.

His chair scraped over the floor as he pushed away from the table and rose. Drawing his wallet from his back pocket, he dropped a few bills onto the table before stalking off. Brody's words were important, but he couldn't just let Angelica slip through his fingers, not again, not after so many years of thinking about her and craving her.

Palming open the door, he stepped out into the noisy street. A quick examination revealed little: no bobbing pale head, no rail-thin figure diving around obstacles or into shops. This one was clever.

Hunter tipped his head back and drew the city's scents deep into his lungs. All around him was that noxious stench, but beneath it was the slight undertone of her musk, faintly sweet...the honey. Chasing after her would likely end in her evading him, but if he trapped her... The corners of his mouth tugged into a carnal grin. He had his prey, now he needed only to hunt it.

He kept his pace slow, careful not to upset the crowd he weaved through. Her scent was so faint, but with every step it grew stronger. It was obvious she'd meant to lead him astray, oblivious to the fact that he could track her across the entire city.

Every step brought her closer; he could feel it. Whatever labyrinth she'd attempted to build, he'd managed to cut through it.

Soft footsteps padded toward him on the other side of the alley he currently haunted. His lips tugged and he slanted against the brick wall. A lithe ball came hurtling around the corner and only at the last moment, when she slammed into his chest, did she rock back.

He studied Angelica's face with apparent detachment, but inside his stomach was churning. Her eyes caught the noonday sun and sparkled like jewels—he'd never seen anything like them in any other woman, not that he'd ever looked. But it was her lips that begged for his attention. It mattered little that they quivered in fear, they were just so plump and ripe. The wolf within awoke the moment her true scent sank into his lungs. Hunter could feel the stirrings of curiosity; the wolf wanted to bury his nose in her and sniff from head to toe, if only to recommit her to memory. She'd been the only one—wolf or human—ever to awaken such a reaction within him.

Wide eyes darted up to his as she leaned against the wall. She appeared shocked, her mouth parting as she drew in her own small breath. "Hunter," she whispered in the meekest voice he'd ever heard.

Ah, she remembered him, something he had not expected. What time they had spent together in the past had been minimal due to Seth, but apparently it had left a lasting impression on them both.

"Angelica," he growled, his eyes closing as he sucked in a steady breath that did little to appease his stirring curiosity. Sure, she positively reeked of the city, but he could still scent that sweet tang beneath it all and with every inhalation his intrigue burned brighter. Leaning into the stone by her head, he scratched at his brow. *Control*, he told himself. It didn't matter how pitiful she looked, shaking in boots clearly too large for her. He was alpha and she'd broken his laws by entering his territory without approval.

"Angel," she corrected him carefully.

A beguiled snort crept from his throat. Angel, with the halo of hair. And *sweet mercy*, her voice was like a caroling nightingale's, softer than he remembered. Hunter instinctively curved closer to her, the tip of his nose sinking into her hair. Her breath hitched, the rhythmic pounding of her heart tightening his pants. A wry smile twisted his lips; his body certainly knew what he wanted. Suddenly he was thankful he'd tracked her previous path and that it had led here—somewhere they were out of the public's view.

Last he'd laid eyes on her, she'd belonged to Seth, a monster in the truest sense of the word, and Hunter had felt nothing but relief when he'd heard she'd managed to escape. For a while his only thought had been getting to her first, before Seth did, but no matter how hard he searched, she'd remained quite elusive.

"Running somewhere?" His tongue felt swollen in his mouth, incapable of forming larger sentences.

He just wanted to fall into her, to hell with the consequences, to hell with Seth. She was a shimmering ball of energy, her wolf craving to be set free. He wanted to give that to her, wanted to take her—he just plain *wanted* her. He'd thought he'd moved on from this fascination with her. With time and distance, he'd been sure of it. Yet that connection he'd felt seemed to have forged a stronger hold than he'd realized. He'd heard whisperings of such a thing—immediate bonds with the one that was meant to be one's mate, but he'd never believed it. Myths, legends spread among the werewolves, except the truth stood right before him. Ten years, and he wanted her just as much now as he had then.

"No," she murmured, the stench of fear crawling over her.

A faint smile pulled at his lips. "You know, a lot of people have been looking for you." *Myself included.*

"I'm not going back." The words fell from her lips without thought and a fluted gasp rose between them as she flattened against the wall, fingers covering her mouth.

The very last thing Hunter wanted was for her to leave. "You like being rogue?" he questioned.

"I prefer 'lone wolf,' if you don't mind," she muttered in a low voice, her brows snapping down.

Lone wolves, rogues, whatever they called themselves, were rare, and the females were far more so. Like their natural counterparts, werewolves craved kinship and relations; they did not survive long in the world without familial support. Their lives became about fighting as they searched for their own territory, and there wasn't much left beyond desert. Female werewolves, while strong, were still no challenge for the males.

"Really. How...odd," he teased lightly, groaning when her crystal-blue depths flickered and her beast peered out at him. His own surfaced and with a deep breath he managed to restrain himself. As alpha, it was expected that he be the epitome of control. But unfortunately, there was something about Angel that had him as unsettled as a new pup.

"I don't like packs," she said, her tongue dragging over the swell of her lower lip.

He forced himself to swallow, his breath catching at the sight of her glistening mouth, before lifting his gaze back to hers. He'd never actually heard the story of all that had happened in her pack, but he had his suspicions, knowing Seth.

"What happened?" he murmured with the hope that she might respond.

Her face crumpled with the distinct tang of pain, a bleak

shadow of despair streaking over it. Clearly there was a woeful tale in her past, one he could easily see she wasn't prepared to share. He knew he could force the issue, but was it worth it?

It was clear if he let her walk, she'd be on the next bus and gone from the city before night fell around them. An option, but the thought of this wolf getting away from him again was more than unsettling—it was downright painful. Slender and petite, she was just as beautiful as ever, with her softly curving face and round-tipped nose. Still, she needed caring for. A few pounds on those bones would do her some good. He could provide that and so much more. A safe haven, a pack—there was so much he could give her, if she was interested. He wanted to bed her—and not just his wolf, but the man as well. For years he'd wondered about her, hoped that she was safe. Not that he could tell her any of this, with the scent of her anxiety and disquiet hanging thickly in the air. If he admitted his interest aloud, she'd tuck tail and run in a heartbeat.

There was something more here, though. Lone wolf, rogue—whatever she wanted to be addressed as, she no longer had ties to Seth. She was packless and free to do as she wished. The first time he'd seen her, time had stopped. There this freshly turned wolf had stood, cowering in the shadows of her alpha, silent and afraid. He hadn't understood even then what it meant, but he'd been interested, absolutely. That night he'd petitioned Seth to transfer her to his pack.

He hadn't known then if he'd wanted her as his mate or not, but he'd wanted her under his watchful eye and the time to figure it out. Seth hadn't listened to a word Hunter said. He'd simply denied the request and the next news Hunter had received, Angel was Seth's mate. The blow had been surprisingly staggering, yet he'd continued with his duty as alpha, the days passing by as he focused on expanding his territory and caring for his wolves, all the while attempting to keep tabs on this girl. Then eight years ago she'd fallen off the map. No one had known where she was or even if she was alive. He wasn't sure why, but he had *needed* to know that she was safe. What scant news he'd managed to scrounge up had given him little to go on and had stopped trickling in altogether two years later.

Here was his chance, his moment to finally bring her into his pack. To offer her a sanctuary, a place where she could be free and protected. Lifting his eyes to hers, he dared to sweep a stray lock of hair back behind her ear. Her eyes flew wide, tracking his movement avidly, but he wasn't fooled by her skittishness. He wasn't the only one suffering from this mad attraction; her sweet scent thickened and her mouth parted sensually when he grazed her cheek.

"I could offer you a place within my pack," he mumbled, a rush of awareness warming his lower abdomen when her tongue darted between her lips, wetting them. Such a simple movement, and how it affected him.

His wolf perked and the man followed suit, a faint chuckle hovering on the edge of his mouth. He wasn't naive; he'd been around long enough to be well learned in the signs of arousal. Shy or not, the signals were still there.

"I don't want a pack," she responded, her voice barely a whisper.

"You may not want one, but you need one." His voice was gentle; he would not force her, though any other alpha would. They would claim her without a second thought, just for being what she was—a mateless female.

"I've gotten by this long without one," she retorted.

His eyes dropped down to survey her body, noting the long, baggy cargo pants that were clearly two sizes too big and the loose top that practically swallowed her whole. Her thin arms hung limply at her sides, the shabby tatters of her threadbare sweater riddled with frayed holes. *Gotten by* was one thing, *living* an entirely different one.

It was obvious she had no intention of even considering his offer, and he struggled with the burning desire to convince her otherwise. It took more strength than it should have for him to lower his arm and step back. He hadn't forced Seth to relinquish her to him and he would not force her now. It was as clear as the shock carved into her face that her independence was important to her. He'd just have to give her a reason to stay.

"You're letting me go?" she whispered, eyes aglow with hope.

He nodded. He didn't *want* to, but he refused to hold someone against her will. If she was going to come to him, it had to be of her own accord. He was a patient hunter and knew enough to let the rabbit find him. At least this time he had the chance to try and win her. Without Seth, the opportunities were endless.

"Just like that?" She was inching along the wall, preparing to bolt.

"No, not just like that," he bit out in a hoarse voice.

He dared a step toward her, pausing when she faltered, the heel of her ratty combat boot catching the loose stone. Hunter swept down and managed to catch her before she spilled to the soiled ground. An embarrassed smile twisted her lips—lips he wanted desperately to taste.

"One would think the wolf would teach me how to balance..." she teased weakly, her eyes refusing to meet his.

There was nothing balanced about being a werewolf, but the words felt far too bitter to speak. Without their unnatural counterparts, he never would have met her, and he couldn't just let her walk away again—not without finally tasting her, at least once. Countless nights he'd thought on how he'd missed his chance, and he knew he couldn't let that happen again. His gaze dropped to her lips, wondering how they would feel beneath his. He had his suspicions, and his mouth watered with the thought of it.

He poised over her and cupped her face between his hands. The faint sound of her breath catching tightened his groin and he bit back the growl rumbling in his throat.

"Hunter?" she whispered as she gazed up at him. "Please, just let me leave. I heard you in the restaurant, Seth is on his way. I need to...go, I need to run, I can't—"

He cleared his throat and relinquished his hold on her, his fingers twitching when they fell back to his sides. Could he just let her go?

"Angel." He breathed her name, swallowing his groan when her eyes softened. How he wanted to tell her no, but that was a death sentence. She'd never trust him then. Instead, he opted for honesty. "Seth is already here. He's been spotted just outside of town. If he's smart, he probably has a couple members of your old pack with him, for protection. I don't see how running will help you this time."

"It has in the past," she argued, but there was doubt in her voice. The pungent scent of her fear drowned out the noxious stench of the city. "Hunter—" She spoke his name as though her life depended on it. "I've been running from him for eight years. Please...I can't go back—won't, won't go back. Please," she begged, "help me."

His eyes tapered as he watched the blood drain from her face. This little she-wolf was pleading for his help, and he *knew* without question he would give it—anything for her. There was only one place he could safely protect her. Seth would learn where she lived, as would any wolf with a nose. Tracking her was the simple part, but taking her...that was an entirely different challenge. "Come," he muttered as he gently gripped her arm and led her out of the alley.

"Where are we going?" she demanded as she stumbled after him.

He muttered something, his thoughts already planning ahead. Her place first—she'd need her things. Then his, somewhere Seth would be a fool to attack. Greed made fools of many, though, and Hunter found he *wanted* that damned wolf to come for her. It'd been awhile since he'd had a good fight, and this was one he'd been dying for.

Chapter Three

The rhythmic pounding of her heart all but deafened her as they climbed the stairway. Just what was she doing, bringing an alpha—*this* alpha—to her apartment? So he could see how pathetic her life was? It'd been his suggestion to collect her things. Yes, she'd prefer to have her clothes, but she didn't like the thought of him entering her domain.

Her experience with alphas was to run rather than trust. They were the same, all of them: possessive, demanding and dangerous. And Hunter was far more dominant than any werewolf she'd ever met. Just the power he carried in his little finger was enough to make her knees weak. Truth be told, that was part of the reason she'd asked for his help, even though it broke her number-one rule: rely on no one.

Her years on the run had taught her many things, such as how to survive in this crazy world as a rabbit among wolves. So why was it that with him she didn't feel like a rabbit?

Reminding herself that she'd begged for his help, she fished her keys from her pocket and grimaced at the sight of her shaking hand as she attempted to unlock the door. There was very little within—a torn couch, a ratty pair of camping chairs and a small futon shoved into the corner. Her lifestyle wasn't exactly conducive to elaborate furnishings. Once, she'd had it all—a life and a future. Now she lived day to day, fighting to make ends meet, all because of Seth.

On the third unsuccessful attempt, Hunter covered her hand with his and guided the key smoothly into the lock. It popped with a soft click and the door swung open with little in the way to hinder it. Oh, but his hand was so warm and firm, and for a single moment she indulged in the whisper of a fantasy, imagining how that hand might feel cupping her breast.

The faint dream shattered the moment his shoulder brushed against hers, and she shook her head clear of such thoughts before following him in. Thinking about such things would do her no good; she needed to focus on evading Seth and not on the six feet of pure muscle stalking around what qualified as her living room.

"All right," he mused as he prowled the length of the room, his fingers dragging over her cracked granite countertop.

Her teeth latched around her lower lip; she refused to apologize for her living conditions. It wasn't any of his business what quality of life she led, though the state of her apartment did leave much to be desired.

"All right?" she repeated as she eased along the opposite length of the room.

His eyes lit up and a small smile spread over his face as he watched her attempts to evade him. "All right," he repeated. "It shouldn't take much time to pack up, so why don't you gather your things together and we'll head out."

Her head spun. "Sorry," she whispered as her fingers found the lip of her futon and gripped the rusted iron bar. "But head out where?"

The resolved thump of his footsteps echoed within her small room as he continued to study her apartment. There wasn't much to see: eggshell-white walls, yellowed linoleum floors and the usual appliances that had come with. It was no expensive mansion, or hell, even a home really, but it was a roof over her head, and that was all that mattered.

"My place," he said with little hesitation.

"Your place," she whispered in a faint voice.

When she'd asked for his help, she'd meant escorting her to the bus stop. Her heart tripped in her chest at the thought of being confined somewhere with him. How many times had she mooned over such a fantasy and imagined him sweeping into her life—bare-chested, of course—to fix everything? Suddenly she wasn't sure if this was reality or wishful thinking.

"Yes, my place."

Her eyes flicked to the refrigerator, where a previously purchased open-ended bus ticket was held in place by a magnet. His gaze followed hers, his mouth crooking into a delicious grin when he read the words.

"You've been running for eight years, Angel," he mur-

mured in that sinful voice that puckered her skin. "Do you
think you can run forever? We can live a long time. One
day Seth will find you." He paused and swung his blazing
gaze back to her. "And I'm not one for hiding."

No, he wouldn't be. She fought against the urge to roll
her eyes. Must be nice not to have to hide.

"So what'll it be?" Her stomach flipped when his voice
softened. "Run, *again*, and keep running until one day
he catches you? Or…" He trailed off, his bright eyes ever
watchful. "Come with me?"

Her teeth found her lower lip and she rolled her tongue
over it as she contemplated his offer. Come with him—
just what exactly did that entail? Her head was all atwit-
ter with the thoughts tumbling around. The idea of going
with him, of following *this* alpha, made her chest tight. It'd
been ten years since she'd reacted so girlishly to *anyone*,
not that he'd known how he'd affected her.

"Seth won't ever stop, Angel." His words clouded her
head. "He wants *you*."

"Why?" she asked in a broken voice. "Why me? I'm…
nothing—a weak little pup—"

A shadow whipped over his face as some errant thought
took shape, the golden light that brightened his eyes silenc-
ing her words. He crossed the length of the room in quick
strides that forced her back until she was flush against the
wall. Such grace and power—every inch of him screamed
alpha. Only when they were inches apart did he stop, his
hands rising to cup her face. Her pulse jumped the moment the pads of his fingers stroked her jaw.

"You don't see what you are," he murmured as his long

finger hooked beneath her chin and lifted until she dared meet his gaze.

"And what am I?" she whispered, both intrigued and terrified by his impending answer.

He smiled and stroked her lower lip with the pad of his thumb. "Beautiful."

One word and her knees went weak. There were no words for the emotions she felt in that moment, and as he began to lower over her, her breath caught and a rush of blood made her fingers tingle. Angelica's head spun, warmth swelling within her body as the alpha's lips shaped around hers, his hot breath filling her mouth. Heat kindled, scorching a burning path across her lips before curling into her heart. For a moment she felt as if she'd go up in flames, and all from a simple kiss. Her mind emptied of all doubts as her mouth parted, their tongues meeting in a slow tangle. She could feel the coiled energy within him, the desire for more, but he maintained a conservative pace, more mindful of her than any werewolf had ever been.

Never had she experienced such a rush from a kiss before; it was liquid ecstasy, an addicting drug that her body now craved. What little experience she possessed came from her human days, and since then, she'd kept her lips to herself as much as possible. The other wolves, the ones that had thought of her as nothing more than a play toy, had never been interested in kissing.

So ardently he fed at her mouth, teasing and tasting his way. Silently she begged for him never to stop, a frightening notion considering they'd only just formally met. The rich scent of his arousal embraced her as tightly as his arms. She shuddered, her stomach leaping at the feel of his erection, large and rigid, digging into her hip. The lack of embarrassment astounded her, and she rocked to the balls of her feet, stretching toward him as she deepened the kiss, exploring his mouth as eagerly as he did hers.

Angel's palms slid up the wide expanse of his chest, which was covered in a soft cotton shirt. Her fingers curled into the small dusting of hair peeking out from the low collar as the pad of her thumb ran over his dark skin. He tasted of wildness and life, and with it came a whisper of freedom. So warm, she found herself drawing closer to the flame, drinking from him vigorously. For the briefest moment, she allowed herself to draw the scent of his pack around her, surrounding herself in the phantom arms of his wolves, of her unfamiliar brothers and sisters. She'd forgotten how it could feel.

Her touch seemed to change something, and the air around them shifted, heating with their passion. A primal growl fell into her mouth as a banded arm wound around her waist, crushing her against him. Together they stumbled, her back pressing into the wall, his fingers diving beneath the thin threads of her shirt. Firm tips grazed over her stomach before drawing up her side. How quickly this was getting out of control, like a wildfire devouring the parched earth. His touch kneaded into her skin and her breath caught when his fingers, after finding her breasts were free and unbound, grazed over her nipple.

Angel gasped into his mouth, her hands settling around the nape of his neck. She couldn't believe the way he was handling her, or that she was allowing it. For years she'd sworn no werewolf would ever lay hands on her again, but this was entirely different. The doubts in her mind dimmed, her need to be touched by him conquering all else. Two strong hands held her pinned to him, his fingers pushing the hem of her shirt up to expose her middle. His thumb circled her hardened nipple, teasing the beaded nub until he elicited a low moan from her throat.

Her shirt vanished to the skilled talents of his fingers, baring her to the chilled air of her living room. He tore his mouth from hers, his lips dragging down her neck and collarbone until they latched around her breast. The sensual press of his hot tongue swirling and flicking over her nipple brought a rush of heat from between her legs. Angel's knees weakened and she grabbed hold of his broad shoulders, taking from him the strength she couldn't muster.

How had she gotten here? Hadn't she been running? A faint thought surfaced, ordering her to get moving. Instead, she shuddered against him, groaning as his teeth closed around the hard nub of her nipple. He pulled the swollen bead into his mouth with just the right amount of force and her knees buckled, nearly spilling her to the ground. For the first time in longer than she could remember, Angel turned off all thought and ordered herself not to be a coward. Was this not what she had fantasized about night after night? Was this not her most secret desire? Right now she just wanted to enjoy the way *this* wolf made her feel.

His hands slid around to her front, fingers dipping into the lip of her pants. Angel stilled until he popped open the button and delved within. Her body screamed for this, to be pleasured and ravished. As though he understood her blinding need, he straightened to reclaim her mouth while his fingers found their way past her damp panties. Her thoughts muddled, the seductive haze making it hard to think beyond all that he was doing to her.

It was the slightest brush, his finger stroking over her pulsing clit, and it pulled her closer to the flame. She jerked against him, wanting nothing more than for him to slide within her and pump until she screamed her release.

The ache of such a want left her a trembling mess when Hunter suddenly stumbled back from her, the sound of his feet dragging over her linoleum rousing open her eyes. She found him wilting against the opposite wall, his brow resting on the drywall. She had no words to explain what had just happened; no wolf she'd ever met could have done that.

With a shuddering breath, he rounded until his back was flat against the wall. The look on his face was so pained, she wanted nothing more than to cross the room and free him. Instead, she took the opportunity to yank her shirt back on and snap up her pants, trembling with the remembered feel of his fingers grazing over her silken folds.

Doubt wormed through her gut and she smoothed her hair down as she fought with her own emotions. She was more than confused. The way he'd followed her, it was more than frightening. But she found that she *liked* it— him watching her as though he desperately needed her. Yet when she'd been about to give herself to him, to break all the rules in her book, he'd withdrawn.

"Forgive me," he growled, his voice thick. "I didn't intend for it to go that far."

Her body felt much the same, a hard knot of hunger, but

she couldn't give in—not after so many years of fighting to keep free. Swallowing, she swept her fingers over her swollen mouth as a shiver shot down her spine. What was happening here was madness. Surely it was too good to be true, that this alpha had just fallen back into her life, now of all times. She pushed off the wall, her wobbly knees hardly able to lead her across the room to the table. Golden eyes stalked her every step, proof of how close he was to shifting, but he made no move toward her.

Angel dipped her head, about to suggest he leave, when his growling voice embraced her. "We should leave."

She paused, silenced by the sound of his frustration. The odd part was that she *wanted* to stay here, more than anything, and explore this new rush of emotion and feeling. There was something in his eyes, something she just knew she could trust. It was *herself* she couldn't trust—not after allowing him to touch her so freely. Even now her body betrayed her, longing to cross the distance and beg him to take her.

Her head dipped in a slow bob. "It won't take long to pack."

What was she doing? *Tell him no! Run!* Her mind screamed at her, scolding her for allowing this to happen, but her heart—and something far more carnal than that—wanted to follow him to the ends of the earth.

She hadn't been kidding when she'd estimated an hour to gather her things. Not forty minutes had passed since she'd started tearing through her dingy apartment and sweeping up what little was strewn around. The challenge had been ignoring Hunter, slanted against the wall, his ever-watchful eyes doing just that. Her luggage had been sitting by her lump of a bed in the exact same place she'd left it the moment she'd first passed through those doors not four months ago. She tore through her apartment like a whirlwind, gathering what few possessions she owned and tossing them carelessly into the suitcase. Such paltry things, hardly worth saving, and when she was finished, she and Hunter abandoned her apartment with little more than the key left on the counter. This was the reason she rented by the month.

His place, he'd said, and her stomach clenched just thinking about it. What was it about this wolf that had her so confused?

A faint scent carried on the wind and Angel tensed, her narrowed eyes studying the shadows for the source. It didn't matter how many times she whipped around, there appeared to be no one following them. Worse, Hunter appeared completely at ease.

The sound of her luggage wheels rolling over the pavement was loud in the dead of night, but Angel ignored it, her ears primed for the more natural sounds of crickets chirping in the tall grasses and the wind whipping through the reeds of the nearby swamp. She could even make out a couple of small mice burrowing through the loose soil and an owl silently stalking them. It was when the wildlife suddenly went quiet that she knew she had reason to fear.

"There's a bus stop just around the corner." Hunter's quiet voice sundered the silence.

Angel jumped and her fingers tensed around her luggage. Yes, there was a bus stop. In fact, it was the same stop where she'd purchased her ticket. For a moment her chest tightened; was he letting her go? Her thoughts wavered, torn between her head and heart. She *should* run—that was the smart thing to do. Sadly, it seemed her brain had little in the way of control.

Hunter turned and slowly slid his arms around her waist, drawing her into his chest. Her heart rate spiked, her lips tingling with the memory of that kiss, and she found herself straining toward him, craving another taste.

His head ducked and the warm press of his mouth found her ear. "Pretend we're saying goodbye," he whispered, his breath pooling against her neck.

Pretend? She tipped her head back and fell into the depths of his eyes as her hand crept up his chest. Who were they pretending for? Her fingers flexed the moment he dipped down, her excitement barely containable. This wasn't healthy, this odd infatuation she had with him. *He is an alpha*—the words chanted through her mind, yet when his lips sealed around hers, she melted into him, her arm sliding around his neck.

The kiss was little more than a brush of lips and she shivered when his mouth dragged across her jaw, settling at her ear once more.

"We're being followed," he whispered.

Her stomach lurched; she should have trusted her instincts. "Seth?"

"Shh," he murmured softly as he threaded his fingers through her hair and smoothed it back behind her ear. "I won't let anything happen to you. But I need you to enter the bus station like you're leaving."

Her breath caught and her fingers latched onto his shirt. Bait. He wanted her to play bait. It must be Seth, then, and her entire body froze with fear.

Aware of her impending panic, he backed away and cupped her face between his palms, his lips crooking into a small smile. A final kiss and he turned and vanished into the shadows.

Surely those following wouldn't believe that he'd just left? The ticket she'd bought had been purchased for the eleven twenty-five bus, only fifteen minutes from now, and it was practically burning a hole through her pocket. She should leave right now, hop on the bus and never look back. Could she do that?

Following his instruction, she wrapped her fingers loosely around the metal handle of the terminal door and swung it open. She quickly slipped inside, only to find a deserted room, the ticket counter closed and locked. Angel fell to a dead stop, her eyes flicking to the departures board. She'd checked the schedule upon arriving in this city and knew it like the back of her hand. Sometime between then and now, however, someone had opted for a new one and, with panic chasing down her spine, she realized she had no escape. The next bus wasn't until five-thirty in the morning.

Sighing, she slumped down into the nearest hard plastic chair, jumping at every little sound. What was she supposed to do now? Sit here and wait for Seth to show up? Hope that Hunter did first? Her life was a mess; she just wanted to board that damn bus and get the hell out of Dodge. Of course, her mind took that moment to flash an image of Hunter, remind her of the sinful taste of his lips. Perfect, just perfect. She couldn't run—they'd follow her scent—and without the bus she was trapped; her only option was to follow Hunter's plan. She tipped her head back, her thoughts drifting away without pursuit, praying for them not to center on Seth.

In the backdrop her sensitive ears picked up on insects scurrying over the walls, pipes creaking and moaning, and somewhere in a back room, a stray animal tearing into the garbage. She tried to focus on those things, lose herself to the sounds around her, but her mind rebelled. The memory of Hunter's touch rose unbidden instead. Her eyes tightened and her face pinched with concern. She should *not* have let that happen. What in the world had she been thinking, getting physical with a werewolf? And not just any werewolf—an alpha. She'd sworn to herself the moment she'd first opened her eyes after her change, after realizing there was a whole other world hidden away in the deep folds of what *had* been her reality, that she would never become one of them. Oh, they'd tried many things to force her beast out of her—things she did *not* want to think about in the dark of night with the shadows pressing in. But it'd never worked, or at least, not in the manner they'd wanted.

Angel ached with exhaustion—she'd managed to complete her tenth hour of work before all hell had broken loose, and her dogs were barking. Her finger ran along the line of her lower lip as she remembered the feel of his mouth on hers, the sweet scent of his breath filling her. She'd wanted *more*; even now her body burned for it. Ten years and the desire now was just as maddening! Her startled laugh rose in the cavernous bus terminal, dancing off the walls with a haunting echo. The worst—the *absolute worst*—had been the desire to comfort him when his face had shifted into that torturous look.

Fool.

She'd been taught never to trust a werewolf, especially alphas. The lesson had been carved into her flesh and bone. And here she'd gone and fallen—

She sucked in a sharp breath, snapping straight in her seat. *Don't say it, pup. Don't even think it. It isn't possible.*

He was a werewolf, a monster. It was as simple as that. She might be one, too, but her human half was stronger, always keeping the beast locked down. She was nothing like them and never would be. If she was being honest with herself, she would at least admit that *he* was nothing like them as well.

Slamming the door shut on those thoughts, Angel slumped low in the chair again and returned to her former position, arms crossed over her chest to hold in the warmth. Who knew how long this little plot would take to play out, and she loathed the thought of simply sitting and waiting. She started by counting her breaths—anything to pass the insufferable time.

Chapter Four

A familiar scent filled her dreams, and even in her sleep, her stomach knotted. It'd been *years* since she'd last inhaled that particular aroma, yet she remembered it as clear as day. She scrunched down into the hard-backed chair and buried her nose deep into her jacket in an attempt to block it out. The odor clung to a shimmering phantom, one that drifted around her and threaded its wraithlike fingers through her hair. Grimacing, she struggled to drive the specter from her mind and sink back into a dreamless state.

It was a task easier said than done.

The ghost grew incensed the longer she ignored it and its body began to shimmer in a furious red glow, its milky eyes staring down at her. Ethereal lips curled back over fanged teeth and from its mouth came a deep thrumming growl, one that roused the hairs on the back of her neck.

Angel stirred and dug her fingers into the sides of her

jacket, drawing them around her with the hope of warding off this nasty chill. In her dream, her eyes lifted to the spirit and widened when a familiar face took form. Features she'd long committed to memory took shape from the wisps of mist: sharp chin, narrow face, long nose and hard, piercing eyes.

She gasped and jerked as she came fully awake, her eyes flying open. The scent lingered and she dragged her hand down her rumpled face, wiping under her nose. It seemed stronger now, and she groaned as she struggled to rid herself of the pungent smell.

Asleep. What had she been thinking? How much time had passed since Hunter left? Rubbing her eyes, she lifted her gaze to the clock nailed above the counter gate. The ticker dragged, thundering from one second to the next. Not an hour had passed, and she slumped back, sighing, forcing herself to remain awake. Such a fool. Stupid, but boredom had taken hold as she listened to the seconds tick by on that dreaded clock, waiting for Seth to make his appearance.

"Still not using your nose properly." A dark, familiar voice rose at her back.

Angel shot up from the chair as if she'd been struck, whipping around at the last moment to find the phantom in solid form, perched in the seat behind her. Those eyes... *oh, hell,* those eyes. It'd taken her years to convince herself that not every man had that same stare, and even longer to overcome the distressing fear that he was always there, always watching.

Seth—her maker and former alpha.

"What?" he mused as he pushed to his feet and stalked around the bench. "No warm welcome for your old lover?"

Her face twisted and she sucked in her lower lip. She'd *never* been his lover—at least not willingly. But to Seth that meant nothing. When he found something he liked, he claimed it without thought of whether it was even his to take. She countered his steps, her eyes darting to the large glass doors, searching for Hunter. Two shadows darkened the entry, and though they were familiar faces, neither of them was Hunter. Had she put her trust in the wrong person?

"Come now, Angel." His words pulled her attention back to him and she shuddered at the sound of her name, breathy and thick with desire. "Do you know how long I've searched for you? Some small bit of gratitude would be appropriate."

She felt the draw, the pull, whatever it was that alphas could do to those beneath them. Her stomach warmed with the thought of going to him, even though she knew she'd be disgusted later. That was always the way of it. She would have liked to think her strength had grown in their time apart. But he was an alpha and she was not.

"Come," he ordered, his rumbling voice full of authority.

She broke at the waist, his words binding her to his will, forcing her into submission. The ground rose up, her hands and knees slamming down before she began to crawl across the squalid floor. Inside, her wolf was howling, struggling in a mad assault to free the alpha's hold, but she wasn't strong enough. *Where was Hunter?* He'd sworn he wouldn't let anything happen to her. Well, something sure was happening.

When she reached his feet, two long fingers curled under her chin and drew her head up until he could spear her with his stare. "This is where you belong, my Angel."

Her head shook without thought, her hair settling around her shoulders. No, she didn't *belong* anywhere. She was her own person, had been her entire life until this man had savaged her in the back of his car.

"No?" he asked, his voice darkening with ire. "You are mine. I allowed you your freedom, but the time has come for you to return home. I need my mate."

Cringing, her head dropped forward once more, a curtain of hair sliding over her face. His *mate*—it was what he'd always claimed her to be, the reason why he'd attacked her, the reason why he'd stolen her life. They'd gone on a single date together; it *had* been going well, up until he'd phased and ripped her to shreds. The first moment she'd awoken with her new eyes, she'd known she would never belong to him.

"No." She finally spoke, her breathy voice a pale imitation of what she usually mustered.

Seth sucked in a sharp breath and not a second later he gathered her into his hands and wrenched her to her feet. Fury darkened his already opaque eyes. His wolf was nowhere near the surface; it was purely the cruel man within that she now saw.

"No?" he repeated, a perverse storm thundering across his face. "*No?*" he roared. She was flung from his grasp, her back driven into the far wall.

A sharp crack echoed through the station, her cheek stinging from the sudden imprint of his open-palmed hand. Gasping, Angel cupped her face, her widened eyes swinging back up to him.

It wouldn't be the first time Seth had resorted to violence, though he'd never dared assault her in public. She bit down on her lip, refusing to give him the satisfaction of hearing her cry out.

"You do *not* say no to me," he spat in her face, his hand held high as though he meant to strike her once more. Instead, his iron fingers gripped her chin and squeezed, jerking her around to face him.

"Now, you will come with me, and you *will* be my mate—"

"No," she stated in a firm voice, refusing to let him bully her further. It wasn't the fear of what he could do to her, but rather the idea of returning with him that terrified her. Just the thought of being *his*, having to obey his every whim and fulfill his every fantasy, made her stomach flip. There was much she would do to keep that from happening.

Seth stared down at her, poised on the edge of strong emotion. The storm burst free, a furious rage sweeping over his face. "You might think you're something else," he growled, his eyes flashing gold at her, "running around with *Hunter*. You think I didn't see you out there? Think I didn't *know? I* am your alpha! And you will obey me, even if I have to beat obedience into you."

His grip on her chin tightened and he pressed her aching head into the wall as his fingers kneaded her jaw. Angel's heart leaped into her throat as she stared into Seth's hardened face. His voided eyes held the promise of torment and pain, but there were worse things in life. He'd taught her that.

What a fool she was, trusting another werewolf, thinking that this time it might be different—that *he* might be different. She'd learned years ago that she could only depend on herself. With a sharp breath, she drove her elbow down into his arm and twisted in his grasp. A startled cry rose between them as Angel shoved him back. Without any thought, her arm shot out, a clenched fist colliding with the side of his head. For a moment she was too startled to move, having never thrown a successful punch before. Her knuckles blazed with pain, fingers trembling as they flexed and retracted like a nervous cat. It wasn't until he rose, his hand cradling his mouth, that she thought to bolt. If she could just shift—

A firm grip ensnared her waist and whipped her around, throwing her back and knocking her head against the wall. Stars burst before her eyes and she crumpled, her legs incapable of holding her up.

"You'll pay for that," he muttered darkly. "Think you can just do whatever you like? A lesson in manners, I think, in how to treat your betters."

Angel couldn't help the crazed laugh that spilled from her mouth. "Maybe you should fetch me one first." She knew the moment the words left her lips, it was a mistake. But she'd rather he kill her than drag her back to the pack.

"I'll not stand for this, Angel," he growled, lips rearing back over his teeth.

Her eyes fluttered shut at the sight of his lengthening

fangs. His wolf was so close, soon it would be over. That was all she could hope for now. No more running, no more hiding, no more monsters in the shadows. Fingers wrapped around her throat and he flexed his grip, the station fogging as blackness crept along the edge of her vision.

Through the brume, a wolf's howl rent the suffocating silence. Angel stiffened at the sound of the symphonic baying. Somehow she knew it was Hunter and relief rushed through her; he'd kept his promise—she wasn't alone here with Seth. A surge of strength straightened her shoulders and her gaze darted expectantly toward the door, waiting for the moment Hunter came into view.

A shadow darted beyond the entrance, knocking into one of Seth's wolves, and she jumped when a splash of blood sprayed the glass. Seth's grip vanished and she sucked in a sharp breath, shuddering as she fought to control her racking cough. He stalked away from her, hardly paying her a second glance when she slid to the ground.

The creak of the door roused her attention and she lifted her chin to watch as Seth propped it open, peering out into the darkness. A faint scent drifted through the door and Angel's breath caught in her bruised throat—oak. She was more than familiar with that distinct fragrance. Seth's nostrils flared as he took it in, and from the white of his eyes, it seemed he also recognized Hunter.

The beast appeared then, phasing out of the darkness, eyes smoldering with green light. His head tilted, taking in the sight of her huddled against the wall, cradling her throat. Enraged, he bared his teeth and whipped back to Seth.

Never had she seen such a large wolf before. At the sight

of him, all slick black fur, she lowered her hands to the floor and began to creep forward, longing for a closer look. Dark as night, his coat caught the dim light of the station, shimmering bands of indigo rippling with his every step. He was more than gorgeous, he was exquisite.

"Hunter," Seth stated, and she heard the slight tremble in his voice.

The wolf's fangs snapped at the air between him and Seth. The sound was sharp enough that even Angel cringed and dragged her knees into her chest. Her eyes wandered past them to the blood-smeared doors. Was that what had kept Hunter? Had there been more than those two wolves, now nothing more than lumps of fur sprawled on the cement? Yet hardly a hair in Hunter's coat was out of place.

Hunter strode forward, his tail erect as he held Seth's stare. When he didn't immediately drop his gaze, Hunter snarled and lunged, about to attack when Seth finally skittered back, his eyes dropping to the floor. The bitter tang of fear perfumed the air and a twisted smile crooked Angel's lips. It was nice, for once, to see *him* fear someone.

Hunter pushed past him, purposely keeping his back to Seth. He was coming toward her and with wide eyes she tucked against the wall, her gaze flicking between the two of them. She didn't fear this alpha, not in the least, and her brow knotted with that realization. In fact, with every step he took, the weight in her chest loosened, and her shoulders rounded with relief. After today, she just knew he would never hurt her, unlike the one that stood behind him.

Hunter stalked across the lobby, his massive paws tracing a wake in the thin spread of dust coating the floor. She stared at the footprints, her keen eyes noticing that his paws were at least twice the size of hers. A common occurrence between male and females, but it made her feel insecure. The wolves she'd once called her brethren had taken nothing but joy in teaching her how pathetic she was. Too small to be anybody, too dainty to be truly fearsome—all traits she'd once thought appealing. But the human world and the *other* world had different standards.

A soft muzzle brushing under her jaw snapped her thoughts back to the present. Seth still stood by the door, his eyes lowered in caution. Hunter's stare trained on her face, watching her for any indication of what was happening behind him. A flash of pink darted from between his lips, wet heat painting up the side of her face. Strangely, laughter bloomed in her stomach, her lidded eyes dropping to his face. For the very first time, in more years than she cared to admit, she felt no fear at meeting another's gaze, and if she wasn't mistaken, Hunter seemed encouraged by this. His lower jaw loosened into a wolfish grin, tongue dangling from his mouth as he panted eagerly. Her own mouth crooked, sharing in this momentous occasion. Her laugh was breathy and high-pitched, but it blended well with his low huff.

The sound seemed to awaken something in the station. Magic crept along her skin, her throat tightening. Her body was a knot of nerves, tingling and thrumming to a voiceless song that only she could hear. The drumming beat came from Hunter, a steady rhythm that called to her. When she dropped forward onto her hands and knees, there was little resistance from her, simply acceptance and an eager need to split her skin that filled her head until she could no longer think.

"Angel," Seth gasped, the heels of his boots clicking over the floor.

As one, Hunter and Angel lifted their eyes, ignoring the unwelcome one. The wolf before her flicked his tail, his paws dancing in the dust, his hunger evident. The call—it was so strong, so resplendent. Even with the roof over them, she could see the heavens above, unbound and dotted with glittering diamonds, all singing their celestial songs. The blood moon waned in the velvet folds, caroling its own ancient woes to the bare, brown earth. And from her lips, a melody slipped out—her howl and hers alone, joining with the primal lullaby.

Hunter dropped back onto his haunches, his head tipped up toward the ceiling. A serene look smoothed over his face as he swayed to the tuneless rhythm.

Angel wanted to weep, it was so beautiful. Never had she heard such a song before and she knew without a doubt it was because of her bond with Hunter. If ten years hadn't weakened it, neither would Seth. She felt it, as strongly as she felt the moon above. Both whispered soft promises, offering her things she'd wished for most of her life—protection, safekeeping and love.

Tears spilled over her cheeks as she met Hunter's gaze, his chartreuse depths watching her so calmly. Shuddering, her head fell forward, sundering their connection.

Never had she shifted in front of another, and the shame of what was about to happen pooled inside her. They would see her at her most vulnerable, and the thought of it stung her eyes. Fresh tears welled over her cheeks and fell to the floor, washing clean the lingering dust that clung to her hands. Angel drew in a long breath. To the rest of the world, she looked like nothing more than a woman on her knees, prostrating before a wolf. But within, wild and primordial chaos erupted. Her skin rippled, her body shifting gracefully as it prepared to phase. Organs shuffled, her bones dislocating with startling cracks and snaps that dragged an aggrieved moan from her parted lips. Her breaths were shallow and uneven, her heart racing in her chest. Only at the last moment did she shut her eyes, the magic plucking her wolf from deep within and yanking it free.

The cry that filled the chilled station was purely animalistic and she slumped to the ground, her eyes drifting open to stare up at the wolf above her. The magic was so strong she couldn't have fought it, and she didn't want to. The universe was offering her something, something that had only ever been whispered about. The mating call had been revered in her former pack; none of them had ever experienced it.

Hunter's wet nose brushed behind her ear, his teeth catching the tip for the smallest moment before releasing it. She felt the pull to rise to her feet, and finally she did. She shook out her fur, scattering the dust motes back into the air, and turned to Hunter, searching his face.

"Angel!" Seth barked at her, his fingers snapping as though she was nothing more than a disobedient dog. Her hackles rose and she bared her sharp fangs, showing that she wasn't his. Never had she so openly rebelled, but there was something about Hunter that gave her strength, whereas Seth had always stolen it.

Her former alpha's face thinned with anger, now burning with the fires of his rage. Not one for hearing *no*, he seemed unable to accept what was happening.

Silence filled the bus station, yet the thoughts in her head were deafening. Hunter eased between them, his head lowered protectively, a low growl vibrating from his throat. A deep chorus of yips fell from his mouth, his challenge riding on the chilled air.

Angel's eyes darted to the man who had dogged her steps for years, hounded and harassed her, abused and debased her until the only option left was to run. Only once had she dared to call one of her pack members to learn what was happening. The news had been staggering. Seth had named her rogue, a word she'd come to loathe since then. Rogue meant beyond the jurisdiction of any other wolf. It meant she was open game, a meal for any wolf that she crossed paths with. It was why she'd been running for so long. But this one, this midnight alpha, had set her free. Hunter had put her needs above the rules, even above his own needs, something she'd never witnessed in any other wolf. The males took what they wanted, regardless of consequence.

Now the moment she'd dreamed about for almost a decade had arrived. After nights spent in Seth's not-so-tender care, days when she'd hardly been able to crawl away as he'd forced himself on her…yes, she was ready for this nightmare to end. Once she'd believed that people deserved redemption and forgiveness. In her human life, she'd believed murder of any sort was despicable, but since becoming a werewolf, she'd developed a whole new set of ethics. Her outlook on life was not so naive anymore. She'd spent years telling herself she was *not* like them, wasn't a coldhearted monster. But things were different now. She wanted him gone—she wanted him dead.

Seth's opaque eyes rose from the cracked floor and stabbed through her, watching with an intensity that burned like a steady flame. Never had she seen such hate in someone, from the clenched fists and curling lip to the scrunched nose.

"This isn't finished," Seth grunted as his shift began to morph his features. "See you soon, Angel," he wheezed as he dropped to the floor, writhing until a large gray wolf stood before them.

Hunter snarled and gathered his strength beneath him, about to strike when Seth dove out of the bus station, his nails skittering over the cement as he retreated.

Fear ran rampant through her gut. It wasn't finished. Angel knew Seth would keep his promise. He always did.

Chapter Five

The cool breeze was a relief to his nose after the stagnant air of the station. Hunter glanced back at the small wolf trailing in his wake, her ivory fur shimmering like the moon within the silken ebony threads of night. Fury and relief washed over him, the stark contrast of both shredding his insides. Her former alpha had laid hands on her; he'd seen the bruised imprint blooming over her creamy skin. How he'd longed to take chase and tear the man to pieces for what he'd done, but that would have left Angel alone and for all he knew, that was Seth's plan—a loathed thought. He was vacillating between warring emotions, equal parts rage and gratitude. And somewhere in the middle was the blessed taste of excitement, rolling and crashing over him in an attempt to drown his rage and irritation.

Angel was following him, and willingly. The sound of her soft footfalls padding through the grass gave his heart reason to beat. She was no longer running. He only hoped she understood that if she came to him, he would never let her go. She was meant to be his mate—they'd both felt the call. Ironic that it had happened the day he'd sat down to discuss such a thing with his second.

As for Seth, if there was an alpha Hunter wouldn't mind seeing taken down, it was him; he'd always been the most difficult, the most troublesome of the pack leaders. His wolves weren't properly cared for, and all the alphas knew it. Yet he also knew that entering Seth's territory to put an end to his reign would constitute war between the packs. Hunter was dominant enough to win, but overthrowing Seth would expand Hunter's territory to an unstable degree. There was little hope that a wolf from Seth's pack would challenge him—years of instilling terror and fear had taken their toll.

It'd been the hardest thing he'd ever done to leave her in that bus stop. Soon after they'd left Angel's apartment, Hunter had picked up the faintest whiff on the wind. Seth and a few of his minions had been following them, quietly enough that had that opportunistic breeze not drifted by, he might not have taken notice. It'd taken a bit of time to find the proper spot where he could sit in the shadows and watch for trouble. They'd stalked the station, ensured Hunter wasn't coming back, and then Seth had slunk inside. The two he'd left outside the doors to guard were nothing, pups compared to the big bad wolf. He hadn't liked leaving them alive, but he couldn't have bodies littering the streets. They'd wake before the morning and likely regroup with Seth. The only question that remained was when Seth would try again.

Forcing his thoughts back to the present, he focused on the city scents fading into the sweet summer night, leaving only the most intoxicating fragrance he'd ever tasted. *Her.* If he'd thought her scent had been strong this afternoon, it was nothing compared to now. She still smelled of the city, but it was an aroma that maddened his soul.

He led her down the abandoned streets until his house finally came into view. Angel lifted her rounded nose into the air, sniffing at the silver gates before them—a deterrent for any that dared to try and infiltrate his home. He stalked over to a small box and nosed the lid open before stepping on a hidden button. The metal swung open gracefully, hardly a catch in the oiled gears. Angel passed through with little prodding, turning around once inside to watch them seal shut.

He could hear her heart suddenly take off, thrumming like a hummingbird, her breath quickening to a shallow pant. The wolf pranced back, her startling blue eyes raking over the bars and up the walk to the entrance. Her scent vanished when a thick wall of panic rose between them, and as he watched, her muscles coiled, preparing to spring forward as she searched for any way out.

It was Hunter's alarm that brought his magic down on him, enabling him to shift faster than he ever had before. He *had* to show her she had nothing to fear from him and he couldn't do that as a wolf. Seconds later, his shift was complete and he found himself kneeling, nude, on the pavement. Straightening from his crouch, he approached her, his fingers slowly combing through the fur of her cheeks, notching them right behind her ear. He couldn't help but chuckle when she suddenly canted into him, her eyes fluttering shut as the softest sigh spilled into the night.

Slowly her heartbeat steadied and her breathing evened out. The moment she was calm, her wolf melted away under his touch, leaving only the woman behind. His lips spread and his hand slid down to curl over her cheek. Her eyes flicked up to his, her face pale under the moonlight.

She rose slowly, her arms sliding over her midsection to shield herself from him, even after all they'd shared earlier. Her eyes were cast to the ground, avoiding his gaze. Hunter's brow snapped down at the sight of her hiding. That behavior had been taught to her. Werewolves rarely shied away from their naked forms. They took them so often, it was like second nature.

Color stained her cheeks when her eyes suddenly climbed the length of his body. He was aroused, erect and throbbing as he watched her, but all he wanted was to chase away the terror creasing her face. She'd felt it, too— the call—earlier tonight in the bus station. It had poured from her soul, the most erotic howl he'd ever heard. He'd felt the drumming and heard the primal song echoing from the moon.

"Angel," he murmured. "I won't hurt you," he promised her. "You *never* have to worry about me hurting you."

Disbelief clouded her eyes. Hunter crossed back to her and cupped her cheek, his fingers smoothing the length of her jaw—so soft, so smooth.

"We're not all like him," he whispered, trying not to

acknowledge how her skin was like creamy silk, pale beneath the blood moon. Her hair fell in ash-blond lengths, curling over her shoulders. She was…remarkable. "And I will do whatever it takes to prove that to you. You *are* safe here. I'll protect you."

She nibbled on her lower lip, a sheepish smile that stole his breath quirking her lips. Her scent was so tempting; he *needed* this. Giving in to his desire, he bent toward her and claimed her mouth, his thumb running down the length of her cheek. He'd tasted her before, yet it didn't compare to now, after listening to the moon's promise that she was his. It took every last bit of his restraint not to spill her down onto the cement and take her right there. More than anything, he craved to see her stretched beneath him, face flushed with want and body quivering with need. He wanted to bring her to the cusp of passion until she howled his name, over and over.

He drew back, drinking in every little bit of her, from her reddened lips and blushing cheeks to her half-lidded eyes. For someone so shy, she appeared to want this as badly as he did. It was almost too much and he swallowed, forcing his heart to slow.

Gentle, he cautioned himself. He just wasn't sure he could be. After meeting her and learning that Seth had claimed her first, he'd never again given thought to finding a mate. Many of his wolves were already paired, but to him, there had always seemed to be something missing.

Pushing those thoughts to the back of his mind, he let his eyes browse the rest of her body. The careworn clothes from earlier had given her an air of hunger, but now he could see she was all curves. His hand fell away from her face, fingers stroking down her soft side and curling around her hip.

His mouth dried at the sight of her, and he watched as unspoken thoughts crossed her face. After what felt like an eternity, she stepped into him, her soft body pressing against his and her arms winding around his neck. Hunter's breath caught, the feel of her bare breasts against his skin sending his blood pulsing. She rolled to the balls of her feet and stretched up to meet him, covering his mouth with hers. He couldn't imagine how hard this was for her, to finally be a willing participant rather than being forced. Giving in to the feel of her warm lips, he poured a silent promise into her mouth that he would never be like *him*.

His hands swept down the soft expanse of her back until they cupped her rear, lifting her into the air. A soft giggle—dear Lord, a *giggle*—filled his mouth as long, lithe legs latched around his waist, clinging to him. He whisked her away, drawing them out of the pale street-lights and into the muted shadows. Out there, he knew no one would see them; they were hidden within the thickset cover of his trees and bushes. Releasing her mouth, his lips dragged down the smooth column of her throat, teeth nibbling, feeling the fluttering pulse beneath her skin. Her taste…he'd never thought skin could be so delectable.

He dropped to his knees in the lush grass, gently lowering her to her back. Golden hair spilled around her shoulders, her body spread like a fine meal before him. He was quick to cover her, his mouth trailing down her collarbone. Her breath caught, fingers clenching in his hair, but it was nothing compared to her gasp when he finally took the peak of her breast into his mouth, lavishing his tongue over her hardened nipple. With his eyes closed, the pads of his fingers smoothed down her flat stomach, caressing her skin as he teased her taut nub. Her head fell back into the soft grass as she arched off the ground, a faint moan rising into the night air.

His hands grazed down her smooth thighs before climbing the inner, more forbidden path. She trembled, her anticipation palpable, and he had to remind himself to move slowly. His fingers grazed her mound, resting there as he reveled at the sound of her quickened breath as she waited for him. He offered the slightest caress, barely even a touch against her center, yet it dragged a low, tuneless moan from her—one that stopped his heart.

He released her breast and moved back just enough to watch her face when he finally slid a single finger between her folds. Sapphire eyes flew open, her lower lip caught between her teeth. Her shuddering breath and the faint blush of color dusting her cheeks sent an electric shock straight to his groin. His hooded eyes brightened with pleasure and he dropped down, claiming her other nipple with just as much fervor.

He was so entranced by her body, his pulse spiked when her fingers suddenly closed around his throbbing erection, moving to the rhythm he set. His mouth released her nipple and he slid down the length of her body, his ebony hair shining in stark comparison to her creamy thighs. Her ragged breath plucked something deep inside and he couldn't wait any longer—he dragged his tongue across her damp sex, delighting in her ardent gasps. The taste of her filled his mouth and with a low moan he suckled and licked his way, working her clit and thrusting his tongue within, listening as her breathing sped. She squirmed beneath him, offering the slightest little bucks, her hands balling in the grass, his name spilling in a half breath from her lips. Oh, it was the sweetest sound he'd ever heard, more divine than her honey-sweet flavor.

Her hips moved beneath him, her panting breath catching every time his tongue teased her nub, the hard length of his cock pulsing when another pleasured moan fell from her mouth. He continued to stroke her, his tongue laving her moist opening. Not another moment passed before she shattered around him, her body coiling as her cries rose into the shadows. He was rewarded with a gratifying whimper, and a rush of sweet ambrosia wet his lips. Her fingers dug into his shoulders, her back arching into him, head thrown into the grass as she rode out her ecstasy. Hunter drew back, pausing for a moment to wipe his mouth before perching over her. He *needed* to be inside her—wanted nothing more than to bury himself deep until he felt her end.

Her eyes lazed open, and for the first time it was her wolf peeking out, golden rays flecking the crystal blue. Mindless want streaked over her face, a daunting need that he felt deep in his stomach.

"Hunter," she whispered, reaching for him. "Please—*please*..."

He groaned, his erection resting against the blessed heat of her tight opening. A small thrust, that was all it would take, and she'd be wrapped around his pulsing length. It felt so natural, this call of the wild thrumming through him. He moved, about to sheathe himself within her, when she pressed her palm against his chest and guided him off. For a moment he was sure she meant to stop and he struggled to tame the beast, to lock it down before he frightened her off. Instead, she directed him to lie down on the damp earth and hovered over him, a shy little smile crooking her lips. She pinned him with a teasing look, one that had his wolf panting, and Hunter stopped breathing. Perhaps he'd given little thought to finding a mate, but now that he had, he had no idea how he'd lived so long without a woman who looked at him like that.

She lowered down onto him, her silken folds conforming to his length.

Hunter's breath hitched, the feel of her sliding over him freeing a torturous groan. A deafening silence hovered over him as he struggled to keep from moving, even as she bent over him, her hands bracing in the dewy grass on either side of his head. He was given a single moment to wonder where his shy little she-wolf had gone when she caught him in a kiss, her tongue moving against his. It was unbearable, this need to have her, to move within her, all while she settled against him.

His arms snaked around her waist and he was about to start moving within her when she suddenly rose and set an agonizingly slow rhythm. Such restraint she showed, far more than he. With every shift, every little maneuver, her warmth grew hotter. He couldn't take it; she needed easy and gentle, he knew that, but his desire for her was too great. He pressed his head back into the grass and closed his eyes as he struggled not to come unhinged, but his resolve weakened every time she pumped over him.

A touch manic, his fingers gripped at her waist. He was about to move beneath her when her pace shattered, suddenly quickening. Her vigor swept him away and his eyes clenched shut. The way she moved over him, with a grace he'd not yet seen from her, sundered his control and he rose to the challenge, hips meeting her halfway. The sounds she made—like music to his ears—the soft sighs and sharp gasps as she gave herself to him. An animal need burned through him, encouraging him to explore deeper. His name spilled from her lips as she tightened around him, her body shivering and trembling. Her hips drove down a final time, pleasure rippling over her face as he gave in to his own ecstasy, lost to the wild rush of sensation. Buried deeply inside her, he hung there, riding out the lingering pleasure, her shallow breath pooling against his throat.

He was no amateur when it came to women, but if this was what being mated was like, he planned to welcome his new life with open arms, so long as she was in them.

Chapter Six

The sound of her softly pattering footsteps was quite soothing to listen to as she moved about his guest bedroom, dressing herself in what little clothing he'd found that would fit her. From there, she'd begun shuffling from room to room, perusing whatever was laid out on his shelves or hung on the walls. There wasn't much left in the open for anyone to study, yet he still enjoyed that she was making the effort to know him.

He settled in and tipped his head back until it rested against the thin wall, choosing to let his thoughts wander without pursuit, lost to the sound of her careful explorations. He could hear her slender fingertips caressing his picture frames, and her steady breath. Such a beautiful sound—no fear, no anxiety. This was how it should always be for her. Quiet comforts with an ease of being around one another.

She turned on her heel, slowly making her way through the hall and toward him at a resolved pace. Slow steps rounded the staircase, her hand gliding down the polished rail. Hunter cracked an eye open, peering out from his thick mop of dark hair.

The moment her gaze swept over him, she jumped, a sheepish smile tugging her lips. "I didn't know you were here," she murmured as her hand dragged her loose hair back from her face.

Hunter rose to his feet, his fingers clasping hers as he led the way to the kitchen. "Are you hungry?" he asked.

An inane question if ever he'd asked one. Of course she was hungry; werewolves' stomachs were bottomless, and hers had been growling since their romp in the grass. Shifts always left him ravenous, as did the more pleasurable acts. He could smell the brackish tang of her newly risen anxiety. The last thing he wanted to do was add to it, but there were still answers he sought.

He opened the refrigerator door with a sharp yank and studied the contents, eventually settling on reheating the protein-rich pasta dish he'd made the night before. Tossing it into the microwave, he busied himself with the challenge of unearthing spare utensils as she slowly settled at the table, her fingers tracing the intricate lines engraved into his coasters. Self-proclaimed bachelor that he was, it took a bit of time to scrounge up a second fork, and the bowl proved even more elusive. As for the drinks, his ended up in a teacup; it was the only thing he could find. He drew to his full height, studying his kitchen. If Angel meant to stay, changes were required, and the thought brought a satisfied quirk to his lips rather than a groan.

"Tell me about your pack," Hunter commented as he caught the fridge door with his heel and kicked it shut before walking into the dining room, his arms overflowing with the steaming bowls, cups and utensils.

She drew in a sharp breath. When he lowered her meal down in front of her, he found her eyes trained on the veneer and her fingers gripping the edge. The bitter taste of her fear overwhelmed the pasta's fragrance, and before he dropped into his own seat, he crouched next to her, smoothing her hair back from her soft cheeks. It seemed this topic of conversation frightened her, but he'd always been a patient hunter, and this was no different. Long, pale lashes fluttered and he was suddenly gazing up at her, her anxiety quelling from his simple touch.

"You're safe here," he assured her as he drew his thumb down her jawline. "With me." Such shadows behind those bright eyes, such nightmares she carried. All he wanted was to soothe her, to abolish what fears she carried, and give her something else to burn with—hope. His fingers swept down her arms until he gathered her shaking hands. When she finally nodded, he felt as though he'd won a battle, and with a soft smile, he shifted back into his chair.

She was the first to drop her gaze, her fingers fiddling mindlessly with her fork as she stared down on the bowl of food before her. "What would you like to know?"

"How many are in Seth's pack?"

"I don't know. I've been on the run for eight years." She released a slight sigh and propped her elbow on the table, resting her chin in her palm. "Eight years. It feels so much longer than that."

He took a bite, the cold metal of his fork resting against his lips. "That wasn't the first time Seth's handled you... like that, was it?"

The fool he was. Of course it wasn't, if her rigid shoulders and timid manner were evident of anything. She was more rabbit than wolf, a behavior likely beaten into her. The thought burned deep, and the metal fork in his hand gave way as he bent it in half.

"It was why I left," she admitted in a quiet voice, a faint smile climbing her lips. "I'd never felt so free as in that moment, so...human," she said with a nod. "I didn't care what the cost was, I had to get away from him."

"But you were his mate." Hunter bit out the bitter words, and a fresh wash of her anger swept through the room. "Surely you saw something in him—"

"I was *never* his mate," she growled, her chin snapping up until she could spear him with a glare. "*Never.*"

Her personality swam in the dark depths of her eyes, burning like a candlewick. "Angel—"

"He forced me to be his mate," she whispered, a coldness devouring that tiny flame he'd spotted. When her eyes lifted, they stared *through* him, fading into less pleasant memories, no doubt, ones he instantly regretted making her dredge up. "If I fought against him, he showed me what it meant to be a submissive wolf." Tears clung to her eyelashes, though they never fell. "For two years I surrendered to him. I did what was expected of me, played the perfect little mate, so that he wouldn't—" Her jaw tightened, muscles leaping as she choked on her words. "But I couldn't. Not anymore. He liked pain with his..." Her voice cracked and faded away.

"Pleasure," Hunter whispered when she couldn't, his ruined fork dangling from his fingers. Suddenly he wasn't as hungry.

Her head bowed forward as she nodded. His fingers itched with longing to touch her, to calm her, but logic knew such a gesture would not be welcomed at a moment like this, not with such brutal memories haunting her mind.

"I ran," she mumbled into her hair. "I almost died in my attempt, but my wolf took over. She showed me how to survive. She kept me alive when I couldn't, protected me when I had no one else."

Silence settled between them, broken only when Hunter lowered his mangled fork down onto his plate with a gentle clink. "You have me now," he whispered. "I...won't let Seth touch you, ever again."

Laughter shook her shoulders, the bitter sound spilling from her lips quite abrasively. "Don't you get it?" she scoffed. "*No one* can protect me from Seth. No matter where I go, he follows. For eight years I've run from him, and for eight years he's always found me. *Always*. Do you understand? He will kill you to get to me. There's no stopping it."

Such desolation in her voice, such devastation. The table rocked back when he surged to his feet and drew her out of her chair, folding her into his chest. "Not if I kill him first," he promised her, his lips burying in her hair. She trembled against him, small drops of wetness dampening his shirt. "You have me now," he repeated once more, his eyes staring out the window behind them.

Hunter hoped Seth would come. And when he did, he certainly wouldn't leave alive.

Angel tipped her head back against the bed frame, staring out the window over the vast land Hunter owned. Eerie shadows whisked over her walls, blending with the silvery night.

Before becoming one of them, her life had been much simpler—happy even. But that had all changed the day she'd met Seth. Whatever hellion he'd changed her into, nature herself seemed to fear her. Never had she heard a forest so quiet as when she stepped into it. It was as though death followed her. Animals took wing, vanishing entirely. So for eight years she'd surrounded herself with cities as a means of evading him, yet he'd always found her. Typically she ran, as she'd intended to today, but perhaps the time for running was long past. Running gave him power over her and she was so tired of feeling weak.

Lost to her thoughts, sleep was proving elusive. No matter how often she dared to close her eyes, his face swam through her mind's eye, twisted with such fervent hate. All she longed for was her freedom, the right to live where, when and how she chose. This life—it wasn't hers; it was Seth's. Something he'd forced upon her with little concern for her desires. He cared little for others and focused entirely on himself, a habit she'd soon learned was typical among *his* werewolves. Perfectly miserable creatures, those beasts, taking what they wanted and when.

She could recall the first time she'd laid eyes on Hunter as though it had been yesterday. At first glance, he'd stolen her breath, something that frightened her more than anything. Another wolf, another dominant—that which she hated more than anything. Wretchedly handsome, but still a monster, like them all. Stunning peridot eyes had swept over her as though she was nothing more than a mutt— a common occurrence for one such as herself. Had she known that he'd actually taken notice of her, liked what he'd seen, she would have—

Angel released a sharp breath, fingers ensnaring the coverlet draped over her legs. She would have *what?* Spoken to him? The very idea was laughable. Seth's leash had been tight then, until she'd all but choked from it. Nothing would have been done; nothing *could* have been done. But now she was beginning to understand why Seth had declared her his mate the very next day.

Kicking back her blanket, she pushed to her feet and began to prowl the length of her room like a wild animal, unable to keep to the bed if she wasn't going to sleep. Her emotional state was far more volatile than normal. Since she'd shifted already tonight, the call of the moon was absent, something she was unaccustomed to, and it was leaving her feeling a touch jittery. If she could only sleep…

After what felt like hours of her feet wearing the hardwood thin, she groaned and spun toward the door. The animal within felt caged; her wolf was howling to be set free if for no other purpose than simply to run. Hunter had shown her to the guest room to rest, but what she needed was to burn off this excess energy scalding her from the inside out.

To hell with this. She rocked to the balls of her feet and silently crept to the door. Not a single soul had bothered her since Hunter had given her the grand tour. In fact, it felt as though they were the only two within the house. Pondering such a thing, she peered down the silent halls, wondering if there was anyone else present.

She tiptoed down the corridor, pausing before the third room on the left. The door was slightly ajar, a dim light permeating the darkness of the hall. Angel paused, her heart quickening with the thought that she might be disturbing him. Would he mind such an interruption, or would he think she was invading his space?

She was about to head back to her own room when she silently scolded herself for being foolish. He'd offered up his house and home, fed and cared for her. When he'd offered his guest bedroom to her, she'd been shocked, expecting him to insist she remain with him. Once again, he'd shown her his caliber and how much he differed from Seth.

Measuring the door, she gracefully slipped within. There Hunter lay on the bed with an arm thrown over his face, his body tense. She could see that he was just as awake as she was.

She dared another step, silently praying that his floorboards didn't creak. The last thing she wanted was to startle an alpha werewolf.

"Mmm, this is a fantasy of mine, you know." A muffled voice came from the covers.

His arm shifted, and it was only then that she noticed the

mangled book dangling from his fingers. Apparently he'd been trying to read, though that appeared to be as much of a lost cause as sleep had been for her. A pinched face greeted her, though a single wry brow lifted in amusement.

"A fantasy?" she finally whispered. "Of a girl slipping into your room?"

The book was abandoned to the pillows and his arm dropped down, drawing her eyes to his chest. "Of *you* slipping into my room. There's more, of course," he chuckled, his eyes brightening. "I could divulge a little, if you'd like."

She couldn't help her laugh. "And you've had this fantasy for what, five minutes?"

"Five minutes, ten years. What does time mean to us?" he murmured in a deep voice before pinning her with an odd look. "I thought you were sleeping."

"I couldn't," she admitted softly. "But if you were trying, I could—"

Her words died on her lips when he suddenly drew down the covers, gesturing to the spot next to him.

Leaning back against the pillows, he watched her carefully. "Well?"

Her eyes flicked to the empty space next to him.

"I promise you I won't bite," he offered with a humorous lilt, "too hard."

Her cheeks burned, the memory of the hard brush of his teeth lighting a fire in her stomach. They'd done much more than simply sleep together in the short while she'd known him. Maybe in here she'd manage some rest.

She stole a glance back over her shoulder, peering down the dark hallway. There was no one else here, and if there was, would that matter? It'd been so long since she'd lain with anyone in a bed, she found the thought rather exciting. Swallowing what fear clogged her throat, she braved the few steps toward the bed and lowered down before sliding her legs beneath the blankets. A heavy arm draped around her waist and drew her against him. There was a brief moment of panic, one she was sure he could scent, yet he didn't utter a single word, simply buried his nose against the back of her neck and held his breath until it passed. Eventually her heartbeat slowed, her breathing grew shallow, and she fell asleep to the feel of his fingers running through her hair.

Chapter Seven

She didn't dare move, caught in the final moments of sleep and refusing to wake, afraid that it had all been a dream. Such memories hovered on the brink of her mind, teasing her with the thought that she'd finally been given a chance to have all she'd desired for so long.

Burying her face into the rumpled pillows, she inhaled a scent that was as familiar to her as her own now. Hunter's distinctly male aroma surrounded her, yet she found no fear in this, nor the fact that during the night she'd apparently discarded her clothes. She couldn't quite remember how that had come to be, nor did she care, though she was a touch surprised that it didn't feel awkward. The last time she'd woken naked in a bed with a man, she'd been human.

Warm fingers grazed her side and the faintest sigh fell from her lips before she could muffle it. His touch was addictive and regardless of her past, her body responded to it. He'd only been back in her life for a short time, yet he'd left his imprint and now she craved him. She knew that she would only bring pain into his life, but the thought of living the rest of her days without him left an aching void in her chest that threatened to consume her. It was part of the reason she held so still—to revel in the dream before it shattered, to give herself this one moment of bliss before everything came crashing down. Seth was going to come; there was no doubt in her mind about that. Until then, this was what she had—stolen seconds, hidden away in his bedroom, safe from the world.

What plagued her was the thought of losing this opportunity to be with him again—to taste him on her lips and feel his body moving within her. As though he could read her thoughts, Hunter's mouth suddenly pressed against her neck, the soft rake of his teeth drawing out a shiver. Oh, but it was such a satisfying sensation, to be marked as his. Without censure, she turned over and found herself staring into the pools of forest-green that were his eyes.

Passion's fire lit within her stomach, and without a wasted breath, Hunter's fingers swept down her stomach, discarding the sheet.

How she ached for him.

It disgusted her, this sure knowledge that Seth would try to ruin their burgeoning relationship when it'd only just begun. Such emotions roused within her, ones she felt incapable of handling. Whatever this was that she felt for Hunter, it was stronger than she had ever anticipated. Fantasies were one thing, but this was real. All she knew was that she *had* to have him. She couldn't just walk away, not again, not without at least showing him how she felt. They'd been parted for so long, yet nothing had ever felt so right to her as being with him had.

"You smell good," she whispered drowsily.

"Do I?" he rumbled in a pleased voice. "And what do I smell like?"

Her eyes fluttered shut as she inhaled. Feeling brave, she ran her fingers up and down his length, listening to his quickening heartbeat. "Mmm, like wolf," she breathed. "Like strength and power." She opened her eyes and pinned him with a glance, struggling with the decision of whether to tell him exactly how she felt in this moment. It might not last, but she at least wanted to let him know that for one minute she'd found happiness. "Like *home*."

Her chilled nose ran a line over his neck and she grinned when she heard him swallow. She'd never felt this way before, safe and secure, and the unbridled *need* that came with it was overwhelming. Moments ago she'd been attempting to make peace with the fact that she couldn't stay, but with his arms closing around her, she knew he'd never let her go.

The small bit of encouragement from her urged him onward and his hands caressed her curves, sliding down her body as he lifted her against him. The feel of his erection pressing against her center nearly undid her and she found herself squirming, desperately trying to fit herself atop him. Grinning, his dark eyes devoured her body as his fingers came between them, just where she wanted them to be joined.

"Patience," he murmured the moment his finger caressed her opening, barely touching her, yet she ached for him.

Trembling, her entire body kindled with the need to feel him pushing inside her and when his finger slid between her folds, she sighed for him, her lashes fanning her cheeks as he began to stroke her. His movements were far too slow for her liking and the realization staggered her. Only in her fantasies of Hunter did she ever awaken like this— as a ball of need that would die if she wasn't touched. It poured from her mouth in a small moan, one that brought his eyes up to hers.

"Angel…" he whispered. "I—"

She didn't know what he meant to say, and her own plea for him to take her silenced his words. "Hunter, please," she begged, writhing against his hand as he stoked her inner flames.

Acquiescing, the press of his thumb came down on her throbbing clit. Gasping, she arched into him, her head falling back as pleasure swept through her body. Her stomach warmed with anticipation, awaiting that moment when the world came shattering down. Instead, he slid another finger inside her, pulling her closer and closer to her climax, as his lips found her beaded nipples. If only every moment in her life could be like this.

Her hand fell between them, fingers closing around his shaft. Sucking in a sharp breath, he swept his other hand up her back and cupped her head, forcing her gaze to his. Meeting his eyes as they touched and explored one another felt far more erotic than anything they'd done so far. With her every stroke, his eyes brightened until finally he canted her head toward him. He made a small and broken sound as he claimed her mouth, his tongue caressing hers in smooth strokes.

She shuddered against him, struggling to control herself, to delay the final moment before her climax took hold. She hovered on the brink of it—it wouldn't take much now to send her over the edge, and as though Hunter knew, his thumb flicked against her, teasing her in a circular motion. The feel of his mouth on hers, of his fingers buried deep within, his thumb teasing her small bundle of nerves—it all proved to be too much. Her orgasm felt like a train mowing her down when it suddenly hit her. She succumbed to the pleasure, her shivering breath falling into his mouth as his fingers tightened against the nape of her neck, holding her in place while he milked her climax for all he could.

Lost to the throes of ecstasy, Angel settled herself over him, wanting nothing more than to draw it out as long as she could. With her hand already there to guide her, she shifted, about to take every last inch of him into her, when Hunter grew impossibly still and tore his mouth from hers, his body turning to stone as his head cocked.

The pleasure racking her body dimmed as quickly as the eagerness faded from his eyes, leaving them as cold as a wintry sky. Her lips parted, about to ask what was wrong, when his hand slid over her mouth, muffling her panting breath.

"Stay here," he whispered as softly as he could, clearly trying to keep her calm even though his wolf was peeking out at her. "Do not leave this room unless I tell you otherwise."

Far too slowly, her thoughts lined up and she caught the sound of a wolf howling in the distance. Oh, she *knew* that howl, and her body tightened against Hunter. It was like having freezing-cold water dumped on her head, and the icy realization sank in that Seth had come, now of all moments.

She swallowed the lump in her throat. *No*, no, she wouldn't just leave him to deal with Seth himself. It was her fault he had come, and it was time she stood up to him—

"Angel," he interrupted her silent tirade. "Do this for me, please. Wait for me here."

Her face crumpled. But before she could argue, he pushed to his feet, the sight of his hard cock snuffing her words.

He'd only taken two steps before the air shimmered and a dark-as-night wolf leaped out his bedroom window, vanishing from sight.

Terror overtook her and without a thought, her wolf rose to the surface. Hardly pausing, Angel leaped out the same window, her paws barely touching upon the earth before she chased after him, refusing to stay hidden away in his bedroom while he fought Seth.

Branches snagged her fur and rocks cut into her paws, but it didn't stop her. Not even the furred side of another wolf brushing against her gave her pause. Instead, they raced together, chasing after the faint howls that rose within the morning light. The wolf next to her pulled ahead, his snowy coloring standing out as he darted through the evergreen pines.

For a moment he paused and glanced over his shoulder to huff at her, his black nose lifting in the air to scent out the direction. Angel yipped under her breath, trusting her instincts—and her own nose—to tell her that this was one of Hunter's. When he turned and started toward the east, she followed suit, hoping she hadn't made the wrong decision. As strong as her mate was, she still feared for him. That thought nearly brought her to her knees. Her *mate*. She knew as much as he that something had happened in that bus station last night, something powerful. But the talk of mates was all nonsense—just mystical gibberish wolves spoke about when discussing the *old days*. No one in her former pack had been *truly* mated—why would she think it was even possible?

But it had happened. She'd felt it when the moon awoke within her, the moment the song left her lips, in the deep thrumming beat that had come from him. It had called her name, whispered into her soul. She'd felt it deep inside, and it was *right*. She was his, but more than that, he was hers, and the realization spurred her legs faster until they burned with the effort.

Clearing the brush, she stopped herself, rocking to a standstill at the sight of Hunter and Seth standing within a small semicircle, staring one another down. The moment she entered the pack circle, Seth's eyes fell to hers. Still in his human form, he stared down his nose at Hunter, a wry twist of his lips doing little to soften his indignation.

"You have stolen my mate," Seth proclaimed to the circle.

Hunter's wolves howled their enraged responses, some

even casting angered looks her way. She knew nothing of his pack, nothing of the numbers he wielded, but there had to be at least thirty wolves present, and only a handful belonged to Seth—she would know *those* wolves anywhere.

Magic curled around her and in the span of a breath, Hunter shifted back to human and stood, gloriously naked before all. How someone could stand nude before an enemy and still maintain an intimidating stance was beyond her, yet Hunter did just that.

"Your mate left you eight years ago," Hunter argued. "I gave you a pass in the bus station, for Angel's sake. I won't make that same mistake again."

Fury rippled across Seth's face and he shot another dark look toward her. "We all do things for Angel's sake," he growled. His fingers rose to his shirt and tore it off. Seth was by no means an unattractive man, but there was something about him that had always affected Angel—his cruel personality, the way he handled her, forced her to do things she abhorred.

"You mean to challenge me?" Hunter laughed mockingly. "Would you like a moment to think this through?"

Seth's mouth thinned and he jerked his chin toward her. "I win, she leaves with me."

Hunter paused, his back stiffening the moment he realized she was here. "You've learned *nothing*," he snarled. "But if this is how you want to do it, Angel goes free if I win and your second takes over your pack. I want nothing to do with that mess of yours."

Angel's breath caught with Hunter's words, her ears flicking up. He could have claimed her right here, made *her* his reward, as Seth had done, but instead he'd guaranteed her freedom should he win.

Seth's eyes tapered but with a sharp nod, he called his wolf forth and fell to all fours in a burst of fur and magic, with Hunter only seconds behind. If their previous activities and his two shifts were weighing on him, Hunter made no indication of it.

Slowly, they began to circle one another, an uncomfortable reticence settling over both packs. Angel's eyes were all for Hunter, watching with bated breath as he hunted her former alpha. His movements were liquid and dangerous, his eyes alight with rage and savage strength. Where Seth made grandiose swipes at the air and menacing growls, Hunter remained silent. It was the quiet wolves that were to be feared. Vicious, calculating—and Angel could see exactly that.

A broken howl from Seth shattered the eerie silence of their pack mates, and she gasped, her claws digging into the soil to restrain herself from rushing forward. Another howl, an unfamiliar one from one of Hunter's wolves. Her wobbly knees shook, her ears flattening against her head as she listened to what was beginning to sound like war breaking out in the small clearing.

Seth struck.

The movements were far too quick to follow and Angel's heart raged against her ribs as her eyes darted over the clearing, struggling to see what was happening. The two wolves began the dance of death, neither willing to back down.

She whimpered when a canid scream found its way to

her ears and a splash of blood darkened the soft ground. Her paws skimmed over the surface of the earth as she unknowingly moved toward them. One of Hunter's wolves leaped before her, his teeth catching gently at her ear before he stepped on her paw. Hunter could do this, she knew that, but she also knew how dirty Seth fought. She couldn't lose Hunter after finally finding him, after so many years of dreaming about him. His soft touches, gentle words, they all turned her knees to mush. For an alpha he was certainly a man of contrasts, and she would *not* lose him to Seth. That bastard had taken *everything* from her; he could not have this.

The two remained locked in their endless struggle and Angel grimaced with every strike Seth landed. Hunter's side was a mess of matted fur and she watched breathlessly as tiny rubies of blood splashed to the ground. Seth was no better, a garish gash having nearly claimed his eye, yet their battle continued, snarling and howling with each lunge, their claws and teeth deadly accurate.

Fangs bared, Seth leaped into the air and came down on Hunter's back, his claws tearing into his side where a glaring wound already lay. Angel gasped and it was only the heavy press of the other wolf that kept her back where she belonged. They didn't understand—this was not Hunter's fight! It was hers, and the cold fear that Hunter might just lose settled into her gut. She couldn't go back with Seth—*wouldn't*—and she knew that if Hunter lost, her life would be forfeited as well. There was no way she could just sit back and watch Seth kill him.

Paws dancing against the ground, she shifted back and

forth, clouds of dust rising from her movements. Anxious, afraid, there were only so many emotions she could suffer.

Hunter shook clear of Seth and turned, his massive paw striking against Seth's jaw. Her former alpha collapsed to the ground, his dark eyes spearing her once before he jumped back to his feet and struck out with his own attack.

Blow for blow, she watched, each strike landing against Hunter met with her own soft whine. It was unbearable. That they expected her to just stand back and watch them throttle and pound on each other was ridiculous. But every time she moved, Hunter's wolves were there, pushing her back with a hardened glitter to their eyes that had turned threatening.

Something in the air shifted and Angel tensed. Hunter shirked to the side, feinting when Seth struck next. Lightning quick, Hunter turned and lunged, his score flawless. Whetted teeth sank into Seth's throat, claws digging into his back. A sharp cry fell from Seth's lips a moment before he crumpled, a scarlet mess now where his throat had once been. Prancing back, she stared down at the dark blood pooling in the grass. A low whine leaked from her lips, the image of Seth thrashing on the ground all she could see, his leg twitching in an attempt to fight off the final throes. Angel couldn't tear her gaze from his voided eyes, the life within already fading. How many times had she dreamed of this moment, pictured his lifeless form sprawled before her feet? Seth had lost. She had won—her freedom, her life, *everything*.

Her chest heaved with unrestrained excitement, her heart soaring in her chest. She found Hunter standing in the clearing, watching her carefully, as though waiting to see what she would do. Time seemed to stop as they gazed across the bloodied field at one another. Her first steps toward him were awkward, her rubbery knees struggling to keep her upright. It was all so overwhelming, she needed a moment to sit and think about all that was about to change.

Had she not been watching him, she might not have noticed the small shift in structure at Hunter's back. One of Seth's wolves—Jordan, if she remembered correctly—lowered toward the ground, his muscles coiling beneath him as he prepared to spring.

There was no hesitation in either Jordan or Angel, no thought that he was surrounded by Hunter's entire pack and that this was a futile move on Jordan's part. All she could taste was her fear as she watched him vault toward Hunter. Angel's heart clenched and without a second wasted, she sprinted forward and leaped over Hunter's back, her paws striking Jordan down. She let her instincts guide her and sank her teeth into the familiar neck. Before this night, she'd never lifted a paw against any of Seth's wolves, knowing what punishment would await her. It was strange to feel fur in her mouth as she shook him furiously. He bucked against her and sent her flying, his claws cutting into her shoulder as she fell, but the pain was nothing compared to the fear of what *might* have happened. She braced, waiting for his return attack, when the wolf suddenly went sailing through the air, slamming to the ground with a shuddering breath.

Between her and Jordan stood a towering inferno of midnight fur, eyes snapping with a fury that hadn't been present when he'd fought Seth. His possessive growl awoke something within her, something she found she *liked*. Lost to these new feelings, she hardly took notice of Hunter stalking across the clearing, his powerful jaws snapping Jordan's neck.

Hunter turned in a circle, his deadly stare narrowing on each of Seth's remaining wolves until one stepped forward. Angel recognized William the moment he shifted back to human. He was one of the few that had always let her be; she knew he meant no harm to Hunter.

"Peace," William rumbled in a voice deeper than she remembered.

He cast Hunter a wary look before finally turning to Angel and taking a knee before her. Gentle fingers fell to her shoulder, and when a small gasp rose from her lips, Hunter was there, butting William back—her guardian standing before her.

With a small nod, William's hands fell away from her. "We all witnessed what transpired here tonight," he began, looking to each of his wolves with a watchful eye. "I will take *my* wolves and leave your territory."

Hunter's head dropped in his own nod.

"Angelica," William murmured with an extended hand. "You can return with us, should you like."

All eyes swiveled to her, Hunter's included. A subdued pain chased over his face, but eventually he nodded and stepped away. Not once did those eyes leave hers and she could see the silent plea within for her to remain with him. But for once, the decision was hers alone.

"I'm sure your family would enjoy hearing that you are

alive and…well." William forced out the last word, a hint of a questioning lingering on it.

Her family. It had been so long since she had seen or spoken with them. A warm nose brushed hers and Angel jerked her gaze away from William, meeting Hunter's verdant eyes, lit with worry. His head cocked and he silently regarded her, his nose lifted into the air as he scented her emotions. Angel could hardly think past the layer of confusion twining in her stomach. This was what she had always wanted and finally the time had come.

But did she want to return to her old life? Or did she want the new one presented before her? Hunter was her mate, she knew that now. There wasn't a doubt in her mind. And with that realization came the knowledge that she could never leave him and that he would never let her go. It was different than with Seth—Hunter would never force her, but he would *die* for her, and she him—as she'd just proved. What more could either of them ask? As far as she was concerned, it was the easiest decision she'd ever had to make. Burying her head beneath his chin, she brushed against his side. Stress poured off his body in waves as he wound around her, rubbing his cheek against hers.

William's chuckle was soft and forgiving. "I thought not," he whispered as he backed away and directed his wolves toward the gates. "Be well, Angelica," was the last thing he murmured before he vanished with his pack.

She hardly heard a word William said as Hunter bowed over her and swiped his tongue across her paw. The feel of his hot breath threading through her fur dragged her attention down where she watched him lick the blood from her foot.

The movement of his own wolves brought both their heads up and with a quick look back at her, Hunter stepped forward and unfolded from his wolf.

Chapter Eight

His hands were on her shoulder before she could stop him, touching and prodding the wound carefully. Anger controlled his every movement and so she held perfectly still. Even kneeling, he was larger than she and her eyes kept falling to the long, hardened length standing tall and proud from between his legs. It was normal to see such a thing—he'd just won a challenge and Angel had shown both packs that she would be his mate.

"Brody," Hunter growled, snapping his fingers at the wolf next to her.

Both she and his second jerked their eyes to Hunter.

"Take the others and leave. I have some…unfinished business to attend to."

The look he gave Angel lit her stomach with desire. She knew what business he meant and her memories flitted to their morning escapade.

Brody's head dropped and with a short bark he turned and left the clearing, a couple dozen wolves following in his wake. Only when they left did Angel dare shift back to her human form, stepping into it with a grace she'd never possessed before.

Pain twisted Hunter's face and the tips of his fingers met the trio of gashes cut into her shoulder. She couldn't help but shiver, the warmth of his digits successfully renewing her desire.

"I told you to stay inside," he murmured as he studied the wound.

"I couldn't," she whispered. "I couldn't just sit there and wait to see who came to find me. I had to know that you won."

Something dark shifted behind his eyes and he turned to her. "To know that you were free," he muttered in a tight voice.

Her breath caught as she cupped his cheek, her thumb tracing his jaw as he'd done to her. "No. To know you were safe. I couldn't—" She paused.

"Couldn't what?" Hunter asked, stepping into her until they were flush against one another. The feel of him throbbing against her was almost too much and her lashes fluttered as she struggled to rein in her thoughts. "Couldn't what, love?"

She broke right there, hearing such an endearing term fall from his lips so easily. For a moment she wanted to sob with relief and happiness that the nightmare was finally over. She wanted to rejoice in the fact that she'd awakened, and with it came a new life.

"Angel," he murmured in a soft voice that did odd things

to her heart. What anger he'd felt before this was gone and was now replaced with an adoration that filled his eyes. "Couldn't what?"

"Couldn't lose you," she bit out.

Pleasure smoothed his face. Without pause he swept down and stole her mouth, kissing her with such passion that it left her breathless. His arms curved around her and a moment later he took her to the ground.

"What are you doing?" She laughed against his lips.

Breaking from the kiss, he leaned back and eyed her with amusement. "I think you know, love."

Excitement hung in the air—the thought of being with him again rekindling the fires from earlier. Only this time she'd acknowledged that he was her mate. Somehow it made the connection stronger, brought them together in a way that neither had understood before this moment. There was closeness, a desire to join completely with one another. And if that was to be this moment, Angel couldn't wait.

With a shuddering breath he lowered over her, his lips falling upon hers and tongue sweeping through her mouth with the utmost determination.

There was no hesitation; desire took hold and Angel met him in equal abandon, her own need stealing away her ability to think. The only capable thought she had was to have him, and his want—the way he fed at her, the way his hands gripped her tightly—seemed just as desperate. All she knew was it wasn't enough; it would never be enough.

Bare to the chill of the elements, Hunter guided her to her knees, settling behind her. His mouth dropped down to the milky skin of her neck, palm smoothing down her back as his hips ground against hers. Heat spread through her limbs, her temperature spiking beneath him, and the erotic aroma of their desire thickened in the clearing. Her entire body ignited in one long lick of ecstasy, his teasing fragrance thinning her already waning control. The hot press of his mouth was deliciously spicy, and she found herself praying for more.

On all fours, Angel crooked a glance back over her shoulder, and the rippling muscles of Hunter's chest stole her breath. His fingers found her opening, parting her, preparing her for what was about to come. Oh, but she wanted—*needed*—him, and he was taking his sweet time, relishing in her. How she wanted to tell him she was ready, that the passion of their earlier moments had long prepared her, but she couldn't make her lips work when his fingers found their way to her center, exploring the sensitive area that brought her into an instant squirm, a shameless pleasure that had her writhing into his hand.

His mouth swept down her neck, dragging over her back, the fingers of his other hand finding her hardened nipples. Aching, her head dropped forward as she offered as much of herself as she could before she reached back, her fingers closing around his steeled length. The groan that rumbled behind her drew a moan from her as she stroked him.

Releasing her, he straightened and Angel looked back over her shoulder, lost to the sight of his parted mouth and shining eyes. Before she could calm her jittering nerves, his strong hands curved around her hips and guided her back, pressing her against him. A silent question filled his face and when Angel's chin dipped, he pushed into her, the thick feel of him almost enough to shatter her control. She shuddered against him in that moment of togetherness, to feel them joined together in this most carnal of dances.

"Angel," he whispered, the gruff tone of his voice bringing her back to reality. Chest heaving, she continued to watch him, his face flushed with need, eyes glittering with lust.

His gaze locked with hers, he set a much slower pace as he began to move within her. They needed this, this heartfelt moment, to show just what they meant to one another. Her breath caught in her throat, Angel's knees deepened into the earth and she permitted him this guilty pleasure, to do with her as he wished, his hips sinuously rocking against her.

Not a moment earlier, she'd wanted him to simply take her, lost to the desperate emotions that had flooded them both, but now, as he moved with grace and purpose, she wanted *this*.

His eyes held hers as his hand swept up her back, fingers sliding through her long hair. Cupping her hips, he turned her around, bringing their mouths together before slowly easing her down onto the ground. A chill from the damp earth raced up her spine, but as he started to move within her again, the world around her faded until only he remained.

The heat of his mouth trailed over her neck, his tongue tasting his way back down to her breast. How arduously he fed from her, savoring each and every moment, even as he continued to fill her, spearing her on his length, over and over.

Angel's head pressed into the earth as her fingers

dragged through his silken curls, kneading at the roots. The sensations were overwhelming—his fingers working her center as he pumped into her, his mouth tasting every last inch of her tender flesh.

A cry built in her throat, her stomach heating with his skilled touch until finally an explosion of colors burst behind her eyes and she arched toward him. When the cry spilled from her lips, his mouth was there, devouring it as she moaned around him. Her body trembled as he continued to thrust, her fingers gripping at the strong line of his shoulders.

She could feel him thickening inside her, pulsing against her walls as pleasure overtook her. A brusque groan fell into her mouth, his chest rumbling beneath her palms. *Now*—she knew it the moment he broke from the kiss and his head fell back. Satisfaction wound through her limbs when his heat settled between her thighs, a different sort of pleasure filling her as she watched the strength of this moment carve his face in rapture.

An eternity they hung in that small drop of time, committing to memory the feel of themselves wrapped around one another. As their climaxes subsided, Hunter wound an arm around her waist and slowly withdrew from her, lowering down into the grass next to her.

"Thank you," Angel whispered.

Laughing, Hunter pushed up onto his elbow and gazed down at her with felicity lighting his face. "No, trust me, thank *you*."

She joined in his laughter, reveling in the sound of it. "No, I mean thank you for everything you've done for me."

"Angel," he murmured, spearing her with a bright glance. "For ten years, you've haunted me. No one ever came close to the memory of you I carried with me. I would have done so much more for you."

Her mouth dried with the realization—she'd already figured out that he would die for her, and that was a frightening notion. The frightening part being that she felt the same way for him.

"Maybe I should have said this sooner, but I—" His voice broke and he swallowed. "I love you. I have since the first moment I laid eyes on you."

Her heart swelled in her chest until it became difficult to breathe. Nodding, she twined her fingers with his and lifted them to her mouth, caressing her lips along each knuckle. "It was the same for me. I just…I was scared."

His arm wound around her waist and drew her against his side as he buried his lips into her hair. "There's no reason to be scared anymore."

A true smile lit her face and she buried herself into his chest. "I know."

With the scent of his skin so close and the heat of his body keeping her warm, she rose up and stole his mouth. This was what she'd dreamed of, and now that she had it, she never intended to let it—*him*—go. Love had found a way through the paths haunted by wolves, and now that she was finally in his arms, she knew she'd never look back. There was nowhere else she'd rather be than with the hunter that had finally caught his prey.

* * * * *

A sneaky peek at next month...

NOCTURNE™

BEYOND DARKNESS...BEYOND DESIRE

My wish list for next month's titles...

In stores from 21st February 2014:

❑ Running with Wolves — Cynthia Cooke

❑ Shadowmaster — Susan Krinard

In stores from 7th March 2014:

❑ Spellbound — Michele Hauf, Nina Croft, Elle James, Seressia Glass & Lauren Hawkeye

Available at WHSmith, Tesco, Asda, Eason, Amazon and Apple

Just can't wait?

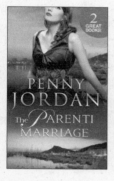

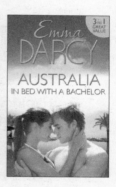

Join the Mills & Boon Book Club

Want to read more **Nocturne**™ books?
We're offering you **1** more absolutely **FREE!**

We'll also treat you to these fabulous extras:

- **Exclusive offers and much more!**
- **FREE home delivery**
- **FREE books and gifts with our special rewards scheme**

Get your free books now!

visit www.millsandboon.co.uk/bookclub
or call Customer Relations on 020 8288 2888